Don't Date the Haunted

Don't Date the Haunted

A Dark Romantic Comedy

HAUNTED ROMANCE BOOK ONE

C. Rae D'Arc

No part of this book may be reproduced, or stored in a retrieval system, or transmitted in any form or by any means, electronic, mechanical, photocopying, recording, or otherwise, without express written permission of the publisher.

This is a work of fiction. Names, characters, places, and incidents are either the product of the author's imagination or are used fictitiously. Any resemblance to actual persons, living or dead, events, or locales is entirely coincidental.

Copyright © 2020 C. Rae D'Arc
All rights reserved

Cover design by: Blue Water Books

ISBN: 978-1-961733-00-8 (paperback)

Published by Bursting Box Publishing
www.craedarc.com
www.facebook.com/c.rae.darc
www.instagram.com/craedarc

For the cynical hearts
who think their lives are tragedies;
a little humor and openness can find
Romances and Adventures all around.

Chapter 1

RUN AWAY WHEN

Lights flicker
It's always storming
There's no cell phone service
Your only light source in a dark room is a single bald bulb
You see the reflection of anyone or anything that's not supposed to be there
Someone was murdered there

- *Oz's Haunting Survival Book*

Alone was a dangerous status in Horror Zone. The last time my fiancé smiled at me was during a mad dash from a possessed scientist. Five months later, the whispers of "black widow" were almost bad enough to chase me out of town like a witch hunt. I'd survived worse Hauntings, but an ominous black cat just crossed my path.

I shooed the cat away from my trailer park mailbox with a manila envelope addressed, *To Ms. Pansy Finster*. My stomach churned at the thought of what was inside.

I shuffled through the accompanying ads for licensed silver bullets, then scanned the trailer park for more omens, like windless chimes, a shadow that was too still, or that condemning cat. Grey clouds blocked the sun, and thunder rolled in the distance, but that was normal in Brimstone, Horror.

C. RAE D'ARC

My neighborhood was quiet. Maybe too quiet. I hurried back to my trailer, avoiding the suspicious eyes that peered between the broken blinds of trailer 14008. I specifically waited until my roommates left for work before retrieving the despised envelope. The gossip was bad enough without anyone knowing that the last of the Chase family named his fiancé as his sole inheritor. No one needed to tell me that I didn't deserve Sean's inheritance. I already knew.

With a deep breath, I lied to myself one more time—Sean's death wasn't my fault. There was nothing else I could have done.

Stories of people becoming disfigured by their lies caused me to check myself: no warts on my long fingers, my nose was still small, nothing more than the usual pimple on my wide cheek-bones, and no new bumps on my head. I pulled my bangs across my face to analyze them. My hair was still black as night and too short to tie into a ponytail. Good.

Reassured, I made another scan of my paint-peeling neighborhood. A loose gate squeaked on its hinges, and yellow smoke blew from trailer 15025's chimney. That probably wasn't good. I quickly crossed the threshold into the safety of my shared trailer and locked my front door behind me. As always, I double checked the lock.

All my lights were on and doors were wide open because Hauntings liked to hide in the dark and behind closed doors. I would remove the doors altogether, but they were also barriers from axes if necessary. My lights were updated every year, so if they flickered or fused, then I knew it was a direct warning.

I dropped the impersonal notices to become a forgotten pile of papers on the laminate kitchen counter and opened the manila envelope. Inside was a bank receipt for Sean's transfer of funds, affirming my new wealth. Each and every penny of

DON'T DATE THE HAUNTED

it taxed my peace of mind. The inheritance was an unwelcome condolence. I didn't want money; I wanted Sean back.

Phrases from my brother's survival book warned, *Don't give anyone motivation to murder you (AKA: the seven deadly sins), by having lump sums of money or too attractive boy/girlfriends.*

How many of those deadly sins took the lives of people closest to me? Sean. My brother, Oz. Even my parents were dead long before I had the chance to know them. A dozen other names flashed through my memory—people who almost survived Hauntings with me, but made mistakes at the wrong time.

Like every resident in Horror, I'd been plagued by Hauntings since I was a child. They ranged from the undead, cursed, monsters, and ghosts to the everyday person gone mad. They struck every six to twelve months and went dormant (to return with more strength later) if they weren't destroyed within a couple weeks. In a way, Hauntings were like final exams. Lots of Horrors relaxed and hardly thought about them until cramming time. A few others, like Oz and me, prepared all year-round.

I survived by following my brother's rules to avoid Hauntings or by having support when evasion was impossible. A few of my personal encounters included sadist foster parents, a werewolf, and unknown demons who murdered my brother.

Five months after the Haunting that killed Sean, my reprieve guarantee was almost over.

A casual glance at the counter mess of papers brought another letter to my attention. Hidden between the folds of a sale circular, it now poked free. The envelope was small, with my name and no return address.

My body tensed into alert mode as my mind echoed again with my brother's voice, *Never ignore anonymous threats from emails, letters, or phone calls. They're the first signs of a Haunting.*

3

C. RAE D'ARC

I opened the envelope with my dagger and pinched the sides inward, careful not to touch the possibly cursed contents. A letter fluttered to the floor. The typed message on lined paper was worse than I feared.

ENJOY YOUR INHERITANCE WHILE YOU CAN.

My blood chilled as I checked the front and back. Nothing else. Every Haunting had its own signature, such as calling cards, certain omens, or specific displays of its victims. This one chose to print its capitalized font on lined paper that was heavily water-damaged.

I flipped open my cell phone and called a housing agent. No one was supposed to know about my inheritance from Sean. That detail would only fuel the black widow rumors. Neighbors ignored my statement of innocence from the Haunting Investigations Unit, a specialized task force that recorded and neutralized the aftermath of Hauntings. The gossip was already bad enough to trigger thoughts of fleeing Brimstone. The hate mail raised my urgency. I needed to run as far away and as fast as possible. My only hope was to escape before the Haunting matured.

Flight first, Oz told me. *If you can't outrun it, then fight it. Learn all you can to fight Hauntings, but never go looking for them. Hunters almost always die, and Hauntings will find you, sure enough.*

A voice recording greeted me.

"Thank you for calling Haunt-Free Housing. 'We help you live.' If you have concerns about your lighting, creaky floors, plumbing, or other fixtures, please press one. If you have questions regarding past residents of your home, deceased or otherwise, press two. If you would like us to send a team to remove Haunted items..."

I studied the cockled threat while waiting for my option. I wasn't ready for another Haunting. If this new Haunting sent me threats before my reprieve ended, it was bound to be terrible by the time it arrived. I needed to get away, but to where? I had no direction without Sean or Oz. No family ties or reasons to stay in Brimstone. Or even Horror.

My head lifted at the conclusion.

Sean and I had been saving money to emigrate from Horror. His inheritance plus my own earnings as a hotel maid meant I had enough for an airplane ticket and a little to spare. I could go anywhere. The whole world of Novel was open to me.

Then, "If you want to talk with an agent about a new residency, press six."

I pressed six.

"Please hold while we transfer you to our next available agent."

A busy beep accompanied my thoughts. I paced down my trailer and checked the bedrooms and bathroom to make sure no surprises were inside or eavesdropping. I shared the larger bedroom with Gretta because Caroline wanted the single room to fill with her sewing/knitting/crocheting supplies. Also, I preferred to have a roommate for extra security.

I was going to miss living here with the sisters. Last year had been a real blessing when I turned eighteen and was kicked out of the orphanage. Gretta and Caroline were smart about Hauntings, but they wouldn't move with me so I could avoid one. That meant starting over in a new town with new roommates. Ugh.

Where should I go to escape a Haunting? Outside of Horror for the first time? I didn't know enough about Western and Childrens to thoroughly consider them. I imagined Sci-Fi, Mystery, and Fantasy were interesting places to visit, but I wouldn't want to live there. Thriller appealed the most to me, but Sean and I had planned to explore his childhood home in Romance.

A busy beep cut short as someone picked up my call. "This is Haunt-Free Housing. How can I help you live?"

"Hi, I need to move. Do you know of a trustworthy residential agency in the Romance Region? Maybe, um, near Heartford?"

My heartbeat quickened with nerves as the housing agent paused. "Yes. Hold on, let me look that up for you."

If the world was an open book, I'd favor the Heartford chapter. Heartford University was where Sean's parents had taught before coming to Brimstone as medical humanitarians during the zombie outbreak three years ago. Sean's inspiration and hand-me-down medical knowledge rekindled my hope after Oz's death. I was tired of so-called friends who wanted a "pansy" to sacrifice when a Haunting struck. I dreamed of being the medic that everyone relied on, and to do more than simply survive as my brother taught. I wanted to help others survive as a paramedic. Sean and I enrolled in the university's renowned online medical program, and I hoped a transfer to campus would be simple.

I could research residential agencies online, but when considering the many unknowns of a new home—on a new continent, no less—I wanted a referral from the most Haunting-conscious real estate agency in Horror.

Haunt-Free Housing gave me a number for Regent Retail, which I scribbled down and dialed after a "Thanks. Bye." I needed to act before doubts changed my decision. Instead of a dial tone, smooth jazz greeted my ear.

What the horror?

My doubts intensified.

Could I really escape a Haunting by moving halfway across Novel? As a born and raised Horror, I never traveled internationally because of the expense. Boats were often shipwrecked or haunted, and pricey airplanes were few and far between. Also, Oz taught me, *A known enemy is easier to handle than the unknown friend or foe.*

As much as Heartford University appealed to me, my cultural knowledge about Romance was limited to movies, books, and Sean's stories. I knew their big life "problems" were generally emotional and didn't stem from demons. Their relationship dilemmas seemed like the opposite of Hauntings. Sure, *The Phantom of the Opera* mishap occurred in Romance, and Sean said there were groups of Romantics attracted to the paranormal. That made no sense to me. I hoped to avoid those in Heartford, since it was in Romance's Contemporary region.

The voice of a young woman interrupted the smooth jazz prelude. "Hello, thank you for calling Regent Retail! My name is Michelle, how may I assist you?" She spoke as though she'd had one cup of coffee too many. I could practically hear her plastered smile through the phone.

"Um, hi, Michelle? I think I want to move to a place near Heartford University, but I have a lot of requirements."

"Oh, I know, don't we all?" She giggled like she inferred some other meaning from the phrase. "Tell me about your dream home."

"Well, I'm moving alone, so I need a place with at least two roommates." I'd been single most of my life, but that sentence was an unpleasant reminder of my failed marriage security with Sean. I allowed myself a deep breath then surged on. "I want a place that requires a clean background check. It needs to be one level—no stairs, no attics, no basements. It also needs to be new so that flooring, plumbing, and doors don't break. Somewhere with a community shower and bathroom would be best."

With each requirement, Michelle replied with a quick "Hm-hmm," or "Okay," but as my list grew, she sounded more hesitant and unsure. I knew my list was unusual, even among Horrors, but I wouldn't reject my brother's research and experiences. At least I left out my requests for sparse mirrors and reliable door locks. Those were easy to remove and replace on my own.

"Ideally," I continued, "it would have two or three entrances and exits, and locking windows in each room. Please no cursed items, toys, or pictures left behind by previous owners. I don't want anything on clearance. I'll pay more for an unhaunted house with reliable cell phone service and WiFi, away from the woods and surrounded by good neighbors." Unlike the cabin with the basement laboratory, where I rescued Sean from the experiments of a mad scientist.

Silence. I worried when people were too quiet on the phone. Was she still there? Had she been taken over by a Haunting?

"Soooo, I don't know what you mean by 'unhaunted.'" Michelle sounded wary, as if *I* was the Haunting. "Like, if a building is condemned from lack of maintenance?"

"If it fits all my other requirements, it shouldn't be haunted."

"What," she snorted, "are you from Horror or something?"

"Yeah. I'm calling from Brimstone."

Silence again.

What happened? Did I give away my current location and future plans to a Haunting?

"Oh," she said. Phew. "That explains your accent."

Accent? I never thought of my hushed tones as an accent. Maybe because my voice didn't ooze with smiles like hers? Maybe she couldn't think of a less offensive way to say, "You're one of those low-class, low-world people who had outcasts and prisoners for great-great-grandparents."

DON'T DATE THE HAUNTED

"What of it?" I would have responded. "That's what makes us survivors."

"Well," Michelle said, slowing her chatter like this was her first time thinking before speaking, "I hope this is a good move for you, and you leave your Hauntings behind."

Me too. I planned to escape my unknown Haunting by surrounding myself with unknown people who either despised or pitied me for my nationality. I hoped it was worth it.

Michelle cleared her throat with a rat squeak, then continued with less enthusiasm, "The cheapest housing in Heartford is—"

"Money isn't an issue," I said. Words I never expected to say. "Again, I'm willing to pay more for something that fits my list."

"Oh, okay. Then, about your dream house…there aren't any rambler houses in Heartford, but what about the Greek Dorms? They're on South Campus and were recently renovated. They require background checks and have many of your other, um, requests. They're three stories high, but don't have any basements or attics. I don't think you'll find any single-story apartments or homes near the university. You know, prime real estate next to campus—if you can't build out, then build up."

"I'll manage—" I grimaced "—if I can board on the second floor and it's not too high to jump from the window or porch. Nobody died before the dorms were renovated, right?"

"Uh, what? Of course not! Why would you think—"

"Never mind, it's great." I cut her off before she accused me of insanity. "How are they with accepting transfer students? I need to move as soon as possible."

"I can email you a link to their websites and applications," she said. "Could I get your email address, then?"

"Yeah." I gave it to her, then thanked her for her housing suggestions.

"Of course," she said. "I can see what else matches your requests, but I highly recommend the dorms. I graduated from Heartford last year and loved the dorm social life. It's where I met my husband, after all."

"Thanks. I'll look for the emails," I said, and hung up.

That was when the reality of my decision struck me with full force. I was moving to Heartford in Contemporary, Romance. Had I gone mad?

First things first, I prepared my emergency pack with pepper spray and a fully charged taser.

Chapter 2

RUNNING

*Always wear clothes you can run in
When you're running, don't get distracted
Have basic coordination and cardio skills
If you fall down, get right back up
Have a clumsy dumb friend (to take the falls for you)*

- Oz's Haunting Survival Book

Panic gripped my throat every time I considered my choice to leave Horror. I only moved without Oz twice before. First, during my forced relocation to the local orphanage after Oz's death, then a year later when I turned eighteen and moved in with Caroline and Gretta. Another year later, I planned to move to a new city on a completely new continent without knowing a single soul. My best source of comfort was to prepare for anything and everything.

For some reason, the godly Supernaturals kept me in their favor as I made rearrangements. I quit my job at the Brimstone Hotel and my manager was happy enough that I hadn't randomly disappeared like so many of her employees. Not only was I accepted into the dorms, but also Heartford University campus. They said they didn't normally accept students this close to the beginning of the semester, but as an international transfer student, they made an exception.

C. RAE D'ARC

When I wasn't packing my limited belongings, I passed the time by running to my local church and self-defense dojo. The jog refreshed my mind, my priest refreshed my spirit, and the dojo refreshed my body. Sleepless nights made the exercise difficult. The passing of each night increased my anxiety about preparing for Romance, Heartford campus, my new home, my new roommates...

I checked the mail after my morning runs for a second warning, but my unknown threat was silent during the week before my move. The silence probably meant I was still safe, and able to avoid it. Whatever it was.

Instead, I received a funeral notice for one of Sean's roommates. Sad to say, I wasn't surprised. He hadn't been the brightest bulb on the block. His death by anaconda Haunting was proof. Everyone knew the nearby river was infested, yet he went fishing anyway.

Gretta and Caroline noticed my preparations to leave. They offered to help me pack and to talk down the gossipers. They assumed the rumors of my black widow status were driving me away. I didn't correct them. Gretta asked about my destination, and I answered with vague half-truths, aching to say more. They were decent friends who actually tried to make meaningful relationships despite the inevitability of death and goodbyes. I couldn't involve them in the Haunting that I intended to escape, especially during Caroline's current Haunting with a barber who had scissors for fingers. The less they knew, the better.

I left a thank you note on the table to wish them well. *Always part ways with people and places on good terms,* Oz taught me. Would I miss Gretta's dry humor and Caroline's random trivia as much as I missed Oz's blank stares of quiet understanding, or Sean's easy smile? Probably not. Still, I cleared my throat of a growing lump as I left my trailer for the last time with my emergency holster bag strapped around my leg, one roller suitcase, and a carry-on backpack.

A small bus drove me from Brimstone to the International Airport of Inferno. I decided to fly because planes were statistically less haunted than boats. If they were cursed with more than gremlins, planes rarely survived for another voyage.

The security entrance to the six-gate airport didn't help alleviate my worries.

"Miss," the bored security administrator said while scanning my bag, "you need to check these items."

"Which items?" I asked.

The administrator opened my emergency pack to remove my taser, revolver, and spare bullets. With a heavy sigh, he continued to unpack my wooden and silver stakes, then my keychain of various religious symbols, pack of matches, pepper spray, and aspergillum.

"Our commercial planes are well equipped for emergencies and Hauntings," he said, then gestured to the holy water dispenser. "Is this full? You can't take liquids on the plane."

My heart sank with worry. "You want me to dump out holy water blessed by the Bishop of Brimstone?" He blessed me with a farewell the day before, and I prayed to the Supernaturals that I could keep the blessing for my journey ahead.

With another tired sigh, the administrator leafed through my brother's survival book, then returned it to my emergency pack with my chalk and bag of salt. "The water device holds less than eight fluid ounces. Put this," he gestured to the aspergillum, "in a plastic bag, then put the rest in your checked luggage."

"Alright," I muttered, unhappy to part with my tools but grateful he hadn't thrown them away. He watched as I followed his instructions, then glanced again at my ticket.

"International flight?" he asked.

"Yeah."

"You'll need to complete the Hauntings examination." He gestured to the side where a woman stood at a boxy computer. A security officer loomed nearby with a heavy-duty rifle. The woman asked for my identification and passport, grimacing with pure jealousy. She probably had plans to travel Novel, but never ventured farther than Horror even with her employee discount.

"Pansy Finster," she confirmed, "please describe your last Haunting."

A small shudder escaped me. "Do I need to?"

"Hauntings lose power outside of Horror," she explained with a dull drone, "but will cross the oceans to follow someone they're currently haunting. To minimize conflicts, we must censor our international flights."

Right. I sent a silent prayer to the Supernaturals that my unknown Haunting threat wouldn't follow me to Romance. "My last Haunting was Dr. Hyde, an experimental scientist who tried to give people kinetic powers by fusing them with poltergeists." I considered how much to say, then swallowed down the emotions that came with the memories. "We started with three of us; me, Sean Chase, and our friend Blake Washington." Some friend he was. He convinced Sean (who then convinced me) to go *looking* for a Haunting because we had gone almost a year without one, and neither of us wanted a Haunting during our high school graduation or following wedding.

"We went camping in the Forgotten Forest," I said. We broke every rule in my brother's book. No wonder it turned to disaster. "Blake disappeared the second night. We looked for him, and caught the trail of Dr. Hyde. Then Sean was taken. I found the doctor's cabin and the basement laboratory. Blake was a possessed corpse, and...Sean was strapped to a gurney."

DON'T DATE THE HAUNTED

I trembled to remember. "Dr. Hyde chased us as we escaped. I shot him in the head and we turned on the sprinkler system to destroy his poltergeist. His body and cabin were burned by the Hauntings Investigation Unit."

"When was it?"

"Five months ago," I said.

She nodded at her computer screen. "Yep, that's what the HIU report says. Thanks for confirming that you're currently in abatement. I need a finger prick."

The security officer with the rifle straightened with particular interest in our next exchange. The abnormally hairy man behind me scratched behind his ear like a nervous dog. I offered my pinky for her to jab with a small needle. She smiled like a satisfied vampire. Whether she smiled for the enjoyment of causing me pain or for the blood that oozed from my skin, I couldn't tell.

"Alive and human," she declared, and the security officer relaxed. The woman waved me onward with a spiteful, "Enjoy your flight."

I clutched my nearly empty emergency pack as I waited at the barren gate terminal. The lights flickered every time a plane lifted from the runway, and no one made eye contact—even the two employees behind the singular shop for snacks and travel gear.

I joined a dozen wealthy emigrants on the small and turbulent propeller plane. Hairy man not included. Based on their formal clothes and various physical features, I guessed none of the other passengers were local Horrors. A collective sigh released as the wheels left the ground. Three people with Sci-Fian tablets cheered. Two others in ripped and bloodied clothes openly sobbed.

For the duration of the flight, I stared out the window, amazed by the views and this sudden change in my life. I had a layover in Mystery, but didn't see much from within the airport. What I did see didn't make sense. Their exit signs ended with question marks. I wanted to grab a late lunch, but the meals were described by only clues. After a bit of problem solving and investigating, I bought a "non-vegetarian, includes gluten and lactose" item: a spam sandwich with sliced cheese. I went through a similar deduction process to find my next flight to Heartford, Contemporary, Romance.

The Romantic airplane was unlike any I'd seen in Horror. It could accommodate over a hundred passengers, and every seat was luxurious, with puffy cushions and computer hookups. I still couldn't relax. I worried I'd lose my luggage, or the person next to me who attempted too much small talk would hijack the flight with a bomb threat. I glanced through Oz's book every ten minutes, checking that it hadn't been stolen or switched with a fake.

Once we landed in Romance, my eyes weren't wide enough to take in the scenes. People lined the terminal exit with signs, flowers, or balloons to greet specific people. I wandered toward the baggage claims, trying to hide my embarrassment from the blatant displays of affection. I couldn't tell if it was a holiday or the result of a mass Haunting attack as emotions gushed over the top. Everyone either wore the cheesiest of grins for a reunion or cried shamelessly as they waved goodbye.

The people themselves appeared alien to me. At five feet and five inches, I was tall among Horror women but became average in Romance. Romantic women were somehow extra curvy with hair that tumbled past their shoulders like soft curls of light. The men's average body mass jumped as many of them resembled the bodybuilder next door (like Sean) or the pompous, rich numbskull. Their skin tones were also redder than those of Horror. These people were blanched pink or sun baked like ready-to-eat meat.

As a whole, I concluded that these were the first people to die in Hauntings. Or they miraculously survived with a lot of luck and the help of others who knew better.

Eager to escape the crowds waiting for a massacre, I snatched my checked luggage then rushed to the exit. I reloaded my emergency pack with my tools and grabbed a city map. From there, I determined the easiest route to Heartford University was via the city bus. Of course, taxis were faster, but I didn't trust them when traveling alone.

I wanted Sean beside me to give me a tour. We were supposed to come here together. Instead, I stared out the window again as the city of Heartford, Romance, swallowed me.

The tallest buildings in Horror were usually fancy hotels with "fourteen" floors and hordes of Hauntings. Homes were wooden or paneled, and businesses were concrete or brick.

Skyscrapers built Heartford's horizon like mountains of unbroken glass and unchipped stone. The structures towered and gleamed in the pink sunset, reflecting lights and colors like a hall of mirrors. A strange artistic beauty emanated from it all. Energy surged through the city, but not with terrified adrenaline. Instead, the lights and activities boasted an excitement and thrill for life.

I wondered if, how, or when I'd ever get used to it.

Pushing the button for the university stop, I exited the bus to find myself surrounded by more unfamiliar buildings. I checked the street signs to confirm the address, surprised by the odd names: Gallant Street and Crossed Lover's Road. My new home was on Gallant Street, but how far down? A small panic built in my chest as I wondered where to go. Tall buildings stabbed the sky in the distance.

C. RAE D'ARC

To my right, red flower bushes framed the monument sign for Heartford University: Where Hearts and Minds Grow Together. It stood in the middle of a too-perfect lawn like a tombstone. Old apartments lined the opposite side of the street with balconies that were far too easy to climb. Down my left, bookstores advertised themselves with colors bright enough to blind someone. A couple cafés and sit-down restaurants spotted the area. I'd never seen such old buildings with cheery atmospheres and maintained decorations.

Every other business catered to weddings. Creepy mannequins modeled ridiculous gowns and tuxedos. The white cakes had to be fake. They were monstrously huge with enough frosting to cause a heart attack. Then the jewelry shops begged to be burglarized, from their simple security to oversized sparkles.

I remembered Sean's elaborate traditions and perspective about marriage. Apparently he downplayed them for me.

My eyes combed the streets for someone to give me directions. Two houses away, a couple stood at a doorway, taking way too long to say goodbye. I didn't mean to stare like a creeper but had to be sure their passionate embrace was with consent. A street musician with a saxophone performed at the next intersection. Either the music wasn't hypnotic, or I was too far away for it to influence me. Down the block, an elderly gentleman shuffled toward a café.

Be wary of kids, twins, and old people (especially when they wear costumes or face paint), Oz warned.

The man ahead didn't wear face paint, and his "costume" was a long brown suit coat with a top hat and cane. He seemed like a better opportunity to catch some directions and possible local gossip. Another rule of survival reminded me, *Leave when your new house has bad rumors.*

DON'T DATE THE HAUNTED

"Excuse me!" I shouted and ran up to the man. "Do you know where the p—uh, the p-si—the P-S-I Dorm is?"

"Why, certainly, young miss," he said with a gentle smile. Too gentle. Too kind. Was it a trap? I gripped my emergency pack, just in case. "You need only to travel two more blocks down this road, toward the Tower." He pointed down the street at a singular skyscraper. "As you reach the Tower, you'll pass the dormitory on your left."

"Thanks," I said, then headed in that direction. I checked over my shoulder if he followed or watched me. He didn't, but continued on his way.

Okay, so maybe it wasn't a trap, but a warning. Elderly people weren't common in Horror Zone since few people survived that long. Then, they either served as sources for information/gossip/warnings, or the Hauntings themselves.

He said 'to-ward' with two syllables. Was there a hidden message in that? To ward off the Tower?

As I reached the Tower's base, I stared up at the dominating giant. The Tower was evil alright. The building didn't appear haunted, but imposed its shadow for two blocks east. All the homes and apartments nearby climbed no higher than four floors, but the Tower went at least a dozen. It had a fresh coat of paint, though I hoped they fired whoever chose the color scheme. Bright orange highlighted the building's balconies and corners against a gray base. A sign hung from a balcony, advertising office rooms and a penthouse for rent.

At least I wasn't living there. I turned my attention across the street, toward my new home. A lush lawn with white aspen trees lined the sidewalk, and purple pansies framed the three-story brick building.

A tall blonde girl sat on the entrance porch bench and waved at me with a grin as big as an evil clown's.

Okay. Now I was officially creeped out.

Chapter 3

LOCATION

Running upstairs to escape will only get you trapped
Basements and attics are *off limits*
Houses that are especially on sale or clearance are probably Haunted
Know the past of your residency—who lived (or possibly died) there before you, and what's underneath the foundation
Beware of neighborhoods that seem *too* clean or perfect

- *Oz's Haunting Survival Book*

My heartbeat quickened with the blonde's enthusiasm as I forced myself to cross the street.

"Ohm'gosh—are you Pansy Finster?" she asked.

"Yes—"

"Welcome to Heartford—I know you'll absolutely love it here!" She spoke without pausing for breath as she threw her arms around to hug me. I stiffened in response. "My name's Tiffany—I'm your Dorm President—I can't believe you only have two bags—they must be stuffed full—here lemme help—ohm'gosh!" She yanked my suitcase with unnecessary force. "That's much lighter than I thought it would be—or my workout's actually working—hah!"

She continued, but I didn't hear. The main entry to my new home had me stopped cold.

DON'T DATE THE HAUNTED

"What's that?"

"What's what—I can give you a tour—do you wanna tour?" Tiffany asked.

"What is that?" I dropped my bag and pointed at the large symbol above the doorway. It was a curly 'U' with a line down the middle.

"Oh—that's the Greek letter for 'Y'—pronounced as 'sigh'—welcome to the Psi Dorms!" she said. She set down my luggage to throw her arms up in the shape of a "Y" as she announced the title.

"It looks like the Devil's pitchfork," I said.

Tiffany laughed and picked up my luggage again. "Ohm-'gosh—I never thought of it that way—hah!—There's nothing to worry about—come on in!" She carried my belongings over the threshold, and what could I do about it? I traded one Horror for another.

This one was brightly lit and colorful like the too-perfect neighborhoods that hid controlling secrets behind false smiles. Was Tiffany secretly a plotting tyrant behind her ditziness? She led me through the dorm main entry which was spacious and decorated in the fancy Contemporary fashions. We ascended a single flight of stairs to room 201.

To my surprise, Tiffany pulled out a key of her own. "You're in the Presidential Suite—hah!—In other words—you're a roommate with me! Come on in—we have a key for you inside."

I poked my head through the doorway and found myself in a newly refurbished kitchen/dining/living room. The front wall was lined with a wide bookshelf and a flat-screen TV, complete with a movie player. There was a fluffy pink loveseat and a matching sofa. It seemed free of Hauntings, but I made a mental note of all the lightbulbs. I didn't know how reliable they were, so I planned to make my own updates.

Tiffany rattled on about the history of the dorms, and I listened for any deaths or tragedies that could spur a Haunting. It was happily uneventful.

She continued on a personal level, "This is my third year here—I love this place so much—I could stay here forever—There are three bedrooms, three toilets, and three shower stalls for all eight of us—so we'll have to share a bit—We plan to meet once a week to discuss events, needs, and updates—are Saturday lunches good for you?—I hope so—they work for everyone else."

I nodded mutely, surprised that she stopped to breathe.

"Perfect!" She clapped her hands together like she was about to start a cheer routine. Then, she pointed to the single door on the right. "I'm in the two-bedroom with Marcellette, so I'm here if you have any questions."

Tiffany carried my suitcases to the room on the far left. Two girls were already inside, decorating their sections of the room. They took the bunk bed, leaving me the single against the opposite wall. "This is the Freshman Room—you're with Emma Morales —who's a local Contemporary—and Miss Appleton from Regency." Tiffany gestured as introduction. "I need to talk to the dorm manager—make yourself at home!" She walked away. I analyzed my new roommates for any signs of Hauntings.

Miss Appleton wore a poofy baby-pink dress that shuffled with her movement. A matching shawl and ribboned hat sat on her desk. I couldn't help but think what a terrible outfit it was to escape from Hauntings. Her bottom bunk was tightly arranged with lace and patch quilts.

Emma, on the other hand, had long, bottle-blonde hair that was curled like the Romantics on TV. She wore tight clothes that were more trendy and expensive than my whole wardrobe. I pegged her as the type of girl who would be more concerned by a blood stain or sliced fabric than the knife wound itself. Her top bunk was a mess of blankets as she used her ladder to pin up pictures of shirtless men and famous Romantics.

I already knew my bedding organization would be closer to Emma's than Miss Appleton's, minus the posters. My spot was shoved in the corner and emitted an odd smell. Then, a flush of water sounded behind the wall.

Ugh, I was next to the toilets?

I missed my trailer with Caroline and Gretta.

Setting my luggage on my bed, I considered how to make the best out of the new situation. There was no way I could return to Horror with a Haunting brewing for me. Also, I already paid tuition and rent for a semester. Despite my first impressions, I wanted this to work. I wanted Heartford University's prestigious paramedics classes. I wanted to make new friends so I wouldn't be vulnerable to Hauntings.

I tried a friendly wave to my new roommates. "Hi," I began. Emma acknowledged me with a curt nod as Miss Appleton pinched her skirts and dipped into a small curtsy. An actual curtsy?

Unsure how to respond, I simply said, "My name's Pansy Finster."

Miss Appleton shrieked. I jumped and glanced around for Hauntings, but her blue eyes literally twinkled.

"Another flower! My name is Miss Heather Appleton. I am positively delighted to make your acquaintance!"

Right. I forgot that pansies were originally flowers, not sissy-pants. People usually trash-talked my name until they learned how hard I worked to survive.

She squealed again. "May we become the best of friends!"

"Nice…to meet you too," I said.

Emma frowned. "Then why can't we call you Heather? Miss Appleton is such a mouthful."

Miss Appleton winced at the flippant usage of her first name, then tapped her forehead as if to smooth the wrinkles.

"Right," she said. "Contemporaries tend to use their first names. If we are to be roommates, that practically makes us sisters. Yes, you may call me Heather," the Regency girl declared, gathering her poise again.

"Cool." Emma shrugged.

"So," I started, "you're both local Romantics?"

"I'm as local as it gets," Emma said, struggling with her outdated poster of Carter Maguire. I frowned at the smaller, updated picture of him—middle-aged, with a rough scissor job that cropped out his family. Emma continued without notice, "My mama and little sis live in downtown Heartford. I always knew I'd come here for school, but I would've loved to go to the University of New Angeles."

"The party school?" Heather asked.

Emma ignored her and continued, "I'm still undecided on my major. I'm thinking of something in Communications, but maybe photography, or modern dance."

"Huh, those sound fun," I said, then turned to Heather. "What about you?"

"My family," she said, transferring set after set of extra long underclothing to her drawers, "has lived in the community of Ferndean, Regency, for over five generations. By attending a Contemporary university, I have followed the forward-minded footsteps of my elder sister, who currently lives in Pemberly City. My mother would prefer that I obtain my MRS degree, and though the idea is not entirely distasteful, my hopes are to major in Home Economics."

"MRS?" I asked.

Emma leaned over her shoulder to explain. "Mrs. degree. Her mom wants her to get married."

I blinked, stunned. Sure, there were a lot of smart men at university, but what an expensive way to find a permanent Haunting partner. I remembered Sean's idealistic perspective of marriage, and our debate about the ceremony. He wanted a grand celebration that would have attracted all kinds of attention. Eventually, I convinced him that in Horror, the smaller the wedding, the better.

"So," Emma bent over her suitcase to reveal ample cleavage, "what about you? You have an interesting accent."

I nodded, accepting the fact that my voice was significantly more hushed and serious than these loud and dramatic Romantics. "I just flew in from Horror."

Heather gasped and Emma did a double take.

"Really?" Emma asked. "Are you, like, a refugee? Isn't it hard to get out of there?"

I hoped to keep Sean's inheritance a secret so the last penny would go toward my education. I said, "Our airports aren't as elaborate as yours, but we have them."

Heather cheered. "How fascinating! You mean to say that Horror has access to Contemporary technology? I was under the impression that most Horror towns are...well, impoverished."

Unsure what she meant by that, I said, "We had what we needed to survive depending on the type of Hauntings nearby. My brother and I moved around a lot to avoid Hauntings, but I spent the last three years in Brimstone, if you know where that is."

Both of the Romantics shook their heads.

I tried, "It's about fifty miles west of Inferno," and their eyes widened with recognition.

"Inferno?" Heather repeated. "The city discovered by Dante? Oh, Miss Finster, I have heard the most dreadful stories about Horror. Such terrible tales of creatures and tragedies! Please say they are fictional and dramatized."

Still stunned by the idea of this Regency girl, I wasn't sure what to say. I was about to quote my brother, to *Never discount a story, because Hauntings attack doubters*, but I was cut off by Emma.

"Those stories are just made up to scare people. I'm sure Horror is super exaggerated. There's no way it's that terrible," she smirked. Yep, she would be one of the first to die in a Haunting if I couldn't help.

"In a way," I agreed. "Horror was a good place to live."

Emma smirked deeper, as if to say, "Of course I'm right."

I added, "Largely in part because the locals with any brains knew that anyone cocky or unnecessarily rude would be knocked off."

Emma narrowed her eyes at me.

"Knocked off?" Heather echoed. "How horrid!"

I shrugged. "It wasn't so bad as long as you followed the rules. But after my fiancé died, I was—"

"You were engaged?" Emma gaped. Her poster of Landon Carter fell without her notice. "And your fiancé died?"

"What a terrible tragedy—Oh!" Heather squealed, and I quickly checked behind myself for Hauntings. Nothing. She squealed with excitement? "Romances almost always bloom after such tragedies!" she said. "How long ago was his passing? Are you still in grieving?"

I frowned. "It was five months ago. If death caused me grief for that long, I'd always be grieving."

"But he was your fiancé," Emma said. "You say that like you didn't love him."

DON'T DATE THE HAUNTED

To their surprise, I shrugged. "I've never been in love, but Sean was my best friend, and we shared mutual trust and appreciation. That was all I wanted in marriage."

The two Romantics gaped. Emma recovered first as she put on a game face, like I'd just offered her a challenge. "Oh, girl, we're gonna fix that."

Heather giggled. "Don't you worry, dear, you may acclimate soon enough."

I stood silently dumbfounded. This place was crazy.

"Speaking of Romances," Emma said, glancing between Heather and me, "I need to teach you two how to do your makeup."

I expressed my confusion with a simple, "Huh?"

Heather blushed and fingered a curl of her muddy-brown hair. "I have yet to explore such Contemporary fashions."

Emma's expression changed to almost pity. "You both look so, um, natural."

I could tell she tried hard to make it sound like a compliment, but I knew she meant "bland."

"I wear enough to keep my face clear," I said. Makeup was a tool to attract and distract masculine Hauntings. Otherwise, I kept mine light because mirrors revealed trouble.

As if the situation couldn't get worse, Heather pulled doll figurines from her luggage to arrange them on her pillows.

"What are those?" I asked.

"Oh, these are from Great-Grandmother Eyre. They are my prized possessions!"

"They'll possess you, is what you mean."

"Whoa!" someone said from behind. We all turned to see a new girl at the door. She had wild brunette hair and wore a multi-layered outfit that frayed like a witch's skirt. I couldn't tell if her style was supposed to be futuristic or vintage. "You're the new girl from Horror, right? Pansy? I'm Brooke Steamings, from Sci-Fi." Ah, that explained her nasal accent with strange intonations. "I've read about Horror," she said, "but you're in Romance now. Unless you brought a Haunting with you, dolls are just toys."

"These are hardly 'just toys,'" Heather corrected. "They are historical ornamented figurines."

"Um, sure." Brooke blinked with a smile.

I stared at them suspiciously and wondered why my roommates were okay with those monstrosities in the bedroom. Emma raised an incredulous eyebrow at me while Heather arranged her dolls with a slightly guarded expression, like she was half prepared to launch herself in front of them if I chose to stake their faces. So much for making friends.

"You know," Brooke said, "you should come with me to International Club. I think you'd like it."

"International Club?" I asked.

"Yeah, it's for transfer students, like us, who are adjusting to Romance. The first get-together's tonight. Why don't you come with me? That way I won't look like a total dweeb showing up by myself."

I hesitated. I'd need more than a counseling group to handle those dolls, but maybe I could meet other Haunting survivors there.

Brooke grinned. "Come on, you'll totally love it! I bet there'll be others from Horror, and you can share your culture-shock stories."

I weighed my options: stay there and debate common securities with my new roommates, or go to a public gathering in the dawning of night. Putting it that way, I'd choose to stay every time. But Brooke shouldn't venture out alone at night. I also considered the company I'd keep: two Romantics who probably didn't know the difference between a butcher and serial killer, or a Sci-Fian and other Horrors. I couldn't be

DON'T DATE THE HAUNTED

alone. I needed friends—people who'd actually have my back when trouble struck.

Chapter 4

FRIENDS

Never be alone
Keep family and loyal friends close
Don't ask new acquaintances too many questions (don't give them reasons to suspect you have outside motives)
Never figuratively turn your back on friends
Never literally turn your back on strangers and enemies

- *Oz's Haunting Survival Book*

Brooke tugged me toward the center of campus. "I really think you'll like it," she said. "University is already an astronomical change of lifestyle, and to think we're doing it on another continent! International Club is for people like us who are shifting gears not only to university life, but life in Romance too."

"What 'gears' did you have to shift?" I asked.

"The total lack of technology, for one thing," she laughed. "It still drives me haywire that the vehicles here can't fly or even travel through speed tubes. And it took a long time for my roommates to understand that I only rent computers from campus. I can't convince myself to depend on a personal machine."

"Why?" I asked.

"Because," she said, and turned to look at me directly, "computers almost always get too smart and take advantage of your information."

I thought for a moment. "Yeah, I can see that happening."

"Thank you!" She threw her hands in the air. "You have no idea how many times I had to explain it to Asher and Ruby!"

"Asher and Ruby?"

"My roommates," Brooke explained. "Fellow sophomores. You'll meet them soon enough."

"Oh," I said, filing the names of those in the bedroom across from mine. "Well, if dolls can go evil, why can't a computer?"

"Exactly, but here people plug in their information willy-nilly! I'm still adjusting too, but that's what culture change needs," she said with a shrug. "Just give it some time and talk it out with people. It takes humility to realize that your way isn't always the only or best way."

I nodded, though I was still convinced that Romance was merely a new Horror—a bizarre, pretentious type of Horror.

For some reason, I didn't feel nervous to walk around Heartford University at night. Maybe it was the friendly chatter of people strolling by. Maybe it was the light that flooded the sidewalks and windows. Maybe it was the bouncy music that blasted from unseen speakers in the distance. We walked between mowed lawns and patches of trees, passing several large buildings made of brick and white columns. Brooke pointed to them and explained their names and acronyms, but I forgot them instantly. I was too busy mapping the campus in my head, and—

Wait, we walked *toward* the commotion of sounds?

Slow, twangy music rang through the campus center's main hall. As we drew near, the music took a dramatic shift into a synthesized tune with a heavy beat.

"Ooh! I love this song!" Brooke grooved her body into dance-walking.

"You know it?"

"Yeah, it's super popular in Sci-Fi," she said.

We signed in at a booth and were given an introductory pamphlet about the club. The person at the booth wore a sticker that said, "Hi! My name is <u>Sharon</u>" with a clip-art sticker of kids.

"That's the club president," Brooke said to me. "She's from Childrens, and if you have any questions, you can ask her."

"Sure," I said, but couldn't think of where to start. I wrote "Pansy" on an introductory sticker and added the Horror Zone sticker of a bloody ax. The room was full of people, conversations, and laughter. I didn't need the stickers to see the variety of nationalities. Horror Zone wasn't a touristy place. People rarely visited due to the reputation of Hauntings and expensive return flights. It was already a shock to see so many cultures at once.

"Hey, look." Brooke pointed. "See the group of people wearing all black? I bet they're from Horror. Wanna go say hi together?"

Her finger was unnecessary to find the small group. They stood out like a black spot in a rainbow. There were only five of them among the throngs of people from Mystery and Childrens. I swallowed a bite of humble pie to realize that the university likely accepted my quick transfer to meet their minorities quota. I yearned to join the other Horrors, as their posture and mannerisms resembled my familiar closed skepticism. Except I couldn't see any of their faces.

Never approach someone if you can't see his/her face, Oz whispered from my memory.

"Maybe in a bit," I said.

DON'T DATE THE HAUNTED

"OK, then I'll introduce you to my friends first." She led me toward the center of the room. Only when she stopped did I realize the hodgepodge of people before me were in one group. There wasn't a single commonality between them.

"'Sup, Hank!" Brooke said to a guy in a cowboy hat. He was tall, with brawny arms, and had dusty brown hair with eyes to match. "It's super to see you! I wanna hear all about your summer job."

"Howdy, Brooke! It was dandy!" he said, and swept her into a muscular hug that probably smelled like hay.

"Brooke!" shouted a few others. There was a woman dressed in a long skirt and a white button-up like a classic grade-school teacher, and another girl who wore the trench coat of a private eye, but the colorful and bulky jewelry of a gypsy. It didn't make sense, so I assumed the second girl was from Mystery. Last, Brooke shared greetings with a man in the fashion of a medieval noble with his leather knee-high boots, blue embroidered tunic, and sleeveless cloak.

Brooke gestured to me, saying, "Everyone, this is Pansy. She's my new roommate from Horror."

"Well, ain't that somethin'?" the cowboy said with surprise. He nudged Brooke. "Ya tryin' to get us someone from every country? All we'd need now is someone from Thriller." He turned to me and reached out his hand. I accepted the handshake, impossible not to notice his rough calluses.

"I'm Hank, from Western," he said with a wink.

The secretive wink set my mind on alert. Nerved from his excessive friendliness, I said a simple, "Nice to meet you," and surveyed the rest of the group.

Next, the medieval noble held out his hand to me, which I took for a handshake. Instead, he kept his hand still while the rest of his body bent in a deep bow. He swept his cloak behind himself to keep it from touching the floor. I got a good view of his thick, dark-brown hair, immaculately parted at the side.

"Miss Pansy," he said. "I am Lord Theodor Fromm, the Trusted, second son of Duke Konrad Fromm of Margen, Fantasy."

I held back a sarcastic laugh. What a title. "The Trusted?" Thanks for telling me who *not* to trust. Especially a Lord. I bet he lived in a mansion with too many stairs, creepy historical portraits, and deathbeds from several generations.

He stood up again and his bluish-green eyes roamed over my face with a sense of curiosity. First the Westerner's wink, then the intense study from this Fantastic. It made me self-conscious and wonder if he also judged me for wearing minimal makeup.

"Do you believe in Love at First Sight?" he asked.

I blinked. Was that an attempt for a typical Romantic conversation? Unsure how to respond, I said, "Nnno," and slipped my hand from his. I figured love was like magic, or Sci-Fian technology. Some things simply didn't work in Horror, or at least not for me.

"Oh," the Fantastic said, a bit disappointed. "What if we introduce ourselves again?"

Hank burst into laughter, distracting Theodor and allowing me a chance to break away. I turned back to Brooke and tried to become instantly and heavily intrigued by her conversation with the school teacher about—toddlers? Ugh, creepy. *The more innocent something appears, the more likely it is to become haunted.*

In my lack of enthusiasm (and caution toward the two men) I overheard Hank slap Theodor the Trusted on the back.

"Smooth, partner. I ain't ever seen ya move so fast. Where'd ya dig up that pick up line?"

DON'T DATE THE HAUNTED

"My words were hardly a pick up," Theodor flustered. "I meant them entirely to become better acquainted. I just want to know what sets her apart from others."

Hank however, winked at his friend and tipped his hat. "Uh-huh, I get ya."

Theodor flustered some more and turned away.

Did he lie to cover his embarrassment? I kept him in my peripheral and watched for other signs of deceit. He stole a couple glances at me. Yep, I definitely wasn't about to trust "The Trusted."

The group of Horror students walked over and I saw their faces. No abnormal disfigurings or malicious expressions. They were clear of Hauntings as far as I could tell. I distanced myself from Brooke's awkward friends, and stepped beside their path.

"Hi, I'm Pansy." I waved.

"Pansy?" one of them scoffed. That was expected.

"Yeah, I'm from Brimstone." I reached out my hand for a shake. The closest student took it, but the rest lingered back.

Yes, these were my people—loyal and cautious to a fault. Finally, people I could talk to.

I mentally reviewed Oz's survival instruction: *When you feel safe with a group, tell them more about yourself (verifiable facts) to show your trust in them. Don't ask a lot of questions (don't give them reasons to suspect you have outside motives).*

I opened my mouth to say more, but the closest student beat me to the punch.

"You're in luck," he said. "We have an open slot in our branch since Isabella was taken by a Haunting."

"She did it for love," a girl said from the back.

The one who scoffed at my name scoffed again. "She was barely outta high school. *Everything* was for love, even inviting the Haunting here in the first place. What she lacked in brains she tried to compensate with drama."

The one who shook my hand shot him a glare. "Shut up, Tyler. I didn't like her much either, but don't speak ill of the undead."

"Plus," one of the girls snickered, "we all know you were jealous. Falling in love with a Haunting…" She and the other girls swooned. The two guys softened, like they imagined it too.

My mind barfed. Hauntings were meant for killing, not dating! Was this my fate if I stayed in Romance? I hoped not, but one point was sure: these were not my type of people.

I raised a hand in farewell. "Well, it was nice to meet you all. Maybe I'll see you in classes." I hoped that when I turned around this strange band wouldn't turn into monsters and come after me. As I did so, however, a worse fear depressed me.

I didn't even get along with the other Horrors. I was still alone.

Chapter 5

COMMON COURTESY

#1 Rule: Stay away from drugs, sex, and violence
Avoid angry drunks and those who do the above
Do to others what you want done to you, because what goes around *will* come back

- *Oz's Haunting Survival Book*

The next morning, I woke up to screaming. A whole women's chorus was in sheer terror. One voice screamed at a higher pitch, like a child's.

I bolted in a tired tumble from my bed, grabbing for my emergency pack. I fumbled a bit as my brain refused to wake up, despite the shrill screams.

My bleary eyes recognized Emma and Heather laying in their beds. Right, I now lived in a dormitory with Romantics. How could my roommates sleep through the tortured screams? Were they dead? I shook Heather's shoulders to wake her. "Get up! Don't you hear that? Who's screaming?"

She stirred with life, and I searched for the source of the screams. They seemed to come from behind the wall. In the bathroom? No, between the walls. How could so many people be shoved in such a small space? I'd scream too.

"We have to get them out!" I said, considering my desk as the heaviest object to throw and break the wall.

"Pansy, OMG?" Emma said, groggily. "Go back to sleep, it's just the water pressure in the pipes. Someone's taking a shower."

The screams leveled out to a single pitch, then shut off as the plumbing adjusted.

Supernaturals! That scared me! Was I supposed to thank my roommates for correcting me, or was I allowed to be annoyed by their laziness? Either way, I was less than excited to have these girls as my new roommates. They didn't seem like the type to become my next best friends and Haunting survivors.

The screaming plumbing was a bad start to my first day of classes.

Orphaned at four years old and bounced between foster homes like a virus, I never even dreamed about attending college until I met Sean. My goal to survive was enough of a daily challenge. Oz and I lived one day at a time, never expecting to see another.

Then, Sean opened my eyes to possibilities I never thought possible. Not only did he want to graduate high school, but he wanted to attend Heartford University, where his parents once taught medicine and health. He wanted to earn money not just to survive the day, but to leave Horror together. I only learned after his death that he had enough to travel alone, but he stayed until I could leave with him.

His death wasn't my fault, I lied again. Still...I lived his dream. He was dead while I attended Heartford University in Romance. I geared myself with my new minimalist backpack and no-games laptop to be the best student in Sean's honor.

My credits claimed Sophomore status, but my online education left me as campus fresh meat. Simple navigation was a challenge even with my nose shoved in a campus map. Heartford University was a whole town of brick and marble buildings. Somehow, none of the white wooden window

DON'T DATE THE HAUNTED

shutters were broken or hanging loosely in the non-existent wind. Ninety percent of the time I mixed which building was which, and all the pristine lawns looked the same—not a blade out of line. I frequently checked my compass as tall deciduous trees blocked my view ahead and behind. The feeling of insecurity gave me all the more reasons to carry my emergency pack everywhere.

The stares didn't help. Students and professors alike gave me wide eyes and double takes like they'd never seen a person from Horror before. Eyebrows raised and paths were cleared whenever I rummaged through my emergency pack in public. I was likewise confused by the common purses full of makeup and touchscreen cell phones.

The classes were another issue. Most classrooms only had one entry/exit. I worried I'd be surrounded by Hauntings, or we'd be locked inside while a raged killer made a break for the "Emergency Only" hatchet. My Nutrition 3010 and Nursing 2270 labs were even worse, with all the heavy equipment and pointed utensils.

My emergency pack only emphasized how ill-prepared I was for the real scare: information overload. Every class felt like a firehose of knowledge sprayed into my face. I couldn't imagine how they expected me to swallow all of it. Each of my professors seemed to think their course was the most important class ever. My class on pathophysiology (which actually could be life saving) had a list of books to buy with homework to do from each of these yet-to-be-purchased books. Couldn't I simply search online for symptoms of mononucleosis?

My Novel History 1501 professor introduced his class with, "If all you plan to do is sleep in my class, then don't bother coming."

"Oh good," Hank said from the seat next to me. "It's a good sign when they look dishoveled and smilin'. It means they're more in'erested in their subject than their looks."

Only then did I notice the professor's hair was a mess and clothes were hastily tucked in. I wanted to ask Hank if he meant "disheveled," but thought against correcting his Western accent.

I was surprised to recognize Hank in my last Monday class, then more surprised when he recognized me back. I hadn't considered our brief introductions to be memorable, but I wasn't about to complain. Even if he was a bit peculiar, I felt more secure to know someone in the room.

"The study of history is more involved than you may think," our professor continued. "It's a quest for fact when so much of Novel seems difficult to believe. You'll see in the syllabus that we'll read from the classic texts of *The Death of Arthur*, by The Round Table, *The Unfortunate Traveler* by Jack Wilton, and the autobiography of Robinson Crusoe. You may already own some of these, but I suggest getting the edition listed, since those include the analysis and editorial notes we will examine."

Hank leaned over again to whisper, "It can get perty expensive, but I also suggest ya get the class edition. It's a real pain stayin' on the same page when ya don't have the same version."

He winked, and I thanked him with a small smile. Would he be my new friend to survive Hauntings with me? I imagined his strength and Western survival knowledge could make him a helpful ally.

Slowly over the week, I familiarized myself with the campus grounds and new roommates. There wasn't a lot of time that first week for scoping out new friends. Sure, professors assigned lab partners and study groups, but loyal friends rarely came from forced alliances. True to Brooke's word, I soon met her roommates, Asher and Ruby. They were best friends majoring in biology, but their similarities ended there. Asher was a self-proclaimed introvert and native to Contemporary, Romance. She wore plain clothes over a comfortably round figure and let her long black hair fall flat.

Ruby, however, was a born and raised red-headed Western. She was 5-foot-nothing, but her active personality made sure that no one passed her without notice.

I also met Tiffany's roommate, Marcellette. Regardless of my efforts not to despise her, I failed so far. She introduced herself as the "Soon-to-be Lady Marcellette of Rochershire." Not only was she engaged and soon to reap the marriage securities that I'd been denied, but she was snooty about it. She flaunted her fiancé's status like she only cared for his money. Also, she constantly wore the expression of someone who stood over a decayed body, enjoyed the smell, and dared you to question her taste.

Tiffany was often gone for meetings as the Psi Dorm President, and Marcellette rarely came home between days with her fiancé. Ruby and Asher often took over the kitchen with their biology textbooks sprawling across the table while Ruby deep fried anything between meat pastries to ice cream. Brooke claimed real estate on the couch as she did homework while listening to synthesized music, then remained in place to play a first-person shooting game when she finished. Heather frequently left the dorm to return hours later with some useless decoration like fake flowers, a vase of fake flowers, or a picture of flowers in a vase. Emma spent most of her time chatting on her laptop or fancy phone while laying in bed like an underwear model waiting for a peeping Tom.

As for me, I crammed for my studies like my life depended on it. Who knew, maybe my life *did* depend on passing those classes. At least, I hoped my Nutrition class would cover how to identify poisons and counter them.

I didn't have any classes on the weekends, so my Saturdays were blank save for my dorm luncheons. Tiffany called everyone to the kitchen exactly at noon. I was afraid to procrastinate on my homework, but after staring at the same paragraph for half an hour, I realized a break could help.

Smells of cheese omelets with buttered toast greeted me from the dining area. When did I last eat a home-cooked meal? My shelves in Horror had been stocked with canned soups and MREs. In Romance, I found a liking to energy bars and grab-and-go produce. The fresh produce here was amazingly flavorful.

I sat between Heather and Brooke with Emma directly across, then waited for others to eat to make sure the food wasn't poisoned or some kind of trap. Tiffany, ever the cheerleader, sat at the head of the table and clasped her hands together at her chest.

"Welcome!" she began. "It's been a crazy week of getting to know everyone—but I'm sure by the end of the semester we'll all be best friends—as long as everyone's calendars are still clear for Saturday luncheons—we can plan to explore our favorite restaurants in town for following weeks—for some quick business there's been a misunderstanding about our hall's rules and regulations—so I'll read over them with everyone here—"

I already zoned out. The rules were posted near every entry/exit, and they were the basic living courtesies. If someone couldn't live even those simple rules ("Midnight Curfew" as the least of them) they'd be the first one dead in a Haunting.

Tiffany concluded her remarks by saying, "Since you're my roommates, people are gonna watch you and your example—Marcellette, are you listening?—Good, so no more making out in the study room—on to more exciting news, it's the Psi Dorm's turn to organize the Fall Masquerade Ball!" She giggled and started to clap. There were other exclamations of excitement around the table, but my reaction was to laugh.

A masquerade ball? They couldn't be serious. It broke practically all the rules of survival. Masks? Loud music? Uncomfortable dresses and shoes? Large gatherings of adolescents? I bet my door lock that it would be at night in a basement or an attic.

Tiffany continued. "Since I'm in charge, I guarantee this year's dance will be the best one yet!"

Wait—"yet?" I leaned over to Brooke. "This has happened before?"

"Totally. It's an annual fundraiser for campus developments," she explained. "The Greek Dorms switch off who's in charge, and the Deltas had it last year. They did a great job, making it steampunk themed. It was totally awesome!"

I couldn't believe my ears. How did they have no cares in the world? Could I ever be so carefree?

Even if I had the crazy desire to commit social suicide with my dancing "skills," I had a hard time picturing the event without a mass murderer. My brain jumbled between the noises of multiple conversations and chewing. At least I had a couple of months to prepare for the upcoming fiasco.

I didn't want to be the first one to leave the table in case an early departure came with a curse. As soon as Marcellette excused herself to go out with her fiancé, I left to finish my homework. I only had one assignment left for Latin 1020, but had no idea how long it would take. Back when choosing my classes, I thought it would be useful to learn Latin, the language of the dead and frequently used in medical terminology. The work load on my desk, however, questioned whether it would be worth the trouble.

Apparently, I didn't need as much time as I gave myself. When Sunday rolled around, all my homework was done and I found myself with nothing to do. I took a stroll through my neighborhood, looking for a classic black stone and gargoyle chapel. Instead, I came across a small coffee bible study. After a half hour, I decided it lacked passion for fire and damnation. Didn't these people know that studying the word of God wasn't enough? It was all about the fight. Attending church wasn't a rule of survival, but church was supposed to be the best place to learn about God and the angelic Supernaturals. What better way to fight the Devil and Hauntings than to side with their counterparts?

I wondered if Heather left town to attend church with her family for an appropriate sermon. Back at home, Emma took up the bedroom with her daily phone call to her mom. I lay on my bed, eyes glazed over the words of Jeremiah and ears half tuned to Emma's conversation. It sounded like she had moved on from the fancy-feet man in her co-ed dance class to some eye-candy in her photography class. Rare moments like these, I wished I had the support and loyal companionship of family.

I missed my brother. I missed Oz's constant reprimands, and even the silly way he spiked his black hair. I missed our sparring lessons and the surprised faces when Oz took down bigger men.

My hand scratched my leg a few times before I realized my subconscious reached for my emergency pack and my brother's survival book. Where was it? I almost always kept it within reach even when it wasn't strapped to my thigh.

Suddenly frantic, I asked for Emma's help to search. She continued to talk away as I scavenged my desk, the drawers, the floor, and my bed (using my phone light to check underneath).

DON'T DATE THE HAUNTED

"Hey, Emma?" I asked for the third time, standing before her to finally catch her attention.

"One second, Mama." She rolled her eyes. "My roommate wants something." She shifted the mouthpiece down to raise an annoyed eyebrow at me. "What?"

"Have you seen my emergency pack?"

"Your what?"

"My emergency pack. It's a leather bag with two leg straps?"

Emma's annoyed eyebrow became bewildered. "You mean the one that's usually tied to your leg like a bad fanny pack?"

"Sure," I said, too frantic to be offended. "Do you know where it is?"

"No," she sighed and lifted her phone to continue her conversation.

Frustrated, I stomped out to search the rest of the dormitory.

My pack sat on the kitchen counter, beside the sink. How did it get there? Had I simply misplaced it? Asher and Ruby sat at the table with their biology textbooks sprawled across. They were too busy with the definition of "hydrophilic" to be culprits of a filching prank. I swiped my pack and wandered to Brooke, who lounged across the sofa. She had a laptop open and a few textbooks to her side.

I asked her, "Did you see who put my emergency pack on the counter?"

"Huh?" she asked. She kept her eyes on her computer screen for an extra distracted second, and I knew she'd been too focused with her homework to notice.

"Never mind," I sighed, and dropped into the armchair beside her. "I thought you said you didn't have a computer?"

"I don't," she said. "This is the school's. I'm renting it for the semester, but I keep all my personal files on a drive."

"Right, of course." I nodded. "What are you up to?"

Brooke sighed and bent her neck over the sofa's armrest to stare at the ceiling. "I have a Historical Records assignment to write a personal memoir. I can't decide whether to set it in my hometown, here, or in a fictional world."

"It's a memoir," I said. "Why would you set it anywhere but your hometown?"

She flipped around to kneel on the couch and face me directly. "Think of how fun it would be to write it based somewhere else. Nancy Drew wrote her autobiographies in the fictional land of the United States, and John Watson wrote the biographies of Sherlock Holmes in the land of England. It's becoming more and more popular to write personal stories based in the world of the classics."

"It still sounds weird to me," I said. "Also, Nancy Drew and John Watson were Mysterys. You're Sci-Fian, and don't Sci-Fians usually write their biographies in their own setting?"

Brooke sighed. "Yes, but they sometimes begin in the fiction world and come here, like the Time Traveler and Gideon Spilett. And, personally, that sounds so boring."

"I wouldn't think so," I countered. "If I ever write my autobiography, I'll probably write it true to the experience, whether I was in Horror or here."

"But you see the complication?" she asked, leaning sideways on the sofa. "You and I are transfers. We don't think like Romantics, so to write our histories here feels totally wrong. I mean, Romance is great, but I don't really feel like I belong, you know?"

I laughed. "It's actually a relief to know I'm not alone to feel out of place here."

Brooke smiled. "That's why I joined the International Club. There's another meeting next week if you want to come."

DON'T DATE THE HAUNTED

I gave a reluctant shrug. "I don't know. I didn't even connect with the other Horrors."

"Ah, I'm sorry about that, but I totally know what you mean," she said with an honest smile. "I didn't really get along with the other Sci-Fians either, but I found other super friends from the club. You can hang out with us, if you want. My friends really seemed to like you."

"Thanks," I said. I wouldn't have done the same in her place. My brother taught me, *The more pitiful a stranger seems, the more dangerous they can be.* And I felt pretty pitiful.

"Hey." She sat up with an idea. "How about I invite them over for some games tonight? Or do you still have to do homework?" Brooke smiled and I couldn't help but feel hopeful. People didn't survive Hauntings alone. I wanted friends to fight beside me, and Brooke seemed capable. She was also friendly in a way that I never appreciated before.

I gave a sheepish shrug. "I guess I stressed over my homework more than necessary."

Brooke laughed, "Yeah, that happens. Midterms will hit and you'll feel super stressed again, then you'll relax until finals. That's the cycle of university life. Anyway, I'll send some messages out and see who's available tonight."

Brooke set aside her laptop and texted her friends. Half an hour later, a game night was planned at our dorm. As it turned out, only Hank, Theodor the Trusted, and the girl dressed like a private eye gypsy were available. They came over within the hour.

The girl introduced herself as, "Truth Locke from Mystery, though I was born in Fantasy."

"Truth?" I asked.

"Yeah, it's like Ruth, but with a 'T.'"

Or it was like…truth.

"I knew you were from Horror the moment I saw you," she said, then flustered. "Oh, I didn't mean that racially, but characteristically—because of who you *are*."

"Huh?" I asked.

She took my hand and fingered my palm like she was reading it, but didn't break her gaze from mine. "Let's see, your parents died when you were young, am I right?"

"Uhhh, yeah." Lucky guess?

"The way you carry yourself shows strong independence," she explained. "But you also seem a little lost. You hide it well, but you're still learning not to rely on someone—an older sibling perhaps?"

Okay, that was freaky. I wiggled my hand away.

"I'd guess a brother, based on your masculine mannerisms and lack of fashion—"

"Hey, Truth!" Brooke interrupted. "You should totally help us find a game to play." Brooke put an arm around Truth to angle her away. As they stepped aside, I heard Brooke whisper, "Remember how we talked about personal bubbles?"

Truth protested, "But her life fascinates me. To be raised by her brother from such a young age, I can only imagine—"

"Just imagine it all in your head, okay?" Brooke smiled, tapped Truth's forehead, then searched around for a change of subject.

Theodor the Trusted stood off to the side. As soon as our eyes met, he glanced away like I caught him in a place he didn't belong.

I mindfully agreed. That place was my personal life and now, thanks to Truth, everyone knew my "tragic" life story. I wanted to shout at them, "My life isn't tragic, I survived! That's what my brother taught me to do, and I've done it!" The dark cynicism of my mind added "so far."

DON'T DATE THE HAUNTED

"Hey, Theo, Pansy," Brooke called, "help us pick out a game."

"However we may assist, Miss Steamings," Theodor said, and joined her beside the TV.

"You're playing games?" a voice said from our bedroom. Emma had emerged with her phone in hand. "Can I join?"

Just then, Hank walked back from the kitchen. Apparently the clinking of glass I heard was the collection of cups and alcoholic drinks.

So, it would be that kind of game night. I moaned.

Hank suddenly stopped with a dead stare at Emma. She did the same back at him. Their eyes widened and their smiles grew. In a flash, it was over.

"Sure, ya can join!" He grinned.

Truth caught my eye and tapped a finger to her nose, like she and I just witnessed a secret. I couldn't tell what though. Maybe I'd ask Theodor as his gaze shifted between the two, oblivious to Brooke's questions about his preference for card or board games. His blue-green eyes then met my brown with a touch of sorrow.

What was that look for? Had I hurt him in some way? Why did it prick my core to think that I caused his handsome face to frown?

I turned away, suddenly focused on my seat and hoping to ignore the strange incident.

Brooke handed Theodor an armful of board games, and he set them on the coffee table. Hank distributed drinks, first to Emma with a wink.

I refused mine with, "Thanks, but I don't drink."

Truth leaned forward, her mouth shaped to an 'O.' "Oh, I see. Your parents drank, didn't they?"

"Yes…"

C. RAE D'ARC

"Your dad killed your mom in a drunken stupor, didn't he? Then...then, he took his own life from the regret! Ohhh."

Silence dropped over us like a thick blanket of awkward. Truth beamed like she'd just solved a puzzle while everyone else shuffled uneasily. As shocked as I was, embarrassment and anger overwhelmed my surprise.

How did Truth guess all that? I had no memories of my parents, but Oz called alcohol "tired juice" in Mom's hands, and "angry juice" in Dad's. At seven years old, my brother became my guardian as we passed between orphanages and foster homes. Oz watched over me until he also succumbed to Hauntings two years ago. Did Truth have so little tact to blurt out my childhood sob story for the whole Novel to know?

Despite her lack of tact, I managed to hold my own. I clenched my teeth from revealing my pain and forced myself to remain stoic.

"Excuse me," I said, no longer in the mood for games. I stood and walked to my room with as much confidence as my ego could muster.

As I left, Emma broke the awkward silence. "Wow, you're good. How did you know all that?"

Truth replied sheepishly, "I'm practicing to become a P.I. The streets say a renowned official will visit here soon and I hope to train under him. I think Theo knows—"

I closed the door behind me and hoped to block out their conversations. Unfortunately, the door wasn't enough to block out the game's laughter and friendly banter. I heard some of my other roommates go out and join, but I stayed alone in my bedroom next to the stinky toilets. I'd been alone ever since Sean's death, but this was the first time I felt so lonely.

Chapter 6

OTHER PEOPLE

Don't be afraid to kill corrupted loved ones
Listen to ominous warnings from locals and elders
If someone's face is slightly concealed,
don't trust or go toward them
Trust the instincts of animals, but stay away from them
(especially if they act weird)

- *Oz's Haunting Survival Book*

A few hours later, I was ahead in my reading assignments and the games finally packed up. As last jokes were drawn out, Heather came home and joined me in the bedroom.

"How was church with the family?" I asked her.

In a surprisingly non-Regency manner, she collapsed on her bed with a huge sigh.

"That bad?" I asked. It was difficult to see Heather so down-trodden. Feeling sympathetic, I set down my textbook. "Hey, no matter what, though, you should continue to go. Church attendance and keeping family close saved my life multiple times."

Heather sighed again. "I do respect my family, truly, but at times I wish they would respect me too."

"What do you mean?" I didn't want to pry, but she seemed discouraged and I wanted to help.

She sat up to kick off her shoes, then yanked off her stockings and let them fall to the floor. "My mother persists that I give up my education and marry a gent from Regency. My brother jests me for 'learning man's work,' and my younger sisters discount my every remark, as though my opinions have been corrupted with 'worldly pursuits.'"

"Supernaturals," I cursed. "Aren't women educated in Regency?" I remembered Sean describing Heartford as a Romantic city with the best of Regency and Contemporary. Situated near the border, Heartford had the technology of Contemporary, but many of the old fashioned mannerisms of Regency. While I appreciated the social reservations of Regency, I forgot about their sexism.

Heather laughed without mirth. "If this campus had been established ten miles north, it would deny women into the colleges. My eldest sister had warned me of this. Some of the professors will grade women more harshly to encourage 'the proper place for a woman is in the home.'" She quoted the last part with mocked poise. "Oh, I do want a husband and family more than anything, but until I meet him, I reckon a man with half a brain would want a wife with one too."

"And if he doesn't, he's not the man for you," I agreed. I felt ridiculous for my earlier brooding. Sure, my whole family was dead, but at least they loved me. I couldn't imagine living with opposition from home. It sounded horrible.

The bedroom door swung open as Emma entered with a refreshed attitude. She didn't roll her eyes or pointedly ignore us. She seemed exhausted, but floated on air like she just woke up from a perfect dream.

She probably drank too much.

"Heather, Pansy, can I talk to you?" she asked.

Was she possessed? Why was she acting different?

DON'T DATE THE HAUNTED

Heather sat up as Emma leaned heavily on the bunk ladder and sighed. "I wanna say sorry for this last week. I was on my period, and I was uber stressed with the move and school. But now I'm a little less stressed with the move because, even though I didn't show it, I am really happy to have you two as my roommates." She took a deep breath. "So, I'm sorry."

Heather nodded. "Your apology is acceptable."

"Yeah, don't worry about it," I said cautiously. I wondered about her motive behind her change of character.

"Good," Emma sighed in relief, "because I thought we could hang out together next weekend. My photography class gave me an assignment to 'go exploring,' and I didn't wanna go alone."

"Yes," Heather said, and scooted to the side of her bed. "There are few activities that bond sisters together like an afternoon outside of the home."

I wasn't sure if I agreed with that, but shrugged anyway. I didn't want Emma to endanger herself by going out on her own. If she offered to make amends I wouldn't stand in her way, and it sounded like Heather needed a friend too.

Never let your guard down, Oz's warning whispered. *The moment you become relaxed around a Haunting is when it strikes.*

I cleared my head and willed myself to befriend someone. Heather wasn't the only one who needed a friend. Even if I was freed from Horror's Hauntings, I wanted to connect with my roommates.

Emma clapped her hands together the way Tiffany did for a cheesy announcement. "So, since it's fall, I thought we could go out to the mountains and—"

"Vetoed," I said.

"What?" Emma asked, startled.

"No mountains. My brother said to never go camping or hiking. Always stay close to civilization and trusted activities."

Last time I went camping, my fiancé went missing, and I found him strapped to a gurney.

Emma showed off her sassy side again and pursed her lips. She put a hand on her hip and swayed her neck as she spoke. "Well then, where would you say we go?"

My mouth opened wordlessly. I was new to this town. I didn't know of any tourist areas or places for photography. "I don't know," I admitted. "Where do Romantics go on weekends?"

Emma rolled her eyes. "Out in nature, away from 'civilization.'"

"My family always attends church on the weekends," Heather's shy voice sang.

"Aha! I bet there's a historical church we could tour!" I said. I tried to sound excited, like my paranoia actually brought out a better activity. Considering some churches, however, I added, "As long as it doesn't have a graveyard or creepy rumors."

Emma raised an eyebrow, unconvinced.

"There is a cathedral on the other side of campus," said Heather. "It has magnificent architecture from the era of Rebirth."

Emma bounced her head back and forth, as though the options were weights on her ears. "Okay. I guess a church could be just as romantic as the mountains for a first date."

"Wha—first date?" I stuttered.

"Come on." She rolled her eyes again. "If we're going out, we might as well take some hot guys along. We'll triple. You said you're not grieving anymore, right?"

Heather did another one of her twinkle-eyed excited squeals. I knew the day I got used to that sound would be the day she squealed from true terror. My freak out was doubled now. When did this become a date?

"Don't people get married in churches?" I asked. "Wouldn't that be a little forward for a first date?"

"That, dear Pansy, is what makes it so romantic." Heather sighed.

I released my own sigh, but mine was exasperated. "It's hardly been a week since classes started. How are we supposed to find dates?"

Emma didn't even hesitate. "There were those guys who were just here. They're from your club, right? Why don't you ask them? I call Hank though. That cowboy's such a hunk, am I right?"

I stared at her in disbelief. "You want me to set you up with him?"

"Would you, really?" she asked, as though I'd volunteered. "I think we experienced Love at First Sight," she breathed as her eyes went dreamy.

I raised a skeptical eyebrow while Heather gasped, "Was it not *True* Love at First Sight?"

Emma shrugged. "I don't know if I could ever commit that much to one person, but—" she paused to sigh and smile at nothing, "—the moment I first saw him, and our eyes locked…it was magical."

Heather's squeal could have alerted a pack of wolves with her shrill pitch and volume. It definitely put me on alert as she literally quivered. With excitement. Weird.

This whole conversation bewildered me since Love at First Sight was a foreign concept to me. Love itself was unfamiliar to me. I understood lust as a motivator for Hauntings. Then there was infatuation, like what I felt for Sean until it grew into familial love, like the "willing to die for you" affection I had with Oz.

"So." Emma pointed at me, snapping my focus back. "You'll contact Hank? I know how those situations can turn out. Don't you dare let him fall for you instead."

I almost laughed. "That would break a rule of survival. Don't give anyone a reason to murder you from envy."

A light seemed to turn on in Emma's mind. "If that's true, you could be the best friend a Romantic could ask for."

The next morning, our water turned into blood.

As if mornings weren't groggy already, my mind was preoccupied with different scenarios of approaching Hank with Emma's request. Ruby chatted at the mirror with Emma as I stepped into a shower stall and undressed. I preferred community bathrooms, but I also liked my privacy. With my change of clothes stowed, I turned on the faucet. Then screamed.

Red liquid poured from the shower head and puddled at my feet. It swirled down the drain and threatened my stomach with a traumatizing memory of Sean's death.

The shower ran for only a second, but it continued to drip red after I twisted it off.

Emma and Ruby's quick response was commendable as they dashed to the outside of my stall.

"Pansy? Are you in the middle stall?" Emma asked.

Ruby swore. "What's this shindy? I thought all the powder was run out. Did you put more in?"

"No." Emma snickered. "Too bad she noticed so fast. We could have pranked two roommates with one trick."

"What are you talking about?" I shouted, wrapping my towel around myself to exit the shower stall as quickly as possible. "Did you know there's blood in the water?"

DON'T DATE THE HAUNTED

"Blood?" Ruby asked. "Naw, it ain't nothin' but punch powder. It dyes the water."

"Who died?" I panicked.

"Pansy, calm down," Emma said. Her efforts to calm herself were overruled by her urge to laugh. "OMG, this prank worked even better than I thought."

At that moment, Asher walked in. Her normally black hair was tinted red. So was her normally pale skin. Emma and Ruby burst into laughter.

Supernaturals, my roommates turned her into a demon.

The red-dyed Asher glowered at them and stalked back out.

Emma and Ruby held their stomachs with laughter as I switched to a different stall. The beginning of my second school week didn't seem any better than my first.

I was sure to be early for my first Novel History class of the week, and smiled as Hank sat next to me again.

"Hey, Hank," I said. "I have a huge and stupid favor to ask you."

He grinned. "No favor's too big for a big-sky man. Wha'dya need?"

My mouth was open, but now that the moment came, I had no idea what to say. I figured it best to say it straight.

"I need you to take my roommate on a date."

He stared at me for a long moment then broke into a jovial laugh. "I had a horse like ya, growin' up. No games, just went straight to the point. Did Brooke put ya up to this? How long has she been bidin' her time?"

My cheeks burned at his horse comparison and misunderstanding. "Uh, actually, it's not for Brooke. It's my roommate, Emma. She played games with you all on Sunday. She's the one from Contemporary."

Hank's eyes widened with recollection, "Ah, right, the blonde. She is a beauty. Sure, I could take her for a spin. Ya think she'd like line dancin'?"

Emma? Line dancing? The idea made me laugh.

"Actually," I said, "we already made plans to tour the cathedral north of campus. Emma needs to take some pictures for her photography class and wanted us to join her."

"Us?" Hank asked. "Yer comin' too?"

"Yeah." I shuffled my feet. When did my life get so awkward? "It's a triple date, except I don't know who else to ask."

"Ya need a man? Huh." Hank seemed surprised and my awkwardness spread. He snapped his fingers. "What about Theo?"

"The Trusted?" I asked, remembering the awkward bow and intense greeting. "He'd probably be better for Heather."

Hank shrugged. "He seemed to take a likin' to ya, but if ya insist. I could ask my roommate, Jake."

Careful who you date, I remembered from Oz's book. *If they like you more than you want, they'll likely become your next Haunting.* I didn't want to scare Hank with my list of questions and requirements, and instead asked, "Tell me about him?"

"We've been roommates since freshman year. He's from Contemporary, but he knows how to respect a lady," Hank said with a wink.

Respect. That was a good sign. "Does he have any obsessive ex-girlfriends or stalkers?"

"Hahah! Girl, ya've got nothin' to worry about."

Now I was worried, but what else could I do? "Sounds great," I said. "Here's Emma's number. She wants you to call her for all the details. And, um, thanks again."

"I'm lookin' forward to it," Hank said, smiling.

DON'T DATE THE HAUNTED

I let out a big sigh of relief and turned forward as the history instruction began. I fulfilled my task and got dates for everyone. Next I just had to survive the real terror of the date itself.

After Emma's apology, it became easier to live and laugh with my roommates. Since Emma grew up near Heartford, she knew some of the tricks of the town. We rode the city bus together to shop for groceries and the less-thought-of necessities (like kitchen towels and cleaning supplies). As the week dragged by, we talked about classes, watched movies, and even walked up to campus together. One day as we left the dorms, Emma's joke about a boy in her dance class was interrupted by a deep voice.

"Ms. Finster?"

I turned toward the caller. A middle-aged man pushed himself from leaning against a tree and walked up to me. He wore a trench coat and fedora hat that shadowed his square facial features and greying dark hair.

"He must be from Mystery," Emma whispered. She eyed him up and down, then lifted a flirtatious eyebrow and half smile. "I wonder why he's here."

I mentally barfed. He had to be twice her age!

He narrowed in on me and stretched out a hand for a formal introductory shake. His hand was icy and clammy, and he didn't let go. "Ms. Finster, my name is Mr. E. Can I speak with you alone for a few minutes?"

"Mr. E?" Emma asked with a swaggering step closer. "What does the E stand for?"

He ignored her and tightened his deathly cold grip on mine.

"U-um," I stuttered out, "can I see your badge to prove you're official?"

Heather nodded approvingly. "A woman ought to be assertive."

With a raised eyebrow, the man named Mr. E finally let go of my hand to open his coat flap and reveal a metal crest. It looked real, though I didn't know enough to spot a forgery. I'd never met an official from Mystery before.

I turned to Heather and Emma. "Don't go too far, okay? Stay in sight."

Heather nodded with a smile while Emma wiggled her head at me, mouthing the word "alone."

Once they stepped out of earshot, Mr. E said, "Normally the Homicide Department of Mystery leaves the Horror Zone to itself since your 'Supernaturals' seem to execute their own definition of justice."

"The Supernaturals bless the righteous and innocent," I said, while thinking "execute" was an accurate word choice for the justice from Hauntings. But he'd said "Supernaturals" with a hint of exaggeration and disbelief.

"As you say." He reached into his coat to pull out a pen and notepad. "I despise working on cold Cases that international departments claim to be closed, but how could I pass up the opportunity to interview a local and eyewitness?" He made a quick scribble on his notepad then bore down on me. "Ms. Finster, where were you Wednesday, March fifteenth, at 1:48 p.m.?"

Chapter 7

APPAREL

*Dress for comfort and function, not fashion
Wear shoes you can run in
Clothes too tight will catch the wrong attention. Clothes too loose will get caught in snares
Keep your hair short. Long hair and ponytails are easier for Hauntings to grab*

- Oz's Haunting Survival Book

My legs tensed, ready to fight or flight. "Are you interrogating me?"

"I'm interviewing you," Mr. E said, like it was entirely different. Though this was my first "interview," I'd seen enough police shows to know better.

"Please answer the question," he said, pen ready. His eyes were like a picture that watched me from other rooms and reported my whereabouts to its vampire master.

Supernaturals! This guy was creepier than a phantom! Maybe if I answered his question quickly, he'd leave me alone sooner. What was it again? March fifteenth?

My blood stilled.

The day Sean and I fought the experimental scientist. The day Sean died.

Against my will, I started to sweat. What was wrong with me? Stop sweating, I'd look guilty! Sure, I blamed myself for Sean's death, but that didn't mean I deserved to go to prison. Probably? If Mr. E was anything like the detectives on TV, he could misunderstand or twist the truth to his own agenda... Whatever it was.

"1:48 in the afternoon?" I confirmed. The fight in the basement laboratory happened so early in the morning, it was still night. By the afternoon, I was home and considered the Haunting finished. "I was at my trailer, taking a shower."

"Are there others who can confirm your location and actions?"

"I don't remember, it was months ago—wait—yes." I ended firmly as details of the afternoon returned. They made me wince. "My roommate, Gretta, was home too."

The Mystery scribbled down some notes, then asked, "How did you know Sean Chase?"

He was my first and best friend after Oz died. He helped keep me sane in the orphanage, fought a werewolf with me, and helped me defeat the poltergeist experimenter, Dr. Hyde. He was my fiancé, the only person to say he loved me and kiss me like he meant it, and the only person to make me wonder if I could fall in love. He was my inspiration to hope for a brighter future. Simply put, "He was my best friend. We planned to get married after we graduated."

"Then you know that your fiancé was a born Romantic? This means the Case of his death is within Mystery jurisdiction, especially since the only person who claimed any information regarding his Case has now transferred to Romance."

Yes, I knew that Sean was a native Romantic. He moved to Brimstone with his parents three years ago, during the zombie outbreak. I met him at the orphanage when Oz died a year later.

DON'T DATE THE HAUNTED

I didn't respond, and the detective flipped to another page. "I'm aware the crime scene underwent a complicated 'cleansing' process of Horror protocol? Please describe it for me."

"Yeah," I said, and regained my bearings. "The Hauntings Investigation Unit has a ritual that attempts to restore areas back to balance and diminish Hauntings."

He raised his eyebrow. "Attempts?"

"Well, exorcism works, but only so long as someone stupid doesn't invite the Haunting back."

Mr. E wrote more notes on his pad. "Thank you. Is there any other information you'd like to share with me about the death of your fiancé?"

"I don't know what you're looking for." I shrugged. "Sean was killed by a poltergeist. End of story."

"How would you describe the poltergeist?"

"Uhh…" I spaced, confused and annoyed by his disbelief. "It was a malicious ghost who interacted with the physical world. They're known in Horror for levitating things, especially sharp objects."

Mr. E flipped through his notebook. "Yes, the HIU report of Dr. Hyde's death was—what's the word—enchanting? Even Mystery's most terrorizing crooks are still human. What's the probability that your 'Hauntings' are just clinically insane people behind costumes and makeup?"

"Depends on the zone, but poltergeists aren't a costume."

Mr. E continued as if he hadn't heard me. "I'm curious why there were so few details about Mr. Chase's death. All it said was, 'Responded to an emergency call. Sean Chase was found dead on arrival.' Care to fill in the blanks for me?"

I blinked a couple times and wondered what else to say. If he read the HIU report, then he knew about how Sean and I defeated Dr. Hyde's Haunting. What he didn't know was how Sean died after. What happened? Well, we finished the

Haunting, but apparently the Haunting wasn't finished with Sean and me.

Before I could respond, a new voice called out, "Good day, Miss Pansy—Mr. John!"

We both looked up to see none other than Theodor the Trusted down the street. He waved. He was definitely talking to us, but who was Mr. John? John didn't start with "E."

Mr. E waved back. "Duke Fromm? No—*Lord* Fromm? How did you get to be a spitting image of your dad? Did your Adventures bring you out to Romance?"

I retreated a step, glad I hadn't said any more about Sean's death. Who was this guy to lie about his name and ask those questions?

Theodor, the man who claimed to be trustworthy, jogged over and thumped Mr. John/E on the back.

"The Adventure of education is ever enlightening. What brings you here, Mr. John? I thought you were done with school." The Mystery grinned from Theodor's tease.

"Is a detective not allowed a side Case?" he asked in a vague explanation. I took another step back to glance at Heather and Emma, grateful they were still in sight. My roommates waited for me a block up the street.

Hoping to not set the men off, I made up an excuse—"I need to get to class,"—and walked away in haste.

Mr. E called after me, "I have a few more questions for you, miss!"

I turned back to shout, "I'm late!" and ran. Mr. E appeared torn, like a business opportunity slipped through his fingers. Theodor also seemed torn, like he had half a mind to chase me, but for reasons I couldn't tell. I didn't give them a chance, and ran harder. I prayed to the Supernaturals that Mr. E wouldn't call this "evading arrest," or something else to detain me.

I tumbled between Emma and Heather, shouting, "Run!"

DON'T DATE THE HAUNTED

"What?" they both asked.

"Must. Hide. On campus," I said between breaths. As worried as I was, it felt good to run at full speed again. How long had it been since I last ran for my life? The wind whipped past, and my adrenaline rush turned into exhilaration.

"Slow down, Pansy!" Emma called behind me. "We're not that late for class!"

I risked a quick glance back. The two men still stood where I left them. I relaxed and slowed to my usual walk.

"Sorry," I said. Heather and Emma nearly collapsed with deep breaths. Emma flipped her hair and shirt to air out any sweat.

"Seriously, what was that all about?" she asked.

Heather whined and massaged her feet. Why did she wear those old fashioned boots anyway? Oz told me, *Always wear clothes you can run in.*

"Sorry," I said again. "I was worried those men would chase us."

Emma gave me a pointed stare that asked *are you serious?* "If you run like that, the boys will never chase you."

I imitated her expression. Did she even hear herself? "I don't want them to chase me. I don't trust them. First he says his name is Mr. E, then it's Mr. John. How can I trust a man who doesn't tell me his real name? And why is he interrogating me about Sean's death? It was months ago, I gave my report, and the case was closed."

Emma's eyes rolled. "His name is Mr. John E. Why can't that be his real name?"

Heather giggled to herself. "Johnnie, how cute."

"And besides," Emma went on, "the man's from Mystery. Nothing they do makes sense. Maybe he's a workaholic, or found new evidence to reopen the case. That's not a reason to run away."

Heather rested a hand on Emma, half to get her attention and half for support as she whipped out a hand fan for her face. "Emma, she had lost her previous opportunity for love. The process of opening one's heart again is unique to each individual."

Emma sighed with another of her classic eye rolls. "Fine, I get it. I don't wanna commit to anyone either. But when you do want the boys to chase you again, take my advice and run slower."

I stared at them, dumbfounded. I couldn't understand them, and realized it was the same problem that they couldn't understand me. The rest of the walk up to campus was spent in silence as I glanced back over my shoulder, sure that someone was watching me.

After what felt like a hundred years, the weekend arrived again. I came home from classes, determined to keep up with my homework. If I had to spend all Friday night locked in my room or the study, so be it. I was in the middle of my history essay on Dr. Frankenstein's explorations through Horror when Emma found me at the kitchen table. She'd spent the last hour or so in the bathroom.

"You're going like that?" she asked me. She wore high heeled boots over the newest fashion of jeans, and her plaid button up was loose with sleeves rolled up to her elbows. On the other hand, I wore a classic black tank top with my favorite green zipper jacket and comfortable sweatpants.

"Where am I going?" I asked, only half listening. I had finally reached the rare mindset to burst through my homework and despised any distractions.

"Did you forget?" Emma asked. "How could you forget when you set us all up?"

I tore my eyes from my laptop to ask what the horror she was talking about when Heather walked in. She wore a pink, extra puffy, full-length dress with a matching shawl and hand fan.

"You're going to church on a Friday?" I asked her. "I thought you only visited your family once a month."

Heather giggled, and Emma dramatically rolled her eyes. "Yes, Pansy! We're going to church because you said we couldn't go to the mountains!"

"Oh…right." I remembered. The triple date. My desire to stay at home with my homework all night increased. A blind date was as appealing as a dungeon full of rats. But I didn't want to give the stranger a reason to be embarrassed or angry at me by standing him up. Anger was a motive for murder.

"Come on." Emma grabbed my hand and pulled me from my seat. "We have fifteen minutes until they arrive. Let me do your makeup. Heather, pick an outfit for her from my side of the closet."

As simple as that, I was transformed into someone else—someone who dressed for fashion rather than comfort, and someone who checked the mirror to catch a mistake of eyeliner, not a Haunting.

I protested in vain. "Dates are meant for getting to know a person. What's the point of it if he doesn't get to know the real me?"

"He won't wanna get to know the real you if he doesn't like a perfected you," Emma replied. I wanted to retort that a "perfected me" was one free of makeup and constraining clothing. It was no use. It would only add fuel to their fire if I admitted aloud that a small part of me enjoyed the makeover. There was a certain appeal to the colorings that smoothened my burnt umber skin and emphasized my brown eyes.

The doorbell rang all too soon. Asher let in our dates, then ran to hide in her bedroom. Tiffany entertained them until ten minutes later, Emma allowed us to emerge from the bathroom, "fashionably late." Everyone was quite handsome, and I would have felt underdressed if Emma and Heather hadn't taken over.

Hank matched Emma's plaid shirt and boots, but his shirt was tucked in and buttoned all the way. Theodor still wore his medieval boots, but changed out his dressy tunic and cloak for slacks and a crisp blue button up. I'd never seen anyone wear such a formal outfit so comfortably, as if that was how he dressed down among friends.

The third man, I assumed, was my date, Jake. He wore a comfortable Contemporary outfit of jeans, polo, and a light jacket. Even for a date, he dressed casual, comfortable, and good for movement. Why couldn't I have done the same?

I shuffled uncomfortably in the extra-long shirt that made for a short dress with a thick ribbon around my waist. Emma and Heather had both decided that none of my clothes were impressive enough for a first date, and it was a fashion miracle that the lengthy one-size-fits-all long shirts and leggings were in style. They wouldn't let me wear my usual sneakers, but stuffed a pair of Heather's flats with tissues to fit my feet. At least I talked them out of heels.

Each of the men reached out their hands for us. I expected a handshake, but instead, they bent over in low bows. Jake didn't bow as deeply, but kept eye contact with me while Hank added a wink to Emma. Theodor was even stiffer than the first time I saw him give this awkward introduction. Maybe because he didn't have that gallant cloak to blow over his shoulder.

At least my roommates seemed to enjoy the formal greeting. Personally, I wanted to squirm and wipe my hand free from any contact.

My date stood and smiled at me. It was an average smile. Not shy, but not cocky, not serious, but not too lighthearted. There was a hint of intimidation and curiosity, but this was a blind date, after all.

DON'T DATE THE HAUNTED

"Jacob Kennington," he introduced. "Or Jake. I think you're in my Latin 1020 class."

"Oh?" I asked, surprised and slightly embarrassed that I hadn't recognized him. "With Professor Magister?"

"Yes, Tuesdays and Thursdays at 11:00," he confirmed.

Apparently, this wasn't as blind as I thought. I wanted to ask him if he'd finished the assignment. Maybe we could ditch the date and have a study night instead.

Unfortunately, Theodor spoke first. "I was told our festivities were prearranged? What adventures await us, Miss Appleton?"

"Yeah," Emma interrupted and spoke to the whole group. "It's not all that far, but these shoes are gonna kill me if we don't take a cab. Come on!"

Hank opened the door for her as she led us outside. I bit my tongue about her shoes comment. If her shoes were so murderous then why wear them? Emma called for a cab in advance, but I didn't see any vehicles. Then, I saw Hank help Emma into a... horse-drawn buggy? I didn't know they made those anymore. There were two, and Emma insisted she and Hank ride in the smaller one to themselves. I didn't like the idea of splitting up, but there was barely room for the four of us already. Heather's puffy dress squished Theodor to the side, bumping his knees against mine as I was squished across from him.

The ride jolted forward, silent and awkward. Even in the open air, it felt stuffy. Jake gave me as much space in my seat as possible, like he was afraid to touch me. For a Contemporary, he sure had a lot of Regency mannerisms.

"So, Jake," I said, breaking the silence of the cart, "Hank told me you're from Contemporary. Did you grow up near Heartford?"

"No," he said. His shoulders relaxed slightly with the casual conversation.

Good. *Help those around you keep calm. A calm person is less likely to freak out or become a Haunting.*

Jake continued, "I was actually born in Regency. Both of my parents are from Rosemary, but my family moved so that I could attend a private school in Contemporary."

"Rosemary?" Heather asked. "My family resides in Ferndean, just East of Avon."

"East of Avon," Jake sang softly.

To my surprise, Heather joined him. "Where my heart doth wander."

Jake perked up and they sang the next line together. "My childhood love grows ever fonder."

Theodor raised a curious eyebrow while I wondered how half our cart burst spontaneously into song like a corny musical.

Heather giggled with delight. "You are familiar with *Melodies of Angels*?"

"I blame my sisters," Jake said with red ears.

Heather beamed. "It is one of my most favorite musicals! I have yet to see the film adaptation, though I have seen it thrice performed!"

They continued to chatter as the buggy jostled over a rock. My knees bumped into Theodor's, and I drowned in awkwardness again.

Eventually, the horses slowed as we approached our destination. Theodor jumped out first, then turned to help Heather down. I was next closest to the door, and Theodor held his hand up to help me out of the cab. I waved his hand away. I could exit a buggy by my—

I stumbled over the threshold. "Crap!"

Theodor caught me in his arms as my face slammed into his chest. One of my hands braced against his flexed bicep. Condemnation, he had some nice muscles!

A smug smile crept up his lips. "It seems Miss Pansy has learned the purpose of the footman's stabilizing hand."

I composed myself and situated my feet again. I wasn't a clumsy person. Clumsiness at the wrong time could kill you. I mumbled to Heather, "Couldn't you pick shoes that let me walk?"

Heather blushed and Theodor went stiff again, taking a conscious step away from me and closer to his date. Ahead of us, Emma and Hank walked toward the Cathedral gate. I moaned to think this horrible evening was only beginning.

Chapter 8

OUTSIDE

Don't go camping or into the woods
Don't go out or open doors at night
Stay around civilization and trusted activities
Avoid large gatherings of teenagers—they're like buffets
for the murderously inclined

- *Oz's Haunting Survival Book*

Theodor's face weakened with discomfort. "We will tour a church? How forward for a first date."

"That's what I thought!" I said. "I only suggested it before it became a setup."

"A setup?" Jake echoed, but was outspoken by Emma.

"The original plan was to go out to the mountains, but Pansy shut that down."

"Why is that?" Theodor asked me. "The mountains around here are most beautiful this time of year."

I had to hold my eyes down from rolling up. How many times did I have to explain? "Because 'this time of year' is also the most dangerous. Nature itself is dying and giving way for Hauntings. Also, staying within the city is a main location rule to avoid Hauntings. No hiking, no camping, no mountains."

"That, Miss Pansy, is one guaranteed way to live an unadventurous life." Theodor smirked. "One must care to travel wisely in the mountains, though nature is often safer and more magical than the human nature of crowded cities."

I stared at him incredulously. "Have you ever been in the mountains?"

"Did you want the literal sense of being 'in' a mountain?" he mused. "Regardless, my answer is yes. The Margen Duchy includes two forests and the Divining Mountain caverns. Margen towns are considerably safer and better policed than most Urban cities, though even our streets have thieves and false magicians. Villains use cities to congregate, though in the mountains, they only ensnare those who travel alone."

"Or pick you off one by one," I added with a point. "Isn't the mountain range between Fantasy and Mystery where werewolves and night creatures originated? And Hauntings aside, what if we got lost, or fell off a cliff? There's no cellphone service, and the closest help is miles away."

"True as that may be, there is considerably less danger during the day," Theodor countered. "Every Adventurer knows that as long as you avoid particular areas, or simply stay on the path, your safety is ensured."

There was some truth to that, and we walked through the cathedral's property gate, so I let the conversation drop. I didn't want to argue on church grounds.

Heather was right about the beauty of the cathedral. It was magnificently built, with marbled column walls and a large dome in the center. It was unlike any cathedral I'd ever seen before. All the churches in Horror were built with dark stone and bordered with gargoyles. Emma recognized its beauty too and snapped off photos of the orchards, statues, and architecture. Heather and Theodor wanted to walk around the gardens. Unsure what to do, Jake and I followed behind.

The stone walkway between the gardens was a cultivated sample of the mountains. We became surrounded by death as burnt yellow and orange trees drooped overhead. Their discarded leaves lay scattered like bones after a carnivorous meal. A small vegetable garden to the side filled the air with the scents of jack-o-lanterns and corn mazes.

To my amazement, Heather purposefully stepped wide to smother the fallen warrior leaves. They crunched beneath her boots and she giggled like an imp...whose eyes twinkled with innocence.

"I do love the autumn." Heather sighed. "The weather is perfect. I love the changing colors, and the air smells of a harvest feast. I hear how Contemporaries enjoy a celebration of costumes, inspired by Horror. Is that true, Pansy?"

I shrugged, unsure how Romantics translated Horror culture.

Theodor answered her with a nod. "Indeed, the dorms host an annual ball where costumes are encouraged. I am curious," he twisted over his shoulder to meet my eyes, "how it compares to Horror's traditions."

"You mean the masquerade?" I asked, surprised to learn that the event that broke every rule had been inspired by Horror.

Jake smiled back. "Oh yeah, that's coming up in a few weeks, isn't it? I didn't go last year, but I heard it was great."

I shrugged again. "I'm guessing it's based on Halloween or the Day of the Dead, which is a pretty big deal in Horror. As kids, my brother and I would go to friends' houses for candy and sweet treats in skull shapes. Some families would visit graves for Supernatural experiences, and older kids would go to costume parties to fight whatever Hauntings would show up." As soon as Oz and I were old enough for Hauntings, we quarantined ourselves from sundown to sunrise. Some people called us "unpatriotic" for skipping out of Horror's most famous holiday. One of my friends even teased me as a pansy for staying home. She was suffocated that night by a balloon clown.

Jake was the only one to respond after a prolonged silence. "Huh."

Near the end of the gardens, an elderly woman and her miniature dog occupied a lonely stone bench. Without a single precaution, Heather approached the woman to coo at her dog.

"She truly is adorable, is she not?" she said, stroking the fluffy little creature.

As Jake and I approached, the dog suddenly growled. The elderly woman jumped. "Nissa! What's the matter, girl? Calm down."

The woman's efforts to calm her animal went ignored as the dog continued to growl and bark at me.

Proof that this outing was condemned. If only someone else believed me.

We hurried by until the little yapper stopped. Heather and Theodor took a short cut and ended up in front of our stroll again.

Movement around the cathedral's base caught my attention. Someone in a trench coat and fedora hat disappeared around the corner. I stared at the spot, waiting in vain for the person to reemerge.

We neared the front of the cathedral, and Jake extended his elbow toward me. He stared at me, expectant, but I wasn't sure why. Was it to display his muscles by bending his arm for flexing?

Heather and Theodor were quiet in front of us, also a stiff pair. Heather turned around. Her expression searched for something, anything, to talk about. She saw me and Jake, and stifled a giggle.

"What's so funny?" I asked, tearing my eyes from the possible hiding place of Mr. E.

She gestured to Jake's extended arm. "Miss Finster, he means to escort you."

"Why?" I blurted. Heather stifled another giggle. Jake bit his lip and let his arm drop.

"I-I'm sorry," I stammered. I didn't know what to say. Sorry, your customs confuse me? Sorry I'm such a terrible date? Sorry, this is my first date since my fiancé died? Yeah, that would kick the distress level up a notch. Instead, my blundering got the best of me. "Sorry, I'll let you open the next door for me."

Theodor burst out laughing, and Jake gave me a funny side glance. "Are you actually from Sci-Fi? I've heard some of the women there can be, uh…"

He paused, probably searching for a nicer word than 'crude.' I saved him the trouble by interrupting him with a nervous laugh. "Hah, no, I'm…still learning about your culture. I appreciate your architecture though." I gestured to the cathedral, hoping to change the subject. "It's whiter and smoother than any I've seen in Horror."

Jake turned to the building. "It's nice. Do you want to go inside?"

"Sure," I said. Subject change: successful. Until Jake opened the door for me to enter first.

Since it was a quiet Friday evening, the priest was available.

"Welcome, good lady and gentleman," he said, swinging his arms wide. "If you need any assistance, please call upon me, Father Roosevelt."

"Thank you, Father," I said. He carried the same air of reverence and peace as the Bishop of Brimstone, but he seemed too friendly and helpful. I tried without success to picture him pounding at the pulpit about hellfire and damnation. I imagined he preached more about what happened to good people, rather than warning what happened to bad people.

DON'T DATE THE HAUNTED

The building itself was unlike any cathedral I'd seen—tall and open, white stone, and full of flower bouquets. Even the stained glass windows seemed brighter.

Whenever Oz and I moved to a new town in Horror, we were always sure to look up the nearest church. Every cathedral was like a museum of its own town. They were generally the oldest and finest structures to show the town's wealth and dedication to religion. The large bouquets of flowers said a lot about the town of Heartford. I wandered around, lingering at the statues of saints, and reading the inscriptions of their service and love for others. Interesting. The Supernatural saints in Horror were all renowned for defeating terrible Hauntings, or sacrificing themselves so someone else could defeat the Haunting.

A corner was lit with rows of candles. Jake and I added two more candles and wrote quick prayers on scrap pieces of paper. I usually only prayed for Oz, but this time I added a selfish note that I'd survive this date.

"Jake," I asked, "do you mind if we sit for a bit?"

"If you want," he said.

I walked toward the front and slid into a pew. Father Roosevelt must have alerted the organist about visitors, as a slow tune piped out.

"This is nice," I said.

Jake nodded in reverent silence.

Yes, this was nice. A simple date of observation and nothing needed to be said. Maybe it wasn't as terrible as I thought.

Heather walked by with her date and she smiled at me. I replied with my own, finally comfortable.

"Ah, there it is." Theodor chuckled.

"Huh?" I asked.

"A smile. I believe that was your first since this afternoon began."

"Well, now it's gone, Theodor," I said.

His shoulders sank ever so slightly from my bitterness. "People who call me Theodor tend to include my full title. If you desire to use my first name, just Theo will do."

I responded with a flash of a smile, then stood to continue down the other side of statues.

Emma entered with Hank in tow. She snapped one photo before Father Roosevelt asked her to put away her camera out of respect. She explained it was for an assignment, but Father Roosevelt was stern on the issue. Emma huffed and called our group outside so she could fulfill her assignment.

Once we were all outside, Emma snapped pictures left and right again. She positioned Hank in different poses around the garden like a stage director.

"Sit on that bench...Put your arm over the side...Try to look less handsome, you're distracting the lens."

I gagged while everyone else chuckled.

"Pansy, it's your turn," Emma said as she aimed her camera at me. I reflexively swung my hand up to block my face from the blinding flash.

"Come on," Emma complained. "Remember, I'm doing this for an assignment. It's not like I'm asking you to smile." She laughed. "Just go stand a little closer to that statue. Hey, Theo! Go stand next to her! Sorry, Jake, but they're matching."

Oh, we both wore blue. I usually matched people wearing greys. With some awkward hesitation, Theo came over and stood by me.

"Theo, I need you to relax," Emma said. "You can keep looking bored though, 'cause that goes with Pansy's I'm-too-good-for-this face."

I immediately changed my expression to argumentative defense.

"Hey, you ruined it, Pansy!" Emma complained.

I started to roll my eyes as Emma snapped a photo. "Perfect! Ooh! Come look!"

Eager to get behind the camera instead of in front of it, I joined her side. She caught the picture as my lips pinched to one side and my eyes angled to the other—at Theo.

Ah, great. How did I end up pulling a flirty face at the wrong date?

"How peculiar," Theo said.

I wanted to moan in shame. Had he witnessed so many of my recent embarrassing moments that one more was simply "peculiar?"

"What is that black blur beside her?" he asked. "Is your camera lens dirty?"

"What black blur?" Emma asked, flipping her camera around. I also checked for the obvious Haunting omen, but didn't see anything.

"You mean you—" He cut himself off. "Pardon me, I must be mistaken."

Emma controlled the next half hour as she took pictures of all of us, as individuals, as dates, as roommates…

My pupils became dilated and half my vision was killed by the flash. I was tempted to return inside with an excuse to talk to Father Roosevelt. A conversation about the sins of Novel sounded more relaxing than Emma's posing instructions. I cursed my blinded vision as I thought I caught the hiding fedora hat again.

Eventually, Emma went camera trigger-happy over the sunset. After another round through the gardens, I tapped her shoulder. "It's getting dark. Do you have enough pictures for your assignment?"

Emma quickly glanced at her phone clock. "Oh, I guess so. Wow, time flies when you're having fun!"

She grinned and made dreamy eyes at Hank. My mind gagged again. I called a cab, and thanking the Father, we filtered out.

As we left, I involuntarily shivered. The rising moon brought a chill with it and the flimsy dress and leggings I'd been forced into weren't enough for the oncoming autumn.

"Jake," Theo called out, startling the Romantic out of his gaze in Heather's direction. Theo gestured toward me. "Your date looks cold."

"Oh, here." His arm twitched, like it was about to go around my shoulders. Then, he seemed to think better of it and simply put his jacket around me. It was light, but warm, and smelled of herbal cologne.

The six of us squished into a van cab. Heather sat in the back between Theo and Jake, her puffy dress spilling over their legs. Emma and Hank took the middle seats and I sat in the front seat by the driver. I didn't mind the separation from my date, but the driver was overdosed with cologne.

Walking us to our front door, each of our dates bid us goodnight. Jake and I shared waves, Theo bowed over Heather's hand, and Hank smooshed Emma in a husky hug.

I shuffled off Jake's jacket, almost forgetting to give it back. I handed it to him with a "Thanks," realizing that had been our most intimate moment from the date.

Good. Hopefully it wouldn't be awkward for every other day in Latin.

Safely inside again, Heather and Emma giggled like little school girls, while I moaned to myself. I wasn't in the mood to finish my history essay or Latin assignment. Funny how neglecting my educational goals felt more like a betrayal to Sean's memory than the date.

Chapter 9

TEMPTING

Use common sense
Don't ever film yourself sleeping
If you think your house is haunted, get rid
of haunted items or get out

- *Oz's Haunting Survival Book*

I was sure to arrive late to my next class of Latin 1020. It gave me the perfect excuse to avoid the awkward decision whether or not to sit next to Jake. I also gave him a quick wave when I entered. Ignoring him completely would have been just as awkward. I ended up sitting by the door, which meant I was one of the first to leave too.

Mr. John/E waited for me in the hallway.

Not again. Why was he here? Did he know my class schedule? Was he following me? Had he actually been snooping on us at the cathedral?

I tried to avoid him by hiding my face in another direction. Jake was at my side, his bag half packed like he'd left the room in a rush to catch me.

He wanted to talk? Perfect. Please distract me from—

"Ms. Finster," Mr. E said, closer than I expected, "may I ask you a few more questions?"

"Can this be a group conversation?" Jake asked.

"Please?" I asked. I didn't want to be alone with this strange Mystery.

"Mr. Kennington, if you don't mind, I need to speak with Ms. Finster alone."

Jake put his hands up in surrender. "Sure, no problem Mr. Neil. Hey, Pansy, I'll catch you later, alright?"

Jake headed off, and I asked, "Neil?" The Mystery and I were alone, but at least we were in a public hallway with lots of rooms and escape routes.

Mr. E/John/Neil waved his hand like his new name was no matter, then pulled out his notepad.

"Ms. Finster, I have a few more questions for you about Mr. Chase's Case. The report says you were the one to alert the police about his death. How did you know he was in trouble if you were busy as you were?"

He was trying to stump me, checking if I remembered and could stick to my alibi.

"Like I said, I was at my trailer taking a shower. I was on the phone with him when the Haunting came, so I knew when he was in trouble."

"First of all, Ms. Finster, I don't believe in the supernatural outside of Fantasy. I am determined to find a completely logical and natural, although possibly horrific, explanation for Mr. Chase's death."

I wanted to argue, to wonder what kind of fool he was to disbelieve in the supernatural. That included all undead/cursed/monstrous Hauntings and the angelic Supernaturals themselves. His dead serious stare kept me silent.

Mr. E clicked his pen to his paper again. "You said you were showering while talking to Mr. Chase on the phone? Yet he was found in his bathroom? Did you often call each other when taking showers?"

"Yes."

DON'T DATE THE HAUNTED

He raised an eyebrow.

"Bathrooms are one of our most vulnerable places," I explained. "We completely undress and Hauntings are often perverts. Shower curtains and cabinets are common hiding places for Hauntings, and they are often revealed by mirrors or steam."

"Okay, Horrors are paranoid in the bathroom," Mr. E said, scribbling on his notepad. "But why did you call each other while you showered?"

If anyone else had asked me that I probably would have rolled my eyes. Coming from Mr. E, however, I had no intention to make him second guess my sincerity.

"It's a safety precaution," I said. "Hauntings generally strike when you're alone and no one can hear or help you—another reason why bathrooms are so dangerous with privacy, and loud fans and water running. We call each other so we don't feel alone. Also, if something does happen, someone has our back. That day something happened. Our call dropped so I called the police."

"Do you always call the police when your calls drop?" he asked, raising his eyebrow higher.

"No, but I had a bad feeling," I said. "Instincts are your best protection when dealing with Hauntings."

"You...had a bad feeling." He wrote quickly on his pad, though his voice was slow and skeptical.

"I don't know how else to describe it," I said, trying not to sound desperate. I needed him to believe me, but how would I convince someone who didn't believe in the Supernaturals or Hauntings? "I know it doesn't make sense, but like I said, you need to trust your instincts when dealing with Hauntings. I'm sorry I couldn't be of more help."

"I'm sorry too, Ms. Finster. You may go now. I'll find you again if I need you."

I sighed in relief, though I didn't doubt for a moment that he could find me again. He knew where I lived and apparently had my class schedule. Even still, I took a roundabout way to my next class as I felt the neck-prickling sensation of being watched.

At least the rest of my classes went smoothly that day. I had my homework done and actually understood what my professors discussed. It wasn't until the end of each class that I realized how much new homework I accumulated. Like a horde of zombies, it just kept coming back. Finally home again, I dumped the contents of my backpack on my desk, then timbered down like a dead man on my bed.

Heather sat at her desk and typewriter. She gave me a small smile of *I'm sorry*, but continued silently on her assignment.

"Oh good, you're home!" Emma burst into the room.

"What's up?" I asked, worried that someone died while I was gone. She smiled, so I assumed not. She climbed up to her own bed and sat with her legs dangling over the side.

"I need the details, girl!" she said. "You zonked out Friday night so I never got to hear what you thought of the date!"

"Seriously?" I moaned. "It was fine. I saw Jake again in my Latin class today."

"Jake is in your Latin class?" Heather asked, peering over her typewriter. "Ah, right, I do remember that was mentioned."

"Yeah, and thankfully we're on friendly terms so it wasn't too awkward."

"Hmmm, friendly terms," Heather pondered aloud.

"If you want to date him, go ahead," I said. "You two seemed to get along better anyway."

Heather smiled and blushed. "I might be inclined to say the same about you and my date."

DON'T DATE THE HAUNTED

"Um—no," I said abruptly. "Theo is trouble. He seemed to point out every embarrassing and wrong thing about me."

Heather squealed that weird squeal that made me check around for Hauntings. "How delightful!"

Emma wiggled her mischievous eyebrows. "Mmm-hmm. He's gonna be trouble."

"Wait." I paused. "How is that a good thing?"

"He's gonna be trouble 'cause obviously he likes you."

That didn't make any more sense. "What do you mean? How could he like me? He went on the date with Heather, and whenever we talked we argued."

"Yeah." Emma stared at me like she was waiting for me to get the hint. "You argued, which meant he was interested in what you were saying, and whenever a guy's interested in what a girl's saying it's because he's interested in the girl."

My stupid brain played with the idea. Theo was interested in me? His bluish-green eyes and half-smile flashed through my mind. There was something intriguing and almost familiar about his scythe-shaped smile.

I shook off the idea. He was a Fantasy lord, for crying out loud. Our backgrounds were too different to even consider an honest relationship. I debated with Emma. "That can't be the rule every time for every guy. Lots of people seem 'interested' in me simply because I'm from Horror."

"Well, I hope it's the rule for Hank," Emma said, bouncing on her bed. "We talked the whole time! He's amazing and I'm pretty sure we were made for each other. I mean, he's a total hunk, but also knows how to make a girl feel like a woman! Do you think it's too early to ask for a second date? I don't wanna wait too long, 'cause I'm sure tons of girls wanna date him."

Heather sighed. "It was rather forward of us to arrange the first date. Should we not let them have the opportunity to arrange the next?"

"But Pansy was really the one to set up the first date," Emma offered.

"Actually," I said, "Hank did everything. I asked him if he'd go on a date with you and then he suggested Theo and Jake."

"Good point!" Emma shouted with an extra high bounce. "So really, Hank arranged everything! Which means the ball's in our court and it wouldn't be too forward to ask them out again this weekend!"

"Again?" I asked. Did I just get pulled into another triple date?

"Although it is possible we may require a buffer before making any rearrangements," Heather said, forgetting her assignment. She peeked at me, like she was asking for permission. Why?

Emma beat me to the question. "What do you mean?"

"Would it not be considered too abrupt to exchange dates?" Heather explained. She turned to me again. "You acquiesced that I may court Jake?"

"Sure." I shrugged. "But you're not pawning off Theo on me." I felt guilty even as I said it. Theo wasn't undesirable. Quite the opposite. He was physically attractive, mentally stimulating, and socially charming. But his awkwardness and attention toward me made me wary.

I knew the saying to "keep your friends close and enemies closer" didn't apply in Horror, but did it in Romance? Either way, I needed an excuse to stay out of Emma's plots.

"If you're planning another date," I said, "you two can double, but I have too much homework to take another weekend off."

DON'T DATE THE HAUNTED

Was that the best excuse I had? Sure, I wanted to study hard in Sean's memory and become the best paramedic possible, but my homework was manageable. Maybe I could plan to be sick?

"No," Emma said, "Heather's right. If you're switching dates, it would be wrong to jump so officially. We need to make the men feel like it's their decision too. Men can get jealous and that can cause problems, so we need to do the switch right."

I gaped at Emma. That was the first safety conscious thing I'd heard her say.

"If you want to be safe," I said, "I can help with that. It should be a comfortable, unofficial setting, like a hangout."

"That's a great idea," Emma said, "and since it's not an official date, we don't need to wait till the weekend too!"

Heather squealed with excitement again. I would never get used to that. "Ooh! Perhaps we could host another game night! I was unfortunate to miss the first one."

"No, that wouldn't work," Emma said. She didn't even act this serious and contemplative when she did homework. "Playing games would make the men competitive, bringing out their jealous side. But maybe we could watch a movie. We have a big screen and Marcellette has a huge collection of movies. We can plot the seating arrangements so Heather sits next to Jake, and can show her interest in him."

I wasn't too thrilled about it happening in our living room. Remembering the game night, I knew the socializing would carry through our thin walls.

I ignored the rest of their conversation and plotting to arrange Heather to sit next to Jake during the movie. Their scheming reminded me of times my brother and I ran through Haunting scenarios, discussing ways to survive life and death situations. The way Emma talked, it might as well have been a life and death situation.

C. RAE D'ARC

I stacked my homework and transferred it and myself to the study room for some quiet concentration. It took two trips. Asher and Ruby already took up two of the computers, but an armchair in the corner was open. The other Psi girls had earphones in, listening to music or discussion videos. I appreciated the silence as I attempted to bury myself in my books.

I had three solid hours of focus this way and finished my assignments in Latin and Pathophysiology. I was caught up in all my classes.

Maybe if I didn't do any homework for the next couple days, I'd have enough to keep me busy during the hangout.

I made that my plan, but came up empty when thinking of how to procrastinate. Was it really procrastinating if it was planned? I figured to watch a movie or read something from the library.

The next day, I received an unexpected email about my transfer credits. I went to the administrations building after my classes to sort out the issue. The line was long with students wanting to transfer classes or complain that their scholarships hadn't gone through. I waited for a full hour, then clogged the line for a half hour as I sorted out the details with a desk assistant. Apparently, my credits in Obstacle Courses 1022 were rejected and I needed another physical exercise class for my generals. Whatever. I'd deal with it next semester.

I returned home, wanting to relax with a light comedy movie. My heart plummeted as I heard male voices and laughter from my dorm.

Supernaturals, my roommates worked fast!

I opened the door to find my fear realized. Everyone talked in the front room as the copyright warning screens rolled through. The sofa wasn't long, but with Emma and Hank cuddling as tightly as Marcellette and her fiancé, all four of them fit.

This was my first time meeting Lord Rochershire, as Marcellette usually hung out at his house, so I took a moment to analyze him for possible Haunting characteristics. He was devilishly handsome with his thick blond hair, big blue eyes, and muscular figure, with a strong rectangular face for emphasis.

Too handsome and too strong. I wouldn't trust him for a minute.

Analysis done, I studied the other occupants. Heather and Jake sat on the loveseat at a comfortable distance from each other. Brooke was half swallowed in her personal beanbag between the couches. To the far side, they'd pulled out my favorite armchair for Theo's seat.

Of course, because life was ironic.

"Hey, Pansy!" Brooke greeted me as Heather announced, "My dear flower friend! You have come home!"

Theo stood. I've read about men standing when a lady entered, but only Theo followed this forgotten tradition at my entrance. Everyone else turned curious eyes or raised eyebrows to his sudden movement. My chest tightened with embarrassment as their eyes followed his focus on me.

Theo's attention flickered and registered the awkward situation. With a slight blush, he stepped to the side and gestured to the chair. "Will you grace us with your presence? You may take my seat."

Smooth recovery. Before answering him, though, I asked the group, "What are you watching?"

"It's my movie," Marcellette sneered, "And you should know, if you want to watch any of my movies, to ask me first."

"*Nearly Dead Newlywed*," Emma answered.

Crap. It was a good movie that I hadn't seen in years. I vaguely remembered the high-action scenes with frequent comic relief and romantic subplot. The temptation was too strong.

"Okay. I guess I could join."

I considered sharing Brooke's beanbag, though it was only big enough for one person. Without another option, I walked across the room to sit in the armchair, muttering a quick "Thanks" to Theo. That put him in the position without a seat. He shuffled his feet, then dropped to the floor and sat cross-legged to my side.

Lord Rochershire scoffed. "A room full of commoners, and the lord sits on the floor?"

Theo tilted his head at the man. "They may be commoners, yet they are far from common to me. I take greater comfort in knowing those around me are comfortable."

Marcellette's fiancé scoffed again. "Ah, you are one of *those* lords."

Theo flashed an exaggerated grin at Lord Rochershire. "And you are one of *those* lords."

Lord Rochershire's eye sockets deepened, and his spine straightened. His mouth pressed tightly into a near-invisible line. Marcellette turned her sharp nose upward and coughed like a rat squeak. Theo looked away first, mumbling an apology. He glanced at me, and shied away as our eyes met.

And awkwardness again. So much for helping others around him feel comfortable.

As the movie began, I forgot the uneasiness. The comedy thriller had jokes and action to distract me. At least, until halfway through the movie, when Brooke stood to leave, saying bye to her friends because she had homework to finish.

As she left, I caught Theo glancing at me again. This time he didn't turn away, but smiled. Something familiar about his smile teased my brain.

I was in trouble—that man was trouble. I knew it!

I turned to my roommates to tell them as much and make an escape plan when I remembered their response to the other time I mentioned "Theo is trouble."

I kept my eyes fixed on the screen for the rest of the movie, trying to ignore the delicious smell of cologne Theo waved at me each time he tossed his head back with laughter. It must have been his first time seeing the movie, as he laughed with genuine surprise and contagious humor. The movie ended with two hours before the dorm curfew, so everyone remained seated to talk about their favorite parts and jokes.

"'My name is Shannon,'" Heather quoted, "'short for shenanigans.'"

"Remember," Emma said, already laughing from the memory, "when Shannon says the wedding will be the death of her?"

"'Good to see yer past the denial stage,'" Hank quoted the response from the movie.

We all laughed. After catching our breath, Theo piped out, "My favorite interaction was when Gary told her 'You are beautiful.'"

His eyes met mine as he said it. I responded with the movie quote, "'You are too...kind.'" Like the character from the movie, I also felt awkwardly complimented and unsure how to respond. Had Theo given the compliment seriously or simply quoted the movie? Even more unnerving, a part of me hoped the compliment was real. I joined the laughter with everyone else a hesitant second later.

Heather mentioned something about needing a drink, but when she stood, Jake offered to grab it for her. They went together to the kitchen area and Emma and Hank decided to steal their spots on the loveseat. There was room on the sofa now, but Theo remained on the floor next to me.

"So, Theodor," Emma asked, "'The Trusted?' Were you named by your parents or as a title?"

"I was titled as part of a noble tradition in Margen," he explained. "On a lord's twelfth birthday, he is titled by the people based on his most prominent characteristic."

Emma yawned with wide exaggeration. "Apparently I can 'trust' you to give me a history lesson for every question I ask."

Theo's light mannerisms disappeared as his upturned lips dampened. Hank frowned and came to his rescue by distracting Emma with flirtatious whispers in her ear. That didn't stop Marcellette though.

"Seriously?" she jeered. "Trusted was—what'd you say?—your 'most prominent characteristic?' Aren't you from a Fantasy Kingdom, where people can, like, tame dragons and be princes of chivalry? But they called you Trusted? Sorry, but I don't think I can 'trust' you to sweep a woman off her feet."

Theo's throat bobbed with a heavy swallow as Marcellette's muscular fiancé laughed at her rude joke. She went a little too far. I felt more than sympathy for Theo; I had empathy about a mockable name.

Standing up for the bullied could put you between mean Hauntings, but Oz said that doing so *will either ensure your safety or your death as a hero*. It was a risk worth taking.

"Hey, Theo," I said, tapping his shoulder. He faced me, wearing an unexpected expression of a cool stone. He didn't appear angry, but neither was he welcoming. I hesitated, and he beat me to speaking.

"I wish not to offend any women of the house with my presence or an abrupt exit. With your permission, I will take my leave."

DON'T DATE THE HAUNTED

"Oh. Um, could I go with you?"

He blinked, surprised.

"Not too far," I explained. "I'd like to stay in sight, but maybe we could talk on the balcony?"

He hesitated, his face guarded but growing with curiosity. "If you desire it."

"For the record," I said, and he paused as he stood, "I think it's incredible to be trustworthy. It's a virtuous and rare attribute, especially around here," I added, loud enough for Marcellette to hear.

His stony expression softened and he teased a small smile. The expression stirred my memory again, reviving a sense of security and something that sent my insides jumping. Jumping with nerves? With anticipation? Or with worry? The undefined sensation came with doubts.

What was I doing? This man unnerved me since the day we met, and now I volunteered to step outside with him? Alone?

I analyzed the possibilities: as "The Trusted," Theo could be the most deceitful Haunting I'd ever met...or he could be my most valuable friend. Either way, Oz taught me to *Know your enemies as well as your friends.* It was time to determine which one Theo would be.

Chapter 10

SIGNIFICANT OTHERS

Be careful who you date
Respect and loyalty are key
Don't date anyone too rich or beautiful
Know your significant others' past, especially if they have exes or stalkers

- *Oz's Haunting Survival Book*

I lead Theo through the kitchen to the back balcony. He passed me to open the door and held it for me to exit first. I didn't like going through doors first, especially when waited upon. Why wouldn't the other person want to go first? Was there a danger beyond the door?

I had to remind myself that it was a courtesy.

On the balcony, I breathed in the fresh air. The dusky sky slightly worried me, but I'd replaced the outside lights. If they flickered, it was a direct warning.

They didn't flicker. Plus, I could see Heather and Jake talking from the dining area. I tapped on the window and waved so they wouldn't forget about us. Precautions secured, I turned to Theo, who leaned his arms over the railing.

Now that we were outside, I wasn't sure what to say. We stood in silence as I racked my brain for a conversation. He stole a couple curious glances at me, probably wondering what

I would say. If only I knew. I thought back to the conversations from before and considered how to get him to talk about himself. People liked to do that, right?

I wiped my hands on my hips and hoped to not offend him with my first attempt of a normal conversation. "If it's okay to ask, why did they call you Trusted?"

"Hah." He laughed humorlessly. "It is embarrassing. I try to wear my name proudly, as if I harbor no disappointment, though even in Romance it seems to be a mark of shame."

His shoulders hunched as he leaned on the railing with his arms, unbearably honest with his humility. I knew exactly how he felt.

"Hey," I said, "I'm *Pansy*. It doesn't get much worse than that from Horror. My only friends growing up were those who expected me to fall behind as sacrifice, or to give up and die like a coward."

He turned to me with a slight smile. Despite everything that made us different, at that moment we understood each other. We knew how it hurt to be told we were useless, and we fought against it.

"And it was only me," I went on. "My parents named my brother Oz, meaning 'strength.' And I got Pansy."

Theo chuckled with a sympathetic nod. "My brothers are Greggory the Wind Master, Dunstan the Night Shade, and Oswald the Fire Breather. Though what am I? The Trusted."

Yeah, a positive spin on that one was hard. I tried anyway. "So you don't master winds, breathe fire, or do whatever a nightshade does. It's not bad to be trusted, especially at the early age of twelve."

He took a deep breath and let it out slowly. "The reason is I cannot fight and my ability is useless."

"Wait." I paused. "You have an ability? Like magic?" That was unexpected.

He hesitated, then with reluctance said, "Yes."

Anything magical in Horror was attributed to the Supernaturals or Hauntings. More often, the Hauntings. Theo's attitude toward his ability, however, made me more curious than wary. Hoping to learn more and to comfort him, I exclaimed with extra enthusiasm, "That's so cool! Can you show me? What can you do?"

"I—" His eyes shifted, then he bent close to whisper, "It is not something I can do. It is something I see."

"Huh?"

"As I said, it is useless."

"How can a magical power be useless?" I argued. "You're talking to a girl with no magical powers at all."

He repeated a few of his earlier motions as he sighed, checked for eavesdroppers, and leaned closer.

"I see auras."

"Really?" I asked. "So you can see character types?"

"No."

"Then you see what people are feeling?"

"No."

"If they're good or evil?"

"No."

I couldn't think of another reason for seeing auras. "Oh."

"It serves no purpose," he huffed.

My positive spins came up short. "Well, hey, you fooled me," I said. "I thought you were from the Fairy side of Fantasy, where only powerful witches and wizards had magic."

Theo paused. "I am. Abilities are rare and mostly hereditary, though my father is Duke Konrad Fromm, the Horse, of Margen. Compared to my brothers with their incredible abilities, I was called Trusted because the city could think of nothing better. My whole family, all of Margen no less, considered my ability a mockery. They treated me as if I was unworthy to receive a useful ability because my entire being was useless."

"Ouch," I said. "But you don't believe them, do you?" Memories of school bullies and orphanage teasing flashed through my mind. Yet through it all, Oz defended me and taught me how to protect myself. If Oz hadn't believed in my capabilities either, my trials would have been unimaginably harder.

Theo sighed and turned to the road. "I am less familiar with the customs in Horror Zone, though in the kingdoms of Fantasy, people are valued for either their magical abilities or skills to fight. As for me? My ability is useless and I freeze in the friendliest competition. I cannot fight. I had the best teachers in Fairy, yet failed to master the simplest attacks. As part of the royal family, I was an embarrassment. I came to Heartford to make something of myself." He turned to face me, his expression determined. "Which I will. With my Masters in Political Science, I will prove my capabilities to serve as a Lord of Margen in a way no warrior ever has."

Wow. That was…intense. I found myself inspired and intrigued by his determination.

Unfortunately, I couldn't think of how to respond. Any words seemed jumbled or insufficient. Unsure of my actions, my hand instinctively reached out to him. My palm slipped next to his, and I smiled. I wanted to reassure him, though part of me hoped he took the gesture romantically. We were outside, alone, in the night, holding hands.

Condemnation, what was wrong with me? I had to say something before the moment became awkward.

"Thanks for sharing that with me," I said.

Okay, that should have worked, but he just spilled his diary to me. He probably expected more than a simple thanks.

Pulling my fragmented thoughts together, I said, "Thanks for trusting me. I understand the value and weight of being trustworthy. And...when you're told something your whole life, it's hard not to believe it. But you fought against it. You say you're not a combat fighter, but you *are* a fighter as much as I'm a survivor of Hauntings. I'm sorry about the circumstances that led you here, but I'm glad you came to Heartford."

He glanced down at our clasped hands then met my eyes. "As am I."

Then, the most bizarre thing happened. He smiled. The idea of him smiling at the situation wasn't bizarre, but *how* he smiled. His expression expanded beyond his lips as it spread through his cheeks, lifted his ears, and enlightened his eyes. His determined grin showed off a hopeful ambition, yet as the expression reached his eyes, I saw a peaceful sweetness. It was Sean's smile.

My heart lurched. Were Theo's lips as gentle and passionate as Sean's?

Oh—that was weird. I let go of his hand and leaned over the railing beside him. I needed a distraction to change the subject. Did he notice my moment of weakness? At least he said he couldn't see emotions in his auras. I took a deep, calming breath anyway. Maybe I didn't need to change the subject, but bring it back.

"So, do all auras look the same?" I asked.

"No."

"How are they different?"

"All auras are blue-green, though they vary in shade and length."

Blue-green like his irises. I shoved down the desire to analyze the depth of his eyes. Rather than acknowledge the intimate thought, I asked, "Length?"

DON'T DATE THE HAUNTED

"Yes." He showed off a hint of that tantalizing smile. "There seems to be no rhyme or reason for their lengths, though most remain reasonably static. Yours, however, is the most variable I have ever seen. You expand and compress to unusual lengths, shifting as quickly as a fairy godmother."

That was unexpected. Somehow, it made me feel vulnerable to think he saw me differently than everyone else.

I kept my face toward the road, not daring to meet his eyes. My brain managed to mumble out, "Huh, that's interesting."

"Yes," he said softly. "It is."

Supernaturals, I could feel that smile on me! Even worse, I could feel his eyes on me too, analyzing my aura, analyzing me.

I imagined what it would be like to see people with glows about their faces. Then, in the midst of all the still blurs, one person was constantly in motion: me. No wonder he had an interest in me. His attention toward me wasn't for a Haunting or a Romance, but mere curiosity.

I dared to glance at him and his hand found mine again.

Was it mere curiosity?

"Thank you," he said.

"For what?"

"For sharing your feelings about your own name. Also for surviving, fighting against it by being uniquely you."

I wanted to shrug it off and laugh like it was nothing. Instead, I found it difficult to hide my happiness from his compliment. We shared shy smiles, somehow understanding each other more than we would ever admit.

"I would," he hesitated, "like the opportunity to become better acquainted. Perchance there is a reason for the variety of your aura?"

"Then your ability could mean something," I inferred.

"Exactly." He grinned, then faltered with nerves as he continued. "Are you available this weekend that we may discuss this further?"

I couldn't tell if he asked me on a date or to be his study partner. All signs pointed to the date as he held onto my hand and his thumb timidly caressed mine. Strange how such a simple gesture could hyper my attention and soothe me at the same time. Was this how the seduction of vampires worked?

Whatever it was, it warmed my core, sent my imagination drifting with delirium, and coaxed my words. "I finish my Friday classes at 1:00."

He smiled again, and my heart raced like the adrenaline rush of a Haunting. I felt alive and anxious for each moment. My mind whirled at different possibilities and analyzed every detail, yet connected nothing. The same questions raced through my consciousness: Why was this happening to me? What did I do to deserve this?

Every other time I'd felt this way, I'd also felt terrified for my life. Everything flipped upside down. For the first time, I wondered why something so *nice* would happen to me.

My adrenaline rush jolted as the back door opened. Voices called out goodbyes from the living room. Hank poked his head outside. "Hey, Theo! Curfew's in five. We better get."

Whatever spell was on us broke at that moment. Our hands unclasped and suddenly became fidgety. Theo returned to his formal posture and I consciously straightened, unaware that I'd leaned in. Hank popped back inside with a knowing smirk.

"Miss Pansy," Theo said, reaching his hand forward, "I bid you farewell."

I met his hand with my own and no longer expected a handshake. He bowed and brought my hand up to his lips for a kiss without taking his eyes off mine. A chill ran up my spine,

DON'T DATE THE HAUNTED

almost like a Haunting shiver. It was weird, but exhilarating. The weirdest part was I liked it.

"Good night," I said, practically breathless.

Theo let my hand slip out with reluctance. He gave me one more of his perfect smiles before he left. I followed inside a minute later, a bit dizzy and lightheaded. With a quick bathroom stop, I caught myself in the mirror.

Who was that silly girl with the stupid daze on her face? And that smile...like all of Novel could crumble to pieces and she wouldn't even care. She looked like a Romantic.

Suddenly, I felt sick. I splashed water on my face and slapped myself a few times. When I left the bathroom, Emma ambushed me.

"Girl! We gotta talk!" She grabbed my hand and pulled me into our bedroom, where Heather hummed on her bed. "You're not getting away from us this time. If you make me wait three days to get all the juices again, I might burst!"

Emma plopped us down on my bed. "First of all, Heather, it seems our hangout was a successful exchange!"

Heather stopped humming and turned away to blush.

"Tell me tell me tell me!" Emma said, bouncing on my bed.

"Mr. Kennington—" Heather paused to blush deeper. "Jake asked if I was courting anyone, and then asked if he could fill that role."

"He asked you on a date?" Emma urged. "Did you hold hands during the movie? Please tell me you at least hugged goodbye!"

Heather's face somehow found a shade redder than before. "Our hands clasped briefly in the kitchen," she admitted.

"You owe us chocolates!" Emma squealed.

"I beg your pardon? Why is that?" Heather asked.

"Haven't you heard of the roommate boyfriend agreement?" Emma asked. Heather looked to me, but I shrugged.

"Well, we should have it anyway," Emma said. "It's just a fun way to celebrate new relationships with each other. First time one of us holds hands with a new boy, that person owes her roommates chocolate. For every first kiss, she owes the others cake. If we get engaged, we gotta take our roommates to a candle-lit dinner."

Heather's blush didn't go away, but it lessened intensity. "I have no qualms agreeing to the terms, though I wager between the three of us, you, Ms. Emma, will likely pay out the most. You and Mr. Hawkins rivaled the physical connection of the engaged companions."

Heather directed the accusation directly at Emma, leaving me out. I held in a sigh of relief. They hadn't seen Theo and me holding hands outside. Still, I didn't want to lie to them by hiding the truth.

The truth always catches up to you, my brother warned, *and lying to people can make them angry. Angry people can turn into Hauntings.*

Taking a deep breath, I braced myself for the ambush.

"I owe you chocolate too," I said, interrupting Emma and Heather's debate about dating ethics. They instantly went quiet and stared at me, eyes and mouths open.

"You—"

"Theo and I held hands while we talked on the balcony," I explained. For some reason, I had to struggle against a shy smile from creeping up my cheeks.

Heather gasped. "But you said—"

"Called it!" Emma jumped on my bed, laughing.

"I figure," I said, "if all of us owe each other chocolate, we could just go to the store together and buy to share."

"I was under the impression," Heather said, "that you were disinterested in Lord Fromm?"

I shrugged like no big deal. Emma didn't notice.

"This is so fun!" she said, bouncing. "This is the perfect beginning for a lifelong friendship! We'll get married together, and be each other's maids of honor! If we're gonna live next door and raise our kids together, I vote we live in New Angeles."

My panic reflected in Heather's face.

"New Angeles?" she said. "I disagree that the capital of Erotica is the ideal place to raise a family."

As much as I agreed, the destination of Emma's make-believe life plans was the least of reasons to freak out. I guessed it was my job to reel this in.

"So we held hands," I said, "that doesn't mean we're getting married." Actually, if I considered all the reasons I wanted to marry Sean, Theo was on the opposite spectrum. Sean had been an orphan who survived a mass zombie Haunting and wanted to be a medic. Theo and his powerful brothers were sons of a duke, for crying out loud. He even admitted to being an embarrassment to his family and to freezing in fights. Sure, he had political skills and charisma, but there was no compromising or talking out of a Haunting. No, even if I was attracted to Theo and his smile made me weak, it was foolish to consider anything beyond friendship.

Then why did that thought depress me?

To my roommates, I said, "I wouldn't say for sure that Theo and I really like each other. We simply understand each other in some ways and are interested in the ways we don't."

"Oh, yeah," Emma said. "Totally know what you mean. I'm kinda nervous. I know Hank and I are gonna run into the Dr. soon, and I'm afraid it might hurt."

"Ooh." Heather pulled a face. "I have heard the examination can be grueling."

"Who's the doctor?" I asked.

"It's not who, but what," Emma explained. "The D.R. is the awful but needed conversation when you Determine your Relationship. It's when you talk together about where your relationship is or isn't going. I really like Hank, and really want to move forward, but..."

"You fear he does not reciprocate your feelings?" Heather finished for her.

"But why?" I asked. "The way you cuddled tonight was like you're already dating."

Emma laughed. "Cuddling is way different from dating. I've cuddled with lots of people, but seriously dated? Hah!"

Heather shrank a little with a small terrorized frown, like her morals were bruised.

Emma continued anyway. "'I like Emma,' said no one ever. I mean, I've only been kissed by five guys before, and they were all non-committal make-outs."

Heather gasped. "People truly do that?"

Emma and I just stared at her, unsure of what to say. I'd heard of the idea, usually done by flirts with death wishes. Poor Heather. How did she make it to university this innocent? I never enjoyed the position of corrupting people.

Heather shyly bowed her head. "Mother says you only need two tries to determine whether or not someone is a good kisser. Divulging yourself in more before marriage is asking for trouble."

That was one way to never break the number one rule of abstinence. Not even Oz's rules were that strict.

Emma burst out laughing. "Oh, girl, you're in Contemporary now. Don't worry, I'll get you updated."

"Or," Heather hesitated, "perhaps the reason your relationships have been unfavorable is because you have not taken them seriously."

Ouch. That was bold. Could we rein this in before it turned ugly?

"Says the VL," Emma smirked.

"I have no shame in my virgin lips."

I shrugged. "It's better than being a lip-slut."

Emma gaped at me like I'd slapped her. "I," she said, taking calming breaths between words, "am *not* a lip-slut. I was lip-ravaged!"

"Sorry, that didn't come out right," I said. "I wasn't trying to call you a lip-slut. But seriously? You were 'lip-ravaged' with non-committal make-outs five times?"

Emma went red and pinched her lips together like she could hide them from my words. She stood and swept her hair around in a dramatic exit.

Heather and I sat still as the air around us grew thick with shame.

"That was perhaps a bit harsh, but I do thank you for defending my perspective," Heather said. "I don't agree with my mother on many topics, but she said relationships in Contemporary are statistically shorter because the people here are too flippant. They are afraid of commitment, and afraid that people will leave them when they discover who they truly are. They are also afraid to take their time, and want to rush to the peaks of their relationships. I do not understand it, and I appreciate that Mr.—I mean, Jake, has underlying Regency mannerisms."

I smiled to her, even though the dramas between Regency and Contemporary confused me. When did my life get so dramatic? I wasn't in the mood to apologize to Emma, so I pulled out my history textbook and decided to bury my guilt in it.

Emma didn't come back into the room for another hour. She cringed when she saw I was still awake in my bed. Actually,

I'd fallen asleep during my studies, but I was awake again, trying to make up for the lost study time. My head was clearer after my nap, and I'd hoped to catch Emma returning for sleep.

"Hey," I said. "I'm sorry. I didn't mean to call you a lip-slut."

Emma took a deep breath and released it. She rolled her eyes, not ready to forgive me yet.

I continued, "I'm still trying to get used to Romance culture. I'm sorry for taking out my confusion on you."

She climbed up to her bed and sighed again. "Yeah, I guess we're all wound pretty tight right now. I need some sleep."

"Okay, goodnight, Emma."

"Night," she said, and rolled over so her back was to me.

I hadn't expected her to accept my apology right away, though it was irritating to add another problem to my life. As if my mind wasn't already overworked from homework and Theo.

Chapter 11

WARNING SIGNS

> Threatening phone calls/letters/emails
> Cryptic messages
> Locals tell stories
> Signs that say "Beware of..." "Keep Out," or "Danger"
> Anything involving blood
>
> - *Oz's Haunting Survival Book*

"If I'm not in my office," my Novel History professor concluded, "you can slip your research paper under the door, but it will be counted as late."

I had my books stashed and my backpack ready to go before Hank even set down his pencil.

"Ya sure seem in a hurry," he commented.

"Yeah, I'm meeting Theo at the library right now."

He smirked. "Yeah, he told me about studyin' his ability with ya."

"Studying," I affirmed to Hank and myself. Not a date. No need to be anxious for a study. Besides, I had my own reasons for spending time with Theo other than the fact that he was handsome and an intriguing conversationalist. Whether he was as trustworthy as he claimed, or a deceitful Haunting in waiting, I wanted to learn more about him. "I'm unique to his ability. We think if we can determine why, we'll figure out what his ability means."

"Yer blush says ya might figure somethin' else out too."

My blush deepened and I turned away.

"I was hopin' to walk ya home as an excuse to say hi to yer roommate."

"Oh, Emma would be ecstatic. Here," I rummaged through my emergency pack and pulled out my keychain of religious symbols, "you can go on the errand to take this to her. Say I wanted her to borrow it as a good luck charm for her test."

Hank's half smile became bewildered, but he accepted my keychain, probably eager for any excuse to see Emma. In the least, my misunderstanding with Emma would be forgiven if she figured I sent Hank to her.

I thought a quick prayer to the Supernaturals that I wouldn't need my keychains for the next couple hours as I stepped away.

The outside architecture of Heartford University Library reminded me of the cathedral, with its plethora of columns and white stone archways. Inside, murals decorated the walls with scenes from across Novel, and live ivy crawled up corner pillars. The grand wooden entry and exit doors were especially clogged with students between class hours.

One boy walked by, speaking extra loudly on his cellphone. "Where in the HUL are you?"

How would I find Theo among all these people in this vast building?

Someone called my name. I turned and found him on the marble steps to the higher floors. He grinned and shivers ran through me. Shivers of excitement. Weird.

I tried to make my way over but struggled through the crowd. With authority like the University president, Theo set his course toward me and others made way. He didn't even notice the curious stares he left in the wake of his regal stroll. His eyes smiled only on me. Reaching me, he slipped his hand into mine to guide me from the crowds and back to the stairs. He didn't let go of my hand when we cleared the intersections.

"One benefit to your unique aura," he said, "is it makes you easy to find in a group. There are empty seats among the law documents. The space is public enough not to raise concerns over our reputations, though hardly anyone wanders through."

I shrugged, less worried about our reputations and more about being trapped alone with anyone. All the same, I was grateful he hadn't reserved a soundproof study room without windows. Circumnavigating long shelves of thick books, he guided me to a corner with a velvet armchair and floral sofa. There were maybe three other students among the shelves and desk cubicles.

"Is this your unofficial study spot?" I asked.

"Most of the time, yes." Theo glanced around, pleased with our open privacy. He set his side pack between the corner of the armchair and sofa, then sat on that end. That gave me the choice to sit beside him on the sofa, or corner to him in the armchair.

If this was a date, I'd sit on the sofa with him, but since it was a study, I was supposed to sit in the armchair. Right? Oz would have told me to sit in the armchair, but if Sean was in Theo's spot, Sean would have expected me to sit beside him. Crap, I was caught between a cushion and a soft place! My mind shouted at itself to stop scrutinizing and sit somewhere before it became awkward!

I sat in the armchair. I preferred armchairs. Oz would have approved. Right?

Theo's smile flickered like he considered an inside joke. Then, he cleared his throat and focused on retrieving a notepad from his pack.

"What?" I asked, nervous that I misunderstood something.
"Nothing of consequence," he said, still smiling to himself.
"Your face says otherwise. Did I do something wrong?"
"No, no." He chuckled. "I merely had the thought that you are by far the loveliest subject to enter my studies."

My turn to look away with a shy smile.

I was spared the need to respond as he asked, "How shall we begin, Miss Pansy?"

"Well," I flipped to a fresh page in my school notebook, and propped it up against my knee. "How about you tell me what you know about your auras. You've seen them all your life?"

Theo shrugged. "Indeed, though I was ten years old when I learned that others did not see them and this was my ability. Some auras range as long as the ketheric, or as short as the etheric body. Yours bounces everywhere between."

"Okay." I scribbled down some words he mentioned and nodded thoughtfully. "I don't know what those mean."

He laughed, a good laugh that could force a smile from even a ghoul. "Pardon me, I forget that only healers and diviners share my deep studies of auras. Etheric body is the innermost aura, emanating just a centimeter from the person. Ketheric is the outer-most, and ranges to about ten centimeters. That length is thankfully rare, as I struggle to sense subtle facial expressions of those with such auras."

"I can imagine." I smirked.

He leaned over his armrest to analyze the outline of my face. "Enlighten me, Miss Pansy. What makes your aura different?"

"I'm a Horror."

Theo shook his head. "I have met other Horrors—granted, not many—though none were as variable as yours. I do recall their auras were darker than the typical Fantastic's or Romantic's, yet I doubt that nationality is the sole reason."

"Darker?" I echoed.

"Indeed. The lightness fluctuates moment to moment, shifting as quickly as a person enters a room. Yours, again, is unique, as you are consistently a shade darker, no matter your situation."

"That sounds ominous."

"It could mean anything." He shrugged. "Though it would be a lie to say it does not trouble me." He leaned farther over his armrest and reached to the side of my face. "If I may demonstrate your lengths…" His eyes focused on what only he could see as his hand waved in and out, slowly back in, then shot outward again.

I tried, unsuccessfully, to not feel self-conscious and wiped my hands over my pants. Why did I sweat like the sixth circle of Inferno? Was Theo my next Haunting after all?

I dared to analyze him back for possible Haunting expressions like lust, anger, or madness. Instead, I found curiosity, a hint of worry, and a lot of something I couldn't define in those blue-green eyes and soft smile. Concern? No. Caring? No, something deeper that mixed the eyes of Oz and Sean.

If Theo was a Haunting, he was the most gentle and respectful one I'd ever met. Not that I was about to let my guard down, but why was I nervous? He was only Fantastic. A very handsome, sincere, *royal* Fantastic.

His hand demonstrating the length of my aura hovered an inch from my cheek. I had the strangest urge to lean into it, to feel his calluses, and encourage his fingers to slide through my hair. His blue-green eyes circled down to my lips, then quickly blinked and turned away.

Supernaturals, were we lost in each other's eyes? I thought people only did that in the movies. Supernatural condemnation, how the horror did this man have such an effect on me? What a weird Haunting…

"Forgive my staring." He cleared his throat. "You must be exhausted from men calling on you."

I consciously straightened and leaned back in my chair. Hoping to lighten the mood, I mimicked his formality. "Quite the contrary. Since the demise of my fiancé, men have stayed clear of me like a banshee."

Theo rocked back. "You were betrothed?"

Oh, right. I forgot who did and didn't know about that.

"Yeah." I bit my lip. "Only for a month. Then he was killed by a Haunting."

"Sorry, that must have been terrible," he said, the most honest condolence I'd received of Sean's death. Suddenly he wouldn't meet my eyes, but found a bottom row of law books fascinating and worrisome.

I grumbled at my lack of tact. Were we back to the awkward stage?

"Forgive me," he said again, "except I must ask for reputation's sake. Have you been…known by a man?"

I blinked, surprised by his blunt turn of conversation. "Um, abstinence outside of marriage is part of the number one rule of survival, because infidelity and lust are the main causes for Hauntings."

"I thought most of Horror had Contemporary standards, and especially if you were engaged—"

"It does," I said, "but Sean accepted my brother's rules. That was one reason I agreed to marry him. Why these questions all of a sudden?"

Theo sighed and met my eyes again. "Please excuse my frankness. I am eager to tell my father about the meaning of my ability, however, if I am to write of our studies together, he will pry for such information. It is one of the 'benefits' of royalty. The honor of my friends reflects on me, and my honor reflects on my family. I admit relief that your personal standards are similar to those of Fairy's keys of honor, despite your different reasons. Also..."

When he didn't say more, I rested a hand on his. He froze a little, but accepted my hand as he continued.

"Before coming to Heartford, I helped Lady Greenwood retrieve her stolen heirloom necklace. It was all delegation, yet I was her knight in shining armor and she, a beautiful princess. Apparently, not *my* beautiful princess. I asked her father for her hand in marriage, only to learn that she did not love me. She had, in fact, already given herself to another man."

"I'm sorry," I said, and truly meant it. Fool of a woman must have ripped out his heart and eaten it like a witch.

"Her family's reputation was soiled, then dragged through the mud," he said softly, like he was genuinely sorry for the woman who hurt him. His eyes met mine, and he shrugged. "What is the past if not for learning? I prefer to focus on the future. For instance," he straightened and graced me with one of his perfect smiles, "when we might continue this venture to determine your uniqueness to my auras. May we make this a weekly occurrence?"

"Sure," I smiled back.

My chest warmed every time I thought about meeting Theo again, but the next day I was bulldozed during my roommate lunch meeting. Tiffany arranged our Saturday luncheon at a local pancake diner and greeted us with her usual cheer.

"Welcome, Psi sisters—ohm'gosh—I have exciting news—the masquerade ball is finally legit!" She pulled out a flier advertisement to show off the official time and place.

Unable to read the flier from the far end of the table, I raised my hand to talk over the excited jabbers. "When and where will it be, exactly?"

"It's three Fridays from yesterday—from seven to midnight—in the Tower's penthouse—it's gonna be lit!" Tiffany announced, squealing with the others.

"Seriously?" I groaned.

"Ohm'gosh—right?" Tiffany said, misinterpreting my surprise. "They have a massive ballroom—it's so pretty—and a full commercial kitchen—ohm'gosh—I'm meeting with the caterers tomorrow—it'll be the greatest of all time!"

The rest of the meeting and luncheon went in a blur as I reeled over the predicament. One thing was sure: I wasn't going, but I saw some problems with that plan.

Problem one: make sure I wasn't asked as a date. That was my least concern. Problem two: Tiffany likely expected all of us to be there even if we didn't have dates, so I had to come up with another excuse not to attend. That idea led me to problem three: I couldn't stay home alone, so I had to convince another roommate that it would be more fun to sit at home with me while everyone else was out partying.

Okay, there was no way I could convince anyone it would be more fun, but it would definitely be safer. I remembered Halloween parties of my youth, staying home with Oz and his salt rings. There were always deaths at the parties, but there were also several people who came and left them thoroughly enjoying themselves.

What would it be like to attend a party without a care in Novel? I tried to imagine the masquerade: music, lights, crowds, and everyone in masks. Unknown identities and expressions surrounded me. I shivered. No, even if they guaranteed no Hauntings, I doubted such an event would let me relax enough to have fun.

The next few days revealed multiple omens of a Haunting as the masquerade boasted constant reminders that I couldn't run away. Posters and fliers of the same decorated masks were everywhere: at home, on campus, between hallways, even on the grocery store bulletins. Their empty eyes stared at me, watching me like spies for Mr. E. The worst of it began a week later as I came home to find the front door spotted with something red. Immediately, my brain went into alert mode. I could run, but where? Maybe if I found a place to hide and watch, I'd learn more about what kind of Haunting it was. I heard muffled voices from inside. Whoever it was, they weren't trying to sneak.

Stepping closer to the front door, my eyes focused on the red spots. They were paper cutouts of lips. It wasn't blood, but I didn't rule out vampires yet. This was the weirdest Haunting ever. Cautiously, I approached my dorm.

"Hello?" I asked, swinging the door open wide and checking the corners of the front room before stepping inside.

"Is that Pansy?" someone asked from the kitchen. There was a path of paper lips leading in that direction.

"Pansy—ohm'gosh—come see this!"

It sounded like Tiffany. She didn't sound like she was in trouble, but I ran anyway.

Standing around the dining table were Tiffany, Asher, and Brooke. Our table was large enough to seat eight people, but the whole thing was covered with more red paper lips. In the middle was a simple piece of paper addressed to Tiffany with guy's handwriting.

"Now that I've kissed the ground you walk on, will you go to the Masquerade with me?"

"Isn't it adorable?" Asher sighed.

"It's freaky," I said. "How did they get inside to hijack our table?"

Brooke put a reassuring hand on my shoulder. "No worries, girl, I let them in. I was home and helped them set up."

"So you know who did it?" Tiffany asked eagerly. "Ohm'gosh—was it Terry—oh, you don't know who Terry is—was he tall with blond hair?"

"I know who it was." Brooke nodded. "But you'll need to discover it on your own. His name's on the back of one of the kisses."

"Clever." Asher smiled.

More like sadistic, I thought. There were hundreds of kisses to check. Tiffany and Asher began pulling the paper lips from the table, checking the backs for the name. Brooke and I set to work on the front door and path.

"Brooke?" I asked, adding another red kiss to our trash pile.

"Yeah?"

"Are you planning to go to the masquerade?"

"Totally! What—are you thinking of ditching?"

I didn't need to say. My face gave me away.

"Come on!" she said. "They do it every year, and it's totally harmless! Okay, maybe the dancing's not totally harmless, but it's all for good fun."

I tried to hide my disappointment. Of all my roommates, Brooke seemed the most capable of handling a Haunting. I trusted her sound mind, and hoped to recruit her to stay home.

The corner of my eye caught movement of a figure in black. My heart skipped a beat before I recognized Asher walking in with an armful of paper lips. Brooke also turned at her entrance.

"Can you believe this, Asher? Pansy doesn't want to go to the masquerade!"

DON'T DATE THE HAUNTED

"Cool," she said. "Neither do I."

"You don't?" I asked. Maybe I shouldn't have been surprised since she openly claimed to be antisocial.

"Yeah, I've got loads of homework to do. My biology classes are taking over my life."

That sounded ominous, but I was willing to take a chance between antisocial Asher and homework versus a too-social masked gathering on the thirteenth floor of a suspicious building.

"Hey, I'll stay with you," I said. "And you like to watch movies while you do homework, right?"

"Yeah, the noise helps me think," Asher said.

"And don't you like corny romances?" I asked. "That's perfect! Will Ruby stay home too?"

Asher paused, picking up another kiss. "Dunno," she said. "She traded one of the hardest biology classes for a painting course. And she actually likes being around people, so not likely."

Well, one buddy was better than having nobody, and there was still time to recruit.

My options of possible party poopers dwindled as more of my roommates were asked to the ball. The next week, I was cleaning glitter confetti from the dorm patio when I spotted Mr. E again.

He stood behind a tree two houses away and made suspicious glances in my direction every minute. One of his hands was propped under his chin like he was deep in thought, except his mouth moved. Was he talking to himself?

Annoyed at his recurring presence, I waved and shouted at him, "Are you going to come over here and talk to me like a normal person?"

His grey eyes met my brown for a full second as he murmured one last thing to himself. Not that I enjoyed the

Mystery man's company, but if he was going to hang around, I preferred him to be in full sight. He rummaged with his trench coat as he approached, retrieving his favorite pen and notepad.

One house away, he greeted me. "Ms. Finster, I see college life hasn't changed?"

I gestured to the rope that led Emma around on a scavenger hunt that ended with the patio mess. "Hank asked Emma to the ball by hiding in a box with his guitar and glitter-filled balloons." How long was he stuck in there, waiting, so vulnerable? Now, Emma plotted her response inside, talking about a box of chocolates the size of a coffin. My words, not hers.

Mr. E tapped his pen to his paper. "You've been left as the cleanup service?"

I nodded, sweeping another group of glitter.

He took a deep breath and I tried to conceal my worries. Would he interrogate me again? Or was it bad news?

"Speaking of clean," he said, "your alibi checks out. Your phone records locate you at home, on the phone with Mr. Chase right before his death. Your roommate, Ms. Gretta Hartless, also confirmed that you were showering during his time of death."

"Oh, thanks for letting me know," I said. Why did I still feel like he was trying to pull something out of me?

Mr. E studied me until I shuffled uncomfortably. "So you're unaware of Ms. Hartless's passing?"

"What? Who? Gretta?"

"The day before her death, your roommate was contacted by Mystery's homicide department to confirm your alibi. She seemed surprised to learn you moved to Romance. Why didn't you tell her where you were going?"

I shook my head. "My roommates and I were on a need-to-know basis. The less we knew about each other's Hauntings, the less likely we could become involved or be tortured for information."

Mr. E's eyes narrowed. "Was it possible Ms. Hartless was tortured for information on you?"

I hoped not. Torture was supposed to put a person through as much agony as possible without killing them. If she was dead, I shivered to think how she suffered.

"How did she die?" I asked.

"She drowned in her bathtub after taking a heavy sedative."

"Oh. That's it?"

His eyes became slits. "Are you disappointed that she wasn't tortured?"

"No!" I said in a rush. "I'm glad it was simple—I mean, I'm not glad that she's dead—but I thought she'd go down fighting, or something heroic. She was a good fighter, strong, and stoic. I'm only surprised she was killed by something so simple."

"Uh-huh?" Mr. E continued to scrutinize me. "Speaking of roommates, did you know those of Mr. Chase?"

"Not well," I said, suppressing my relief at the change of subject. "We were already Haunting partners before Sean moved in with them, so he was labeled as the weird one who'd rather spend time with me than get drunk and hit on strangers. His roommates definitely didn't grow up with the same safety precautions of Hauntings. I wasn't surprised when the one was killed in the boating accident."

Mr. E lifted a suspicious eyebrow.

Oops. Wrong comment to make with the wrong person. Time to backpedal.

"I mean, he was like a drug addict who rode his motorcycle without a helmet. It was surprising he lived past adolescence."

Mr. E's eyebrows nodded for him and he flipped through his notebook. "Did any of Mr. Chase's roommates dislike him, or have any reason to hurt him?"

It was a good theory, but barked up the wrong tree. I shrugged. "I don't think so. Sean was friendly with everyone, and the only person involved with our last Haunting was killed earlier that week. Sean's roommates had nothing to do with the crazy doctor or the poltergeists he harvested."

Mr. E wrote some notes in his notepad. Flipping it shut, I relaxed to know the worst was over.

"Thank you, Ms. Finster," he said. "You've been very helpful. Would you mind answering one more question?" He pulled out a piece of paper. "Does this mean anything to you?"

Typed in all caps large enough to cover the lined and water-warped page were five simple words:

YOU CAN'T RUN FROM ME

My breath caught in my throat and my strength drained from my feet.

"What is that?" I asked.

"Do you know why this was found among Mr. Chase's belongings? It was printed recently. None of his roommates claim to know anything about it. Have you seen this before?" he asked. There was his condemning interrogation tone again.

"No," I said, not daring to say more.

My legs liquefied and I struggled to stand firm. It didn't help that Mr. E seemed to loom over me as he stepped closer. "Do you know who wrote this?" he asked.

My mouth worked up and down, but no words came. It was written by the same Haunting I fled. Why was it in Sean's belongings? Its first threat referenced Sean's inheritance, so maybe it was using and abusing our connection. If I couldn't run from it, did that mean it followed me to Romance?

"Ms. Finster?" Mr. E asked again.

DON'T DATE THE HAUNTED

"I-uh..." I stammered like someone guilty though I felt like a victim—possibly the next victim. How could I make him understand? "I might be in danger."

A hand landed on my shoulder. I shrieked and nearly jumped out of my skin. Theo stepped around me, wearing his shoulder pack like he was on his way to class. We'd met a couple more times each week to determine that his auras did not mean a person's lifespan, honesty, fighting skills, or a dozen other possibilities. We were sure they meant something, but still had no idea what.

"Good afternoon, Pansy," he said with that infectious smile. It faltered when he saw my face. "Are you alright? Mr. John, what were you discussing? This damsel is distressed."

Theo put his arm around me. Half of me hoped the gesture was affectionate, not simply protective.

"Ms. Finster just gave me alarming news," Mr. E said, keeping his eyes on me. "If you think you're in danger, would you accept a protection program? We have a safe house—"

"No," I cut him off. *When someone offers you protection, they usually want you alone and an excuse to carry a weapon around you.* "No, I'm safe at home. I want to stay here."

"If you insist," Mr. E said. He tipped his hat in goodbye. "You'll let me know if you think of anything else? I'll keep you updated and keep an eye on you. Take care, Lord Fromm."

I swallowed and tried to ignore the fact that his eye on me made me less comfortable.

"My flower," Theo said, and my insides warmed at his term of endearment, "are you unwell?"

"I'm fine," I lied with a deep breath, and waved a hand like it was nothing. "As long as Mr. E leaves me alone."

"Pansy." Theo stood tall, but I could tell he was nervous. His arm trembled as he removed it from my shoulders and stood before me. Did he suspect Mr. E too? It would be nice to have someone on my side.

Even as I considered the odd pair we'd make for investigating an investigator, Theo spouted words in a quick stream. "I appreciate that you are the practical type and do not require extravagant query demonstrations. Nevertheless, I desire you to accede my offering and proposal."

I heard the words, but none of them made sense to suspicions against Mr. E. Despite his verbose diction, all I could say was, "Huh? Proposal?"

Theo flushed. "Allow me to begin again." He flustered with something in his coat pocket then extended it to me with a simple explanation. "I commissioned this for you."

My eyes widened as he revealed a delicate necklace. A gold chain held a red and black pansy pendant. It was beautiful, but not too dazzling to create envy. The chain was too dainty to choke me, and just the right length to not flop around during a sprint. It was perfect.

I picked it up with one hand as my other reached for his. "It's beautiful. What's it for?"

"I understand you are unaccustomed to escorts, however…" Theo cleared his throat like a gentleman, then swooped into a bow. "Miss Pansy, may I be your escort to the masquerade?"

"Uhh…" Brain. Dead. What just happened? He asked a question. I needed to answer. "I'm not going."

Theo visually tensed like I'd punched him in the stomach. He straightened slowly, and didn't make eye contact. His hand started to slip away, but I held tighter.

"It's not that I don't want to go," I rushed to explain, "but I can't."

He met my eyes. "What do you mean?"

I prayed to the Supernaturals that he'd understand. No one else understood me though. My words couldn't sound like a lame excuse for rejecting him. "It's dangerous. It goes against every rule for survival. If I go, a Haunting will be there, I'm sure of it."

"Haunting," he repeated slowly. I could almost see the magic currents of his brain working. "In Fantasy, I think we refer to those as Adventures. A new problem arises every year and it becomes a Hero's duty to vanquish it. Pansy, if you suspect a problem at the ball, then should you not have all the more reasons to attend?"

At least he tried to relate. I squeezed his hand, pleading to the Supernaturals again. "Theo, it's not an Adventure. People *die* in Hauntings. If one followed me from Horror, the masquerade would be the best time and place to strike because it breaks all the rules. I would be vulnerable, then everyone else attending would be in danger, depending on how the Haunting attacks."

Theo carefully considered my words as his thumb grazed over my hand. "We are a month into the semester. If a Haunting followed you, why has it waited this long to come after you?"

"I don't know. Maybe it's still gaining strength, or maybe I lost it by moving to Romance, or maybe it's waiting for me to be vulnerable, like at the masquerade."

"Alright, then what is the probability that a Haunting followed you?"

I chewed on my bottom lip. There was the new letter found by Mr. E, but he only said it was written "recently." Did that mean yesterday, last week, or last month like my first letter? I shrugged. "Fifty-fifty? It either did or it didn't."

Theo's smile dawned like a sunrise. "I like those odds."

"Theo," I complained, "fifty percent is still a failing grade."

"Not if life adjusts to the curve."

He didn't make this easy. His hand continued to caress mine as he held me with his smile and eyes. I wanted to accept his invitation. I wanted to join my roommates. I wanted to know the feeling of being carefree.

"I can't risk it," I said. "Every moment during a Haunting, you and everyone with you is ten seconds away from death."

"Is that not the way of life?" he asked. "Are we not always ten seconds away from death?"

That was...an interesting argument.

"My flower." He stepped closer with a questing version of his perfect smile. "I was rarely the Hero of Adventures, so I learned to see life as a constant Adventure. You call yourself a 'survivor' of Hauntings, and I reckon it is because you see life as a constant Haunting. You, of all people, should know the dangers of just going outside. Right now we stand beside a road in the middle of a university city. How many ways could our lives end in the next ten seconds?"

I paused to consider his challenge. I counted several ways, mostly involving each other. How many weapons did I carry with me in my emergency pack? Almost every one of them could be turned against me.

"Every breath we take is a gift, granted to us by the gods," he said. "If our very existence is a possible peril, what difference will it be to attend a possibly perilous ball? At least let me be by your side. Would you let me be your sidekick for the evening?"

He took another step closer. It didn't help that he gave a good argument and wore an appealing cologne. His thumb curled around my hand, sending shivers of desire through me and fogging my judgement. Condemnation, it was tempting.

"I can't," I said, half regretting it already. "I can't risk putting everyone in danger, especially you. Anyone I've ever cared about is dead because of Hauntings. Please, don't add yourself to that list."

His eyes flashed with hope before they turned downward. "I see. Regardless, I hope you keep the necklace."

"I will," I said, eager to keep our friendship/relationship/whatever we had. "Can you, um, help me put it on?"

His eyes snapped back to mine and his expression softened. He made me feel warm and safe, like coming home after a dangerous Haunting fight in the woods. His fingers slid across my hand as he lifted the necklace. He stepped behind me and the nearness of him set my heart racing. With gentle hands, he worked at the clasp. I shivered as his fingers grazed my neck, brushing away the ends of my hair to set the chain in place.

Could I persuade him to stay with me during the masquerade? Probably, but I shouldn't in case the Haunting came for me at home. I was an idiot for rejecting him. Heather and Emma would never let me hear the end of it if they knew. How many women would swoon for the chance to dance with this handsome gentleman?

An unfamiliar pain rose in my chest at the thought of Theo going to the dance with someone else. I tried to convince myself it wasn't jealousy, but worry for his safety because of his connection to me. Regardless, it meant I cared about Theo in a way I wasn't ready to admit.

Chapter 12

ESCAPING

Never split up
Don't expect phones or cars to work
But make sure your phone is always charged, and your car is always in perfect working condition

- *Oz's Haunting Survival Book*

One week before the masquerade, we had our Saturday luncheon at home with Sci-Fian take out. The star noodles, moon potatoes, and sentient cow were garnished with a special spice. There wasn't much room on the table for food as white masks, paints, feathers, and a variety of other crafts covered every surface in the kitchen.

"Ohm'gosh—I'm so excited!" Tiffany said with one of her cheerleading claps. "I bought sooo many supplies—who else is excited to make their masquerade mask?—You can match your gowns—I know some of you don't have dresses yet—maybe making a mask will give you ideas."

I pushed my mask to the side and focused instead on keeping my noodles on my fork. The last time I saw a full white mask like that, it had a chainsaw serial killer behind it. Apparently, my fourth foster mother was an extremist against school bullies. No one else mocked my name for a whole year after that.

DON'T DATE THE HAUNTED

For the rest of my roommates, this was the best luncheon ever. Even Asher started a mask, though her plans were to stay home and watch romcoms with me.

For the first ten minutes, each girl debated with herself about how far to cut into her mask. I didn't see the point of a mask that only covered around the eyes. That hardly covered a person's identity. My plate was already empty, but I didn't want to be the first to leave the table.

My roommates joked and laughed as they played with the supplies. No one planned to make theater or sporting masks. Instead of blood, warts, and deformed features, these masks were colorful, fun, and even sparkly.

Could I make something so cheerful and carefree? Could I hide my troubles and pretend to be someone else? Someone who didn't check over her shoulder every block for a snooping Mystery detective? Someone who could return the affections of a Fantasy lord without doubts?

Picking up a pencil and crafting blade, I decided that it couldn't hurt to simply express myself creatively. I worked my mask's frame to be larger than the others', covering my full frontal and the length of my nose. The incisions became studious as I reviewed my medical terminology and Latin by cutting my mask below the cheekbones—or zygomatic bones—*zygo-* meaning pair in Greek, and *-matic* from Latin's *medi* for middle.

Unfortunately, the homework mindset cramped my artistic intentions. I had no idea how to decorate my mask. My creative juices were specialized in crafting weapons from everyday objects, not glitzing up face obstructions. I didn't feel particularly cheerful about the whole idea, so I grabbed the black paint.

As the paint dried, I analyzed the others' masks with colors, glitter and designs. I was disappointed with my own. The masks were for a ball, after all. Not that I knew much about masquerade masks, but I thought it safe to assume they were different from the Reaper's.

I considered how to glamorize my mask as my fingers pet the pansy necklace at my sternum. I wore it every day since Theo gave it to me. Its black and red colors became my muse. With some advice from my roommates, I glued red gems under my mask's eyes and small white feathers on top (the supraorbitals), like eyelashes. Feeling creative, I wired lacework over the eyebrows and up over the edge (to the coronal suture). I attached more white feathers with a dash of red, resulting in a bird-like mask. It was elegant enough, but dulled in comparison to Heather's mask.

Hers resembled a glittering crown with eye holes. She laced the top with intricate gold wiring and nested jewels. She also hot glued lilac lace to a headband to give her tiara/mask a second level.

Emma's mask, on the other hand, was more like a piece of lingerie. It had black lace with thin pink ribbon bordering the hourglass frame around her eyes. She also gathered a small handful of pink feathers and black fish-netting.

"You're putting all that on your mask?" I asked.

"No," she said. "I'm also making a black pillbox hat. I'll use the netting to make a classy veil."

A knock on the door interrupted all conversations. My roommates glanced toward the front room, but apparently no one expected visitors. Eventually, Marcellette set down her whiskered cat mask and stood.

"Is it your fiancé?" Tiffany asked, working her mask with a fake mustache, glasses, and bushy eyebrows.

Marcellette shrugged. "I told him I have plans every Saturday at noon, but maybe he has an update from our caterer."

DON'T DATE THE HAUNTED

Unscheduled visitors were always a cause for alarm. It was difficult with the busy crafting and chatter, but I tuned my ears toward Marcellette as she opened the door. The door closed and Marcellette returned, holding a poster.

"Asher has an admirer!" she said, smiling, though her eyes said she didn't care.

At the top of the poster were the periodic table elements of Arsenic, Hydrogen, and Erbium to spell out the blocked letters of [As][H][Er].

What followed was so cheesy that I almost puked a quesadilla.

"Are you made of Copper and Tellurium?

Because you are [Cu][Te]!

Will you go to the Boron, Aluminum, Lanthanum [B][Al][L(a)] with me?"

Ruby giggled, jumping from her chair to analyze it. "Who's it from? Is there a name?"

"It must be someone from my chemistry class." Asher blushed.

Brooke pointed to the bottom of the poster. "There are two more elements down there."

"Beryllium and Nitrogen," Asher read. "Be and N—it's Ben!"

"Is he the shy one you told me about?" Ruby asked.

"Ohm'gosh—how will you answer?" Tiffany grinned.

Asher blushed. "I guess I'll have to finish my homework early. I need to grab my periodic table to see how to spell out 'yes.'"

A chorus of excited squeals and laughter broke out. Everyone was thrilled except me. Asher was my only recruit, and now I'd lost her. My mind grasped for my options. Go to the haunted dance, or stay home alone all night. Neither option sounded safe.

As everyone crowded around Asher for suggestions on where to buy a dress and other accessories, I sat at the table, lost in thought. A light in my peripheral blinked as heavy electronic music played.

"Brooke," I said, "your phone's ringing."

Brooke reached over, her smile excited for Asher, but her eyes transitioned to confusion. "It's my mom," she said, then answered. She left us for the quiet of her bedroom.

She didn't return as the rest of us finished decorating our masks. Asher decided she needed to start over, now that she was attending the ball. Ruby sat and talked with her, and I subconsciously added more feathers. My mind was elsewhere, freaking out about my predicament, while also concerned for Brooke.

It was nearly dinner time as the crafts were slowly cleared away. My mask was a full feathered bird of black, white, and red with accented rhinestones on defining lines. We moved Brooke's mask and crafting tools to the corner so she could finish when she returned. She had brown and gold paint with some gear stencils and a glass eye cap. I couldn't erase Brooke's expression of surprise and worry before she left. She was my friend, and I wanted to help.

Knocking on her bedroom door, I cracked it open and peered inside. Brooke was at her desk, holding her head up with her hands, staring mindlessly at her phone.

"Brooke?"

She jumped, startled from her trance. "Oh, hey," she said. "What's up?"

"We cleaned up the crafts, but your mask is still on the table," I said. "We left out the tools you were using, but if you need anything else, Tiffany said to ask her."

DON'T DATE THE HAUNTED

Brooke blinked a few times, then released a depressing sigh. "I won't finish my mask. I probably won't make it to the ball."

"Huh?" I asked. Would Brooke be my new party-pooping friend?

She didn't reply right away. She leaned back in her chair and stared at her side of the bedroom. She shared with Asher and Ruby, but I liked Brooke's side of the room most. She had her own shelf built from piping to hold various books on lands and cultures. On her wall were several quotes from historical texts and random inspiration. I found a new favorite every time I read through them.

But something was off. Her large luggage cases that were normally stored under her bed were pulled out and open.

"'I must not fear,'" she said, quoting a post on her wall. "'Fear is the mind-killer. Fear is the little-death that brings total obliteration. I will face my fear.'"

"Paul Atreides," I said, recognizing the speaker. "What did your mom say?"

Brooke took another deep breath. "My dad's working for a space launch to exile many criminals, including a super dangerous mutant who killed dozens of people and destroyed a whole town." She paused to gather her words. "If my dad was leading the project, I wouldn't worry, but he's average cannon fodder for this Experiment. My mom and family's worried the mutant will escape and my dad will be caught as collateral damage." A tear broke free from her eyes and she croaked, "I'm—" She cleared her throat and began again. "I'm leaving tomorrow for home."

"Supernaturals, I'm sorry," I said, sitting on the floor by her luggage.

Brooke shook her head. "Experiments can be super beneficial for the few scientists, inventors, or teams, but there's always the chance it'll be fatal for dozens of uninvolved citizens." She paused to face me directly. "To be totally honest, I was jealous of the Horrors' Hauntings. From what I know of them, they only impact a handful of people at a time. In Sci-Fi, our Experiments can alter the lives of hundreds, not including their families."

"Your Experiments are a bigger scale," I realized. "But Horror also has Mass Hauntings every couple years. How often do your Experiments happen?" I asked, hoping to find a light.

"About every year. Since they're on such a large scale, we're only on the Lead Team about twice a decade," she said. "Some scientist, inventor, or team creates a way to benefit our realm. Soon after, some evil or corrupted group twists the Experiment to wreak total havoc for that team. The team usually scrapes out with some damage, but the casualties on the side are astronomical."

Brooke cleared her throat again and turned her head away to wipe her eyes. I reached over to wrap my arms around her. I didn't know what else to do. Sure, I lost both my parents, but I was young. I didn't remember what it was like to lose a parent. The closest experience I had to relate was losing Oz. That had nearly crippled me.

With Brooke sitting in her chair, our hug was awkward. I held on anyway, knowing there was no better comfort I could offer than understanding. Eventually, Brooke sniffled and pulled away.

"Be safe," I said. "Even if the Experiment is fine, you should have this time with your family. I'd give anything to spend one extra day with my brother."

Brooke responded with a simple, sad smile. "How did your brother die?"

I hesitated, unsure how much to say. I didn't like talking about it, and there was no use crying over the past. Except

Brooke didn't ask the question to pity or understand me, but to understand the death of a loved one.

"I'm not really sure," I said. "It was two years ago. He normally walked me home from school, until one day he didn't. I ran home and found him in our apartment. It looked like he barricaded himself in the corner with all our furniture. Everything was torn up, and Oz was..." I closed my eyes and failed to banish the image of my brother's bloody corpse. With a hard swallow, I explained, "He'd been jumpy for a long while and said demons were stalking him, but from the scratches on his body, I figured it was some kind of werewolf. I faced one a month later and hoped it was the same as I silvered its heart."

Brooke was silent for a moment, as though paying her respects to my brother. "Did you wish you could have done more?"

I sighed. "So much I thought I'd go insane. My therapists encouraged me to carry his legacy instead of his burden. This book," I said, pulling out my brother's survival book, "this is his legacy, and I'll share it with anyone who will listen."

Brooke didn't say anything, but took a deep breath then let it out slowly.

"Do you need help packing?" I asked.

She shook her head no. "But will you sit and talk with me while I pack?" A small smile teased her eyes. "Word in the stars says you know my international friends better than I do."

I inwardly groaned. I still felt bad about turning Theo down for the dance, but realized the conversation would be a nice distraction for Brooke. I forced a smile and a blush saying, "I've studied with Theo every week about his ability, and Hank's great at explaining our History assignments. I owe the friendships all to you since you dragged me out to that first meeting. But Emma should really be the one thanking you. She's convinced Hank's her soulmate."

"Yeah, I super didn't see that coming." Brooke laughed, and suddenly everything seemed a little less dreary.

Everyone came out to say goodbye as Brooke left for the airport the next morning. She'd be back in ten days with a load of makeup homework.

I gritted my teeth as I smiled to wave goodbye. I told her to go. What kind of friend would I be to ask her to stay and brave the possibility of a Haunting with me? And that frustrated me. Brooke was my friend, and probably the most capable among my roommates at surviving a Haunting. She could handle weapons. She understood death and fear. And I told her to go. Besides, I had no proof that there would be a Haunting during the masquerade.

Each of my roommates wanted to show Brooke support through hugs, well wishes, and last second farewells. We were the most unified as we all waved goodbye, even though Marcellette lingered on the porch with Lord Rochershire. I was pretty sure Mr. E watched our farewells from a window in The Tower. Creeper.

Soon after, everyone seemed to break apart. Tiffany went berserk over preparations for the ball, traveling back and forth to the Tower and shops for decorations. Marcellette hardly came home to sleep between outings with her fiancé. Asher and Ruby were either busy in the kitchen with homework or out shopping for Asher's ball gown. Then, Emma began acting like Marcellette, preferring the park or some other place to be with Hank. Heather and I found ourselves hanging out in the front room simply because no one else was home to take over the TV or couches.

A few days later, the family room was our new habitat. I even used it for my studies with Theo that week as we determined his auras did *not* show fears, knowledge of Hauntings, seriousness of mood, or (to my great relief) attraction to

Theo. Instead, he observed that my aura spiked less often, holding at the shortest possible length, and grew darker with each passing day. Whatever that meant.

One afternoon, I was practicing my Latin, joking about the sounds of words and phrases with Heather while she cross stitched a garden with a pink tree standing tall off to the side.

The door's lock jiggled and I reflexively reached for my emergency pack. I relaxed incrementally as Emma entered.

"Hey," I said. "Where've you been all morning?"

"Huh?" she asked. "Oh, I was at the park, working on a project."

"Again?"

Emma had a secretive smile on her lips, like she giggled about an inside joke with herself. Something was off.

"Didn't you wear that yesterday?" I asked. Emma never went out in public wearing the same outfit two days in a row. "Did you not come home last night?"

"OMG, Mom, I'm an adult and can go wherever I want," she said dramatically. "I had the most amazing night, but neither of you would appreciate it, because what have you been doing? Homework and cross stitching?"

"This is my homework," Heather said. "My Life Skills teacher assigned us to create a piece that defines us."

"That's interesting," I said, feigning interest when my attention was wholly on Emma's possibly dangerous "amazing night." "Emma, you weren't alone, were you? Did you stay somewhere else, or were you at the park all night?"

"What, Mom, you want to know?" Emma asked, her voice quickly escalating with a weird mixture of sarcasm and excitement. "Good! Because I'm bursting to tell someone! Hank and I slept together last night!"

"What?" Heather and I shouted together, sharing horrified gawks.

"Come on, you sticklers!" Emma whined. "This is Contemporary! People do it all the time, and it's not like we didn't use protection."

"And then they die!" I shouted. "Having sex out of wedlock is the number one lure for Hauntings! A condom won't protect you! They know what you do at night; they *own* the night!"

At the same time, Heather said, "The media does not portray the people as a whole! Simply because a concept is popular does not make it right!"

Emma rolled her eyes. "Seriously, you've been here for over a month now. You two have really got to get with the times."

"The Horror Zone is contemporary too!" I shouted. "Sure, all the best Haunting defeats are centuries old, but you never break the number one rule of abstinence!"

"You don't get it!" Emma shouted back, now a mixed mess of anger and disappointment. Tears dripped from her tired eyes as her cheeks speckled red. "You're not in Horror Zone anymore! This is Contemporary, Romance! Sleeping together is the highlight of a Romance! It's an emotional and physical climax that you get to share with someone special! I just wanted you to be happy for me!" Turning away, she ran to our bedroom and slammed the door.

Heather and I simply sat there, stunned. In our silence, we heard Emma's muffled weeping. Crap. Yeah, my reaction had been less than thoughtful, even if it was out of concern for her safety. Condemnation.

Slowly, I walked over to the bedroom door. I took a deep breath. She was right; we weren't in Horror. If we were, she'd already be dead.

Praying to the Supernaturals for understanding, I cracked the door open.

"Go away!"

A pillow was thrown at the door, but her distress made for bad aiming.

I didn't know what to say, but I didn't want her to be upset with Heather and me. If anything, we had to sleep there too. I quietly sat on my bed and eventually Emma peeled her tear-stained face from a soggy pillow.

"I wanted someone to be happy with me. It was a dream come true, but—but—" She coughed on a sob.

But?

"What's wrong?" I asked.

"But it's a peak, not a resolution."

"Huh?"

"Romances are divided by peaks." She paused again to hiccup and sniffle. "First dates, D.R. tests, first kisses, proposals, and making love are all peaks. Usually there's a problem that comes up after these major peaks, especially first kisses and making love."

I waited to respond to let her know I considered her words. "Kind of like how Hauntings come when you feel most at peace. I can understand that."

Emma shrugged. "Sure. Well, Hank and I hit a major peak, but something's coming! I just know it! We've had such an easy Romance but problems have to show up sometime! And the longer we've gone, the more I'm afraid it'll be big! It's all been so wonderful, I don't want anything to change!" She started sobbing again and buried her face back into her pillow. This time, I climbed up to her top bunk and sat beside her. Unable to embrace the prostrate woman, I simply scratched her back like Oz would for me. I hadn't cried that way in a long time, but I understood the dread.

Life was supposed to be hard, right? So whenever it seemed easy, I couldn't truly enjoy it because it wasn't meant to last. I remembered a quote on Brooke's wall: "If you want a happy ending, it all depends on where you end it."

"So," I began, hoping to lighten the mood, "you kissed, right? That means you owe us cake?"

Emma turned her head toward me to smile behind shy tears. "Yeah. Lots of cake."

Chapter 13

EMERGENCY PACK ESSENTIALS

Gun with extra gold and silver bullets
Silver and wooden stakes
Holy water and religious symbols
Pocket knife and multi-tool
Matches, compass, first aid bandages, map of area

- *Oz's Haunting Survival Book*

Screams woke me before the crack of dawn. I bolted upright in my bed and suppressed my urge to scream with them. It took me a good minute to clear my mind from my nightmare and remember it was just the plumbing. My roommates and I stayed up too late the night before. We enjoyed Emma's red velvet cupcakes with a chick flick and choked on laughter when the delirium of the night hit us.

My momentary freak out disrupted Heather's sleep. She pulled her extra pillows over her face and moaned, "It is probably Tiffany. She did mention an early departure for the masquerade."

I checked the time. Early was right. Who showered at 4 a.m.? What else did Heather say? The masquerade?

Right. The masquerade was today. I buried my face in my pillow, thinking my life was a nightmare. I wanted to go back to sleep, where I could at least control my dream of Sean threatening Emma with a water gun, and Mr. E dropping my proof of innocence down a never ending stairwell.

A few hours later I woke up to the busy sounds of my roommates playing dress up. The dreaded day was here. Tiffany appeared to be moving out with all her makeup, a miraculously contained dress in a bag, and a bunch of fancy decorations she'd stored who-knows-where. She had a bagel in her mouth and a sack lunch in hand as she stepped out the front door.

"Come when you can to help set up!—Ohm'gosh—it's gonna be amazing!"

Marcellette left soon after without any explanation.

Asher and Ruby locked themselves in their bedroom, hoping to get all their homework done before the event. The rest of us scoffed, but left them alone to try.

My first obligation was to check my emergency pack. Revolver with one bullet loaded (not in the immediate cartridge), plus several extra gold and silver bullets: check. Matchbook: check. Aspergillum: check. First Aid kit: check. Wood and silver stakes: check, check. Keychain of various religious symbols: check times seven.

Then, I prepped my desk with my homework and music player. While everyone else would be out dancing, having a ball of a time, I'd sit alone at my desk with history and nutrition homework. I already dreaded my fate. At least I finished my Latin assignments in advance. I figured it unwise to practice the language of the dead on a night of trying to avoid the undead.

Crap, I was going to be so bored. In my case, boredom could lead to anxiety and depression. Staying home from parties had been a lot easier with Oz or Sean.

DON'T DATE THE HAUNTED

I remembered Theo's words: *If our very existence is a possible peril, what difference will it be to attend a possibly perilous ball? At least let me be by your side.*

How badly I wanted him by my side. I did want to go to the dance. If I was about to die, I wanted to go out on my own terms: fighting and defiant. And if I wasn't about to die? Then I'd regret rejecting Theo even more than I already did.

A storm brewed outside, slamming wind into the walls. Trees outside my bedroom creaked like a skeleton stalking through an old house. I tried to focus instead on the chatter and laughter of my roommates as they prepared for the ball.

The bathroom was a madhouse as my roommates showered and pampered their faces. I ate lunch and waited to take my own shower until all the stalls were available, hoping our water heater adjusted again. Thankfully, Tiffany and Marcellette hadn't used all the hot water. I jumped in while only Emma and Ruby remained by the sinks and I sang so they would hear me.

"I slay monsters and demons, Hauntings and Horrors
  Slaughtering laughter from abhorring torturers
  But I'm also a Horror backed in a corner
  Innocence gone, am I also a murderer?"

Ahhh…I needed this. The warm water fell on my head, seeped to my skull, and tumbled down my back. I closed my eyes and willed myself to relax.

Thankfully, the hot water was adjusted as I soaked extra long. The heat loosened my muscles, and the cleansing routine calmed my mind.

Heather's voice joined Emma's, and the decibels raised enough that I could follow their conversation.

"OMG, yes! Girl, I've been waiting all semester to do your makeup! I don't know if I have your colors, but I saw this video online how to lighten foundations. Sit down and lemme get my stuff!"

Squeals ensued. I jumped, but recognized the laughter behind the shrills.

How could they laugh so carefree? A Haunting might come for me, and they acted like there wasn't a care in Novel. Ignorance really was bliss, I grumbled to myself.

At least they were happy.

That thought made me pause. If I went to the dance and brought a Haunting with me, they may escape or die happily with friends. And if I stayed home? I'd die tonight, alone in my room next to the stinking toilets, freaking out every time the wind creaked. Supposing a Haunting followed me in the first place, I couldn't guarantee its focus would remain on me if I was safe while my friends danced with omens.

Emma and Heather chatted and plotted about the dance. Jake asked Heather to the dance a day after I rejected Theo. Still, my roommates jabbered on about the possibilities of dancing with a handsome stranger, then the Romanticism of discovering who he was behind the mask. The whole idea sounded stupidly dangerous to me.

That was the final straw. They needed me. Whether or not a Haunting followed me. Whether I brought danger with me, or they endangered themselves at the dance. They needed my support. And I needed their friendship.

With a final rinse, I ended my shower and toweled off. I stepped from the behind the curtain and paused.

Heather had a natural beauty with her curly brown hair, milky skin, and heart-shaped face. Emma's makeup simply emphasized what she already had: big blue eyes, full cheeks, and an innocent smile.

"Supernaturals, Heather," I said. "You're seriously pretty."

Her blush became genuine. "You truly think so?"

Emma smirked. "You're a babe. Jake's gonna trip over himself when he sees you."

I smiled to agree, and Heather giggled.

"Oh, Pansy, allow Emma to dress you next!"

"Ooh, can I?" Emma clapped her brushes with excitement. "I've been dying to try something with your colors!"

"Please don't die," I said.

Emma swooned backwards with her hand to her forehead. "It would *kill* me if you don't let me play with your face!"

She and Heather laughed. My own smile cracked.

"Okay," I said. "I can't have you dying over something so silly when I can help."

My roommates squealed again.

Emma smashed her brush into her pallet with extra vigor. "Lemme finish with Heather while you dry your hair."

My hair was still slightly damp when Heather jumped from her seat and waved for me to take her place. Emma brandished her brushes like a torturer with her incision tools.

She continued the image as she bent close to my face and said, "Now, hold still."

My smile broke into a laugh. Four eyebrows shot up.

"Sorry," I said between laughs. "You have no idea how creepy you are, which actually makes you innocent."

Emma blinked. "No one's called me innocent since I was in elementary school."

"Which makes it even funnier!" I laughed harder, and my roommates joined.

Eventually, Emma bore her brushes and makeup at me. "Shut up and give me your finger. We're gonna start with some primer."

I sat obediently and refrained from turning toward the mirror. Emma went over the process that had way too many steps to remember as Heather combed through my hair. My

Regency roommate sectioned off my bangs to weave my short hair back into a braid. She curled the remaining pieces with an iron as Emma swept another brush over my cheeks.

Emma murmured, "You have no idea how lucky you are. You don't have to tan or dye your eyelashes. Your lashes and brows are naturally long and thick. Like, there might be one or two hairs I might pluck, but your brows are pretty much perfect, girl."

"Um, thanks?" I said.

"Don't talk," she chided. "It moves your face."

I smiled and made it worse.

After another five minutes, my Contemporary roommate closed her face powders and rummaged through another bag of eyeshadows.

She muttered, "Isn't your mask red, black, and white? We'll have to really make your eyes and lips pop so they can compete with your mask."

She then asked me to open and close my eyes so many times I saw spots. Next, she handed me a palm mirror to apply my own mascara three times. I struggled to keep my mouth open in the right position as she traced my lips with liner and a gloss the shade of dried blood.

They turned me around to face the mirror. I gaped at the stranger before me. She was beautiful, exotic, and glamorous. I didn't need the mask to hide my worry lines and suspicious eyes. I was already someone new. Emma and Heather had turned me into someone ready for a party.

"Condemnation," I said. "My face and hair are so fancy, my clothes look dreary."

Heather clapped her hands. "Would you like to try one of my dresses? Ooh! I know just the one!"

She dashed away to our bedroom. I followed Heather to her side of the closet as Emma pulled a dress from a bag.

"I bought the perfect dress," Emma said, "but I'm gonna need your help putting it on. Regency clothes have way too many layers."

I quickly agreed as Heather pulled out two of everything I could never need.

"First," Heather said, "we have the chemise. You may prefer the combination, which sews the chemise, drawers, and petticoat into one piece."

Emma nodded. "That's what I have. How am I supposed to put this thing on?"

Heather became the instructor as we struggled to find the right holes. The entire piece was basically a dress on its own.

Then came the corset. I couldn't imagine how they planned to breathe—not to mention dance—in the constraints. I helped lace up Emma and Heather, but refused my own.

"I'll just wear a bra," I said. "I don't think I could dance in one of those contraptions."

Heather squealed and Emma blinked.

"Hold the phone," Emma said. "Operation Dress Up worked? You're coming to the dance? Should I alert the media?"

I shrugged, trying to downplay my change of mind. Heather was already rummaging through her closet.

"I could lend you one of my dresses! Ooh, this dark red would adorn your mask perfectly!"

With a deep breath, I accepted the dress that was made for fashion first and dexterity last. Heather directed us into our crinolines, which Emma quickly termed as "butt expanders." We were finally to the dress itself, which included skirts, bustles, drapes, and bodices.

At least the open neckline let me breathe. Heather's burnt red dress created a wide frame to highlight my little pansy necklace. The dress was surprisingly not uncomfortable, though the skirts were heavy and I'd need to hike them up to run. On the positive side, the skirts were long enough to cover my running shoes. Emma and Heather were fashionably disgusted, but there was no way I would force my feet into heels. They relented when I proved all their shoes were too big or too small.

A knock on the door sent Heather to the front room. Emma fussed five extra minutes over her hair, then went to join. With my roommates busy talking to their dates, I hefted my skirts to strap my emergency pack around my thigh. Maybe if they didn't see it, they wouldn't need it. With another deep breath, I stepped from the bedroom to join my friends.

My roommates were stunning beside their dates. Heather wore a full gown of shimmering ivory lace to match her sparkling tiara mask. Jake's simple black suit was made fancy by a single off-white handkerchief poking from his breast pocket. Emma's dress was bright pink with an outside corset and a pin-up to bring her skirts to mid-thigh on one side. Hank wore a tuxedo with a frilly pink vest and bowtie.

I stepped slowly into the light. "May I join you all for the masquerade?"

Heather beamed like a proud parent. "Of course, dear Pansy. Perhaps you can go—how do Contemporaries say—'without a partner?'"

"Stag," Jake said.

"Right." Heather beamed. "No need to limit your possibilities to find a Romance. Come with us. Theo is also attending stag. May she accompany you?" She gestured to Theo as he emerged from the back of the group.

My heated cheeks could have branded a prisoner. My anxious heart pounded as Theo stepped forward. He wore a thick papered white horse mask over his head with intricate cuts and folds for seeing and breathing. He was dressed in a

DON'T DATE THE HAUNTED

dashing white tailcoat and matching cape that shimmered from certain angles. Underneath, he wore a colorful jockey vest. He lifted his mask, revealing a shy version of his tantalizing smile. His hair wasn't combed as usual, but a little frazzled from the mask, like an attractive contemporary style. He hid his blushed cheeks by bending into a courteous bow.

"If it pleases my flower, I would be honored to escort her."

Heather sidled up to whisper to me, "His hopeful partner had discourteously denied him. After all the courage and anticipation he put forth to ask a woman, the inconsiderate fool refused! Can you believe it?"

"What an inconsiderate fool," I said, dazed. I reached my hand forward and hoped to seem as regal as he. "The honor would be mine, Theo of the White Horse."

His eyes raised to meet mine, a little surprised. He straightened and offered his arm to escort me as his smile grew into its full bloom.

My heart stuttered and said I was in more trouble than ever.

Chapter 14

CURSED ITEMS

*Don't touch or live by anything that could be cursed
Avoid dolls, clowns, and anyone wearing masks
Go on the offensive against dolls or things that look creepy
Never own a record player (unless you want to hear it change by itself or repeat over and over)*

- Oz's Haunting Survival Book

"Pansy!" Tiffany shouted when we walked in. "I'm so glad you made it—ohm'gosh—Heather, your outfit is gorgeous!"

Seeing the decorations, I almost turned around and left. Somehow, I hadn't noticed the Who Dunnit Crime theme in the advertisements. Yellow caution tape curled around the Tower's glass elevators and up to the penthouse ballroom. Tiffany and her "tall and blond hair" date sat at a check-in desk to collect tickets and entrance fees. It was decorated in smoky vintage tones to create a private investigator's reception room.

The ballroom doors were wide open, allowing me to see the mess we were about to enter. The room was large enough for a couple hundred dancers, and it was almost full. There was an extra tight clump of people by the DJ.

The whole scene was a juxtaposition. The room architecture was regency themed, like a palace with marble columns and mirrors all along one side with gold frames. The Mystery decorations of magnifying glasses and bleary suspect photos transformed the place into an investigation scene. On top of that, a ball of mirrors hung from the ceiling to reflect the flashing colors of lights, swirling and dancing crazy with the music.

"And ohm'gosh," Tiffany said through her fake disguise mask, "if you find Marcellette—tell her to stop making out with her fiancé—I mean—it's awkward—and I need help with the snack bar—she promised she'd help tonight—then she ran off after the first song."

I made no plans to search for the girl who mutually despised me. I scoffed beneath the blasting music. "Separating from the crowd to indulge in lust? Yeah, that's a sure way to attract a Haunting."

"What was that?" Theo asked.

"Nothing."

Right then, a gust of wind blasted open the eastern doors, banging them hard against the walls. The storm had reached a new level. The hanging ball and chandeliers swung and girls squealed as their expensive hairdos blew apart. Some couples nearby ran to the rescue and barred the doors closed again.

"I thought we locked that door," Tiffany's date commented.

"Pansy?" Theo asked. I met his eyes before glancing down to his arm where I clung onto him like a leech.

"Oh." I released his arm and stepped back a little, embarrassed at my unconscious instinct to grab him while the storm tore through the penthouse.

The temptation to suction myself to him came again as we stepped over the threshold and into the ballroom. The music was loud and rambunctious, and every beat threatened the architecture. The crowds jumped together, shaking the walls and floor. My skin prickled with chills despite the sweaty air. There was a shift in the atmosphere, though I couldn't tell if it was from entering a Haunting's domain or from the energy of everyone in the room. My uneasiness was distracted by Theo as he lifted his mask to rub his eyes.

"Are you okay?" I asked. I had to shout to out-speak the music.

"Yes." He blinked hard. "These lights do a number on my eyes."

"What's wrong?"

"Just a black smudge in my vision." He rubbed his eyes again. "There, it is no more. Will my flower allow herself to relax?"

I surveyed our surroundings. With the normal room lights off, the only lights available flickered with swirls and colors. The mirrors on the ball and walls flashed with shadows and indefinable shapes. With the caution tape and body outlines, this place was a crime scene waiting to happen. We were surrounded by masked young adults who laughed, drank, and danced like Novel didn't have a care.

It was insanity. My mask wiggled on my face as a reminder that I was a part of it.

"I've rarely been more freaked out in my life," I said, "but if I'm going insane, I might as well make the best of it."

Theo chuckled. "I feel rather fortunate that you were dressed and willing to accompany your friends this evening. What changed your mind?"

I shrugged, unsure how to describe his influence on me without sounding corny. "I realized you're right. If a Haunting had followed me from Horror, it probably would have struck by now. Also, even if the Haunting followed me particularly, that doesn't mean it won't target my friends by association. The best way to protect them is to stay near them."

DON'T DATE THE HAUNTED

Theo smiled. "How heroic of you."

Heroic. Sure, if that was what you called suppressing every urge to hide in a corner. I stayed with my group of friends as we joined the dance floor. We passed Asher and Ruby with their dates. Asher never acted so awkward, trying to dance but not knowing how. Ruby had her own version of awkward, dancing freely like a buzzed bat let out of a cage. Both of their dates matched them perfectly and I smiled, glad they were enjoying themselves.

Emma and Hank went immediately to the middle of the throng, jumping wild and pumping fists into the air with the rest of the crowd. If it wasn't to music, I would have thought this was a mob rally.

But no one was angry, I reminded myself. Everyone grinned, laughed, and shouted for joy.

I caught Theo's curious gaze and nervously smiled. He smiled back, and I started to bounce on my feet. I wasn't much of a dancer, but thankfully, it didn't take talent to jump in one place and pump a fist in the air.

Surrounded by people and trying to dance, my insides tightened with nerves. I didn't know most of these people, but some I recognized and wasn't sure how. Were they in my classes? Were they neighbors? Either way, it seemed as though every set of masked eyes judged me for my slightest actions. I was a bit embarrassed for wearing improper shoes and hoped others didn't notice the bulk of my emergency pack tied around my leg.

I did a clumsy imitation of some dance moves. My friends laughed and I joined them, making a fool of myself.

Jake offered his hand to Heather, saying, "We're all friends here. There's no need to be shy. No regrets!"

She blushed. As soon as she put her hand in his, he spun her into a dip.

Theo and Jake laughed with good humor as Heather squealed in surprise. My reflexes thought to rescue Heather from her squeal, but my attention was diverted as Theo twisted me into his arms.

Supernaturals, he had strong direction!

For the first time I was glad my mask covered my face as my expression slipped into awe. Theo pulled some moves of his own. His dancing had an old fashioned folky flair, but his posture and fluidity of movements were regal. I failed an attempt to copy him. He took my hands to show me the motion step by step.

By the time I finally grasped the movements, the music changed. The heavy beat was replaced with smooth strings and the fast talking melody became a gentle duet.

Theo stepped closer and grinned a joyous version of his perfect smile. The expression reflected on my own face.

"Miss Pansy," he said with a slight bow, "I dare not to monopolize your time. However, if I may, it would honor me to have this next dance."

For all his etiquette, I probably broke every rule as I laughed and grabbed his hand. "Shut up and teach me to dance."

Theo grinned, timid and excited, then led me from the bulk of the crowd so we could dance as a couple rather than a group. My muscles tensed.

"Seriously, I'm not a great dancer," I said, thinking that was the understatement of the year.

Theo took my hand in one of his and wrapped around my side with his other.

"Never you wilt, my flower," he said. "Think of dancing as a sparring match—I step, and you react. In ballroom dancing, others only see you through me, and my job is to magnify your beauty." He showed off a dazzling smile, then pulled me in so my body lined with his. He leaned down to whisper in my ear, "Though you are truly beautiful on your own."

My heart stuttered from the compliment and I almost missed the first step. The sensation of his body pressed against mine was a little intimidating, but the proximity made his movements easier to follow. I sensed his steps as he took them, and moved with him to keep us from stumbling. This way, Theo led me into twists and turns, directing me through crowds so we miraculously didn't bump into others. Reaching a small clearing, he simplified our dance until we swayed in a small circle together. My concentration shifted from following his movements to the way he held me.

"What is it about you?" he asked.

"Huh?" I asked, distracted by the dreamy sensation of his touch.

"Your aura," he explained, "is darker and shorter today. If I just knew why."

Whatever it meant, it felt nice. I stopped thinking about the masks, the horde of strangers, and my inability to hear or sense anything five feet away. I focused on the peculiar feeling to be in sync with this man. A warm impression of comfort surprised me: Theo's arm around me, my hand in his, his blue-green eyes peering into my brown. I…felt…

A hand grabbed my shoulder, jolting us slightly. It was Mr. E. He seemed to appear from nowhere.

"Excuse me, Lord Fromm," he said, "but can I borrow Ms. Finster?"

"Is this a cut in for a dance, or may you speak after we finish?" Theo asked, returning to his proper etiquette.

"Lord Fromm, didn't I ask you to stay uninvolved?" Mr. E asked. "Ms. Finster, must I use force, or will you come alone willingly?"

"Always alone," I muttered. "I swear, you want more private conversations than a significant other."

"Mr. John," Theo said, his jaw firm, "can this not wait?"

"What makes you think I haven't already waited?" he asked, taking my arm with one of his dead frozen hands.

"Stay close," I whispered to Theo as Mr. E pulled me away.

"As you wish," he whispered back. I slightly melted with his sincerity.

Mr. E led me off the dance floor, toward an empty side room. The door was wide open, but I didn't want to be alone with this man and his icy hands and interchangeable name. When he noticed my resistance, he paused. Examining the crowd, he must have decided we were far enough away to talk.

"What are you doing here?" I asked. My mind was still a little lost in the memory of Theo's comforting arms. This man's coldness had no comparison.

"You don't know?" Mr. E asked. "Regardless, I acquired a warrant to search your mail, and I'm led to wonder how often you receive letters with no return addresses? I thought maybe it was a query to tonight's ball, but why wait to ask until today? Will you open it?" Mr. E asked, handing it to me.

"You stole my mail?" I snatched the envelope from his hand and removed a piece of lined, water-damaged paper...with typing.

I'M HERE FOR YOU

"Do you recognize the resemblance to the letter I showed you?" Mr. E asked.

"It's here," I whispered, letting the paper fall from my fingers. I shrunk back as if to back myself away from the past.

Mr. E loomed over me. "Ms. Finster? Who's here? Who sent it?"

Panic gripped me. I let my guard down and it came for me. I wasn't safe. Nowhere was safe. Were my friends safe? If a

DON'T DATE THE HAUNTED

Haunting was after me, they might be endangered because of me. I needed to get back to Theo and my roommates.

"I need to go."

I tried to bolt away, but Mr. E grabbed my arm with one of his icy hands. "Do you think I'm done? If you refuse to let me help you, then maybe you can answer some questions for me?" He pulled out his favorite little notebook before continuing. "What do you think the forensics found from your fiancé's crime scene?"

My breath caught in my throat. Why did everything he say sound like an accusation?

"Why," he asked, "did they find your DNA all over his bathroom supplies?"

Oh. Because it *was* an accusation.

"His bathroom supplies?" I repeated. "I've been to his trailer before. I mean, we were engaged, for crying out loud. So I had to use the bathroom during one of the hundred times I went over."

"Your standard procedures, uh—what did you call them?" He flipped to an earlier page in his notebook. "'Ritual that attempts to restore areas back to balance and diminish Hauntings.' Is it always so complicated and desecrating?"

I shrugged. Exorcism wasn't pretty, but some things couldn't be scrubbed away with bleach.

"After all evidence was collected," he explained, "everything was drenched with water, then with oil, and incinerated? How does your zone ever expect to solve murders if they deface the integrity of the crime scene?"

"Could you stop calling it a crime scene?" I asked, losing my patience. "Sean was killed by a Haunting! There's no one to arrest! If anyone, the experimental doctor's at fault, but he's dead! Why are you talking to me about this? I came to the

Romantic Region to get away from the judgements and rumors!"

His eyebrow lifted. "Oh, I checked your 'Haunting' report. If you destroyed Dr. Hyde at 3:35 in the morning, then who pushed Mr. Chase to his death at 1:48 in the afternoon? All of his roommates' alibis check out."

"Mine does too; you said so yourself." What more could I say? Yes, we killed Dr. Hyde, but that didn't mean the Haunting was over.

"I said your phone records confirmed you were in your bathroom on the phone with the victim about the time of his death. Ms. Finster, your deceased roommate said you took an extraordinarily long shower that day. Also, your check up at the hospital the following week stated faded injuries that weren't reported in your 'Haunting,' including a scratch on your arm and a bruise on your neck. The cremation records said that Mr. Chase's body was beaten and singed. Now, will you tell me the truth, Ms. Finster?" He paused to lock his eyes on mine, inches away, bearing into my soul. "Why was your DNA found at the crime scene?"

Blank. Nothing. I was at a complete loss for words. Condemnation, it was hard to think in an interrogation! I could tell the truth, but a man who didn't believe in Hauntings wouldn't understand.

"So, I went to his trailer that day. What of it? I was in his bathroom because…" I breathed heavily, wondering if it was worth trying a lie. I closed my eyes shut, knowing I'd be punished the moment the words escaped my lips, especially after my condemnation of Emma the other day. "I used his bathroom earlier in the day because we, um, had sex."

I heard Mr. E's pen click, and I dared to open my eyes again. "Why didn't you say so in the first place?" he asked.

DON'T DATE THE HAUNTED

"You were engaged, right? That's all too common in Contemporary areas."

I was flabbergasted. He didn't condemn me? He didn't treat me like a lost child—he rolled his eyes! "But we weren't in Contemporary, Romance! We were in Horror! Premarital sex breaks the number one rule of survival from Hauntings! It's as good as a death sentence to sleep together, even if you are engaged!"

Some dancers snickered and whispered "oh dear" from nearby. My outburst was a little louder than necessary, and I suddenly wished we'd gone into the separate room to talk. Thankfully, my mask hid my identity, but then my eyes met another's.

Theo.

He knew me, and based on the uncovered parts of his expression, he heard me too.

Oh, horror. "Wait, Theo—wait!"

Ignoring Mr. E, I chased after Theo's departing figure through the crowd. Luckily, he was tall and that shimmering white horse head stuck out like peacock feathers. I noticed someone in a familiar cat mask and dress stood alone at the kitchen door, neck stretched back, mouth open, and chest heaving. I didn't have time to analyze as Theo slipped between the crowds. I only had one more line of people to break through when he stepped between the doors to the outside patio.

The doors closed on my face. I yanked them open and spotted Theo alone by the banister, staring out to the city. The building blocked most of the storm, but my hair and dress billowed around me. I removed my mask to keep it from blowing off.

I couldn't see Theo's face. My brother's whispers that saved me during all those years of Hauntings screamed at me, *Don't approach anyone if you can't see his face!*

I did anyway. I cautiously touched his shoulder, half expecting to see a monster beneath his mask. What I saw instead was almost worse. He removed his mask to reveal a single tear rolling down his cheek.

"Theo." What could I say? I could deny my words to Mr. E, and say I lied to an official investigator. That definitely wouldn't help his trust in me.

"Pardon my exaggeration of emotions. This is not Lady Greenwood again. I know this is different," he said and I cringed, remembering how his first love betrayed him and left dishonor on everything she touched. "What distresses me is not that you loved another man. It would be unfair for me to expect otherwise, except…you lied to me."

His words hit me in the gut the way a punch never could.

"Theo." I rested my hand on his, wanting to comfort him, but realizing how much my exclamation to Mr. E must have hurt him. How could I explain? In Theo's perspective, I either lied to him about being a virgin and tricked him into spending time with me, or I lied to an official detective to possibly cover up a murder.

Theo turned toward me, but refused to meet my eyes. His gaze instead landed on the pansy necklace he gave me. A sad smile teased his lips as he reached to finger the pendant. "Perhaps I should have known better. Pardon me for any distress I caused from my advances. You must have loved him immensely if you were willing to accept a death sentence through your actions of love."

"Or—" I began, then felt like an idiot for trying to excuse myself. "Never mind."

"No, please tell me," he said, leaning in.

DON'T DATE THE HAUNTED

"I—" For the second time that night my breath was caught in my throat, but for a completely different reason. While Mr. E made me feel like a mouse caught in a trap, Theo made me feel... everything. It was corny and pathetically vague, but I didn't know how to describe it. Even as my heart broke to see him torn, I wondered if this was love. Did I lose it before realizing that I had it?

I scrambled for words, desperate to make it right. How could I explain that the only way I honestly loved Sean was for survival? Not even other Horrors understood my paranoid need for security. I felt more desire for Theo after this short time of knowing him. How could I explain what made no sense to my own mind? I wanted to tell him everything, but how could he trust me?

I had an intense desire to kiss him. Would that say all I wanted him to know? Or would it only confuse him? Probably the latter, but I started to lean in and closed my eyes.

Or I thought I had. Nope. My eyes were still open, but the Tower went suddenly dark. The lights cut out. There were a couple squeals of surprise from inside, and my instincts went into alert mode.

"We need to get back inside," I said, grabbing Theo's arm. "Where are the others?"

"It is just a power outage." He breathed with surprising relief and his arm relaxed beneath my grip. "This is not my brother's Night Shade ability. The lights should return soon."

"It's never 'just a power outage.'" I guided us into the dance room, not bothering to retrieve our dropped masks. The music still played, but was stuck on repeat.

"—here for you—here for you—here for you—"

I glanced up at the DJ, who fumbled with his controls. The lyrics that were meant to be consoling became a threat.

Goosebumps chilled my skin and my eyes were insufficient to detect the Haunting in the darkness.

The lights flickered back on and the music resumed. There was a choir of sighs and a couple chuckles as people resumed their conversations and dancing.

"See? Just a—"

"We need to find the others and get out of here," I cut Theo off.

My roommates and their dates spotted us first, since we were revealed while they were hidden behind masks. They called us over, and I hesitated. I gestured for them to lift their masks first. They did, laughing, like it was a joke.

As we approached, Theo mused to himself, "How interesting."

"What is?" I said, half listening. The other half of my brain analyzed all possible exit routes. Jumping out the windows or off the balcony were exits, but not the best route when thirteen stories above ground.

"Everyone's auras are more shaded than before."

"Huh," I said, then rushed to my roommates. "We need to go! Now!"

"What?" Heather asked.

"I agree!" Emma said. She swayed like she'd had two drinks too many. "Let's blow this joint. But first, I need the bathroom."

"No!" I said urgently. "No splitting up and no bathrooms. We need to get somewhere safe. Is there a police station nearby? Where's Mr. E when you need him?"

"Pansy, you do begin to scare me," Heather whined.

"There's nothing to be afraid of," Jake said, taking the excuse to put his arm around her. "Seriously, Pansy, you need to relax. We probably just blew a fuse. It happens all the time."

"No, time is the problem," I said. "The timing was perfect. It paused the song to the same lyrics as my third letter, and it was right as Theo and I were about to—We need to go." I realized I was speaking out loud and blushed.

Dragging my roommates by the hand, I pulled my group toward the elevators.

"What's your hurry, Ms. Finster?" Mr. E stood by the exit with a frown, like he suspected I was in the middle of a hit and run.

"Just the person I need!" I said, my relief surprising both of us. "We need to get everyone out of here as fast and orderly as possible! A Haunting is here!"

His face went from concerned to skeptical. "Could you describe this 'haunting?' And how do you know it's here?"

A scream echoed through the ballroom. More cries and shouts followed.

"That's how I know! We need to get out of here," I said again, pulling my roommates past Mr. E.

"Oh, no you don't, Ms. Finster. I'm going over to investigate, and if you're not here when I come back, I will arrest you on charges of fleeing the scene of a crime."

As the Mystery went to investigate, Theo pulled me aside. "Pansy, what is happening? Are you alright?"

"Yeah, I'm fine." I released a deep sigh to prove my words. I needed to prove it to him as much as to myself. "I'm just suspected for killing my own fiancé, and our normal 'ten seconds till death' is now closer to three."

Theo's eyebrows contracted. "How could Mr. John consider such a crime?"

"Look, I know you have no reason to trust me anymore, but please, *please*, trust me that there's a Haunting here, and I will do everything I can to get you and everyone out alive."

He studied me for a breath before nodding. "I trust you to do what you think is best, though are you positive you feel alright?" He leaned toward me with worried eyes.

"As much as I can at the moment," I said, trying to remain calm. We couldn't sit around and wait for an investigation! There was no time to waste during a Haunting!

"You…" Theo paused. "Your aura. It is unnaturally dark."

"We don't know what that means."

"Yes, though ever since the power went out, everyone's auras went darker, as yours is now."

"You think it's a warning?"

"I know not." He shook his head. "Though it seems foreboding. Can you promise to be cautious?"

"I'm always cautious," I said, "but don't make promises during Hauntings. They're only broken or kept to the grave."

Theo didn't seem satisfied with that but realized it was the best I'd give him.

Mr. E didn't return. Instead, a crowd grew around the place of investigation. If it was a Haunting attack, I needed to learn more to fight it. I wandered toward the edge of the crowd.

Drawing nearer, I couldn't see between the bystanders, but I heard Marcellette.

"I didn't cheat on you! Why does that even matter when *I was almost killed?*"

Chapter 15

INVESTIGATING

Don't call out for "friend or foe" if you hear an unnatural sound. It only gives away your position. Hide or run
Never go toward the sound, but don't totally ignore it either. If you must inspect, do so with a friend and a weapon
Leave investigations to detectives

- *Oz's Haunting Survival Book*

I stood at the edge of the ring of people craning their necks to stare and wonder. Marcellette and Lord Rochershire stood near the kitchens. They both sobbed. Marcellette covered the side of her neck with one hand as she reached for her fiancé with her other. Lord Rochershire kept his arms folded and back turned on her. As soon as she touched him, he shuddered and shrugged her off. Her hands clenched and she threw them both down to her hips. On her neck were three red spots lining down her neck. Three embarrassing hickeys.

"I swear," she shouted, "I don't know how it happened!"

Lord Rochershire growled. "Surely. You are too drunk to recognize someone kissing you, that you fabricated some ghost story!"

"There was no one!" she cried. "As soon as I realized what was happening, there was only a knife hovering above me! It was floating in the air! I swear, I was alone!"

Mr. E stood with his arms spread wide to the crowd. "Don't you people have something better to do than gawk? The situation is under control. Why don't you go dance?"

I stepped back from the circle to analyze the situation from outside.

Had a Haunting followed me after all? If so, why did it attack Marcellette? I knew Marcellette more as an acquaintance than a friend, and maybe said a total of two words to her fiancé. Was it a warning? Did she have her own Haunting? Unlikely.

I reviewed the facts: the Haunting followed me from Horror. It plotted until the masquerade to attack. It waited for the opportune moment when I was vulnerable and surrounded by others. Whatever it was, it was sentient and cunning.

What was it?

Mr. E likewise tried to piece the clues together as he accused Lord Rochershire. "How many drinks have you had yourself? Is it possible you saw your fiancée's marks and became enraged enough to threaten her?"

"How dare you accuse me—"

Mr. E mowed over him with more accusations. As relieved as I was to have Mr. E's interrogations turned on someone other than myself, my nerves tightened. Marcellette had hickeys. She said a knife hovered over her in the air.

Supernaturals. I wasn't simply followed by a Haunting. My last Haunting against Dr. Hyde and his jarred poltergeists had never ended.

I leaned my back to a wall and struggled to measure my breathing. I pitied everyone else at the party. They had no idea what was happening.

Even without the full truth, a few dramatic people fainted and were carried off to the side. Several people were in denial, thinking the lovers quarrel was an arranged act for the Who Dunnit theme. Everyone's horrified eyes were glued to the investigation...except Theo's. He inspected the crowd itself and frowned with calculating eyes.

Someone called my name. I turned to find Emma.

"Could you help me with Heather? I think she's trying to faint into Jake's arms," she said, exasperated. She avoided eye contact and worked her jaw in her struggle to not be an angry drunk. The turn of events required a clear mind.

Emma led me to Heather, then dictated the duty to gather details to Hank and Jake. Heather gave up her fainting act as soon as Jake walked away.

"I would have thought," she pouted, "that my friends would assist my obvious attempts to fall into the arms of Mr. Kennington."

Emma scoffed. "Hate to break it to you, but you're a terrible actress."

My roommates traded tips in the art of wooing as my attention wandered again toward Theo's analyses of the crowd. I wondered aloud, "Why does Theo look so confused?"

Emma stopped to stare at me, mouth gaping. "The dance is crashed by Marcellette's drama, and all you're wondering is why Theo's confused?"

I stammered with my words, unsure how to respond.

"I knew it!" Emma exclaimed. "You've become a Romantic!"

"What? No!" I said, unable to hold back my angry blush. Emma and Heather, however, took the reddening of my cheeks to mean shy embarrassment. Despite our situation and surroundings, they giggled like imps, plotting my fatal romance. "I'm a Horror," I said. "When people are hurt, we can't focus on the pain, but who the attacker might go for next. I'm simply worried about him."

"And a Romantic focuses on her heartthrob," Emma smirked. "Like, check out how genteel my Hank is, offering to help the detective anyway he can."

Heather sat up and swooned. "Did you hear that, Emma? How Pansy worries about Theo! All Pansy wants for him is to be happy! All she wants for herself is to be part of his happiness."

"Sounds like somebody's in lo-ove!" Emma said, pursing her lips and wiggling her head.

This was getting out of hand, and I was all too aware of the possibility of someone like Theo or Hank walking over and hearing the incrimination.

"That's ridiculous," I said, unable to completely deny my feelings. "If anything, I'm in love with his smile."

"Ah, I can see it now." Heather sighed. "You: in love with his smile. You want to see it always on his lips, hear it in his laugh, smell it in his breath, feel it and taste it in a kiss."

I blushed and turned my face away from them, knowing if I said anything else, they'd turn my words. They were worse than lawyers and more accusatory than Mr. E. The man himself stood by the arguing couple, talking on a police radio.

"I'm putting this building on lockdown. I need an investigation team, and some back up—"

"You're locking us in here?" I shouted at the man.

He cupped a hand over his radio and shouted back, "Ms. Finster, this is a crime scene and everyone here is a suspect, particularly you."

"Everyone here is going to die if we don't get them out immediately!" A few people cried out and squealed at my outburst. I didn't care. They needed to know the danger they were in, and if we had to revolt against authority to find safety, so be it.

DON'T DATE THE HAUNTED

Mr. E narrowed his eyes. "Is that a threat, Ms. Finster?"

"What?" I couldn't believe it. Why wouldn't he listen to me? Could my worst fears be realized, and Mr. E was the Haunting through ignorance or deception?

His narrow eyes grew more suspicious with each step closer to me. "How did you know something was coming? Were you involved with the threat against her life?"

Probably, but I didn't want to admit that straight to an official who didn't believe in Hauntings. How could I make him understand?

"Based on what you've said..." I gulped. "I'd guess she was threatened by a poltergeist."

"A what?"

"Poltergeist," I repeated. "I told you about them before. They're not like regular ghosts. They can levitate objects, and trip, hit, and—" I paused for emphasis "—bite."

"Are they vampires or something?" Mr. E asked with one eyebrow raised in disbelief.

"No, they don't suck blood or anything, but this one is strong enough to create hickeys. Their most powerful and dangerous trait is to possess people who have given into one of the seven deadly sins. It's also one of their weakest points, since possessing someone makes them tangible and vulnerable to ailments of the body."

Mr. E blinked slowly. "How does a smart woman like you believe in such nonsense? Even still, you evaded my question, so I'll ask again, Ms. Finster—how did you know something would happen?"

As much as I wanted to deny and plead innocence, I couldn't. Even if Marcellette did have her own Haunting, why was she attacked during the perfectly eerie timing of my own? Mr. E's smile crept up his face the longer I hesitated.

"Ms. Finster, when will you tell me everything you know?" His glare bore into mine, and I realized that no matter what I said, he wouldn't trust me.

"I don't actually know anything," I said. "But I'm pretty sure they were targeted by the same Haunting that sent me a letter similar to the two you showed me."

"Why didn't you tell me about this when I showed you the first letter?"

"Because I knew it would point more suspicion on me!" I burst. "Mr. E, I swear I didn't do anything, even if this might all be my fault. Either way, I need you to get these people out. They have a record book of everyone here if you need a list of suspects. I need you to trust me on this one thing; if you don't want any more people hurt, get everyone to safety."

"Has it ever occurred to you, Ms. Finster, that if you want trust, you need to give it first?"

I blinked, and the Mystery sighed.

"Don't you know I've kept tabs on you because of the Haunting Emigration Watch?"

"The what?"

"I thought every Horror paid for it as part of their emigration?"

"What?" I asked again.

Mr. E took a deep breath, then recited, "Section 13.06.3 of Horror Emigration Law states that all emigrants of Horror are to be assigned an aid to watch over him/her in the case of a crossover Haunting. If after one year, the emigrant experiences no trial of Haunting proportions, the said emigrant is declared cleansed. In the event of a life-threatening act, it is the assigned Watcher's duty to assist the demands of justice."

What the horror? Somewhere in Mr. E's recitation, my mouth dropped open, and I struggled to close it. "I guess that explains why leaving Horror's so expensive, but aren't you here to interrogate me about Sean's death?"

"Interview," he corrected. "What kind of Watcher would I be if I didn't search your background for past incidents and possible future issues?"

"Okay, but wait a second. You were watching me to make sure a Haunting didn't follow me. But you don't even believe in Hauntings!"

"You're my first Watcher assignment," he said. "My commander thought who better than I could make sense of Horror's Hauntings and why Mystery is forbidden to enact justice on that continent? Now, you say a Haunting is here? As your Watcher, will you let me aid you in bringing justice to these threats?"

I chewed on my bottom lip and sorted the new information. Mr. E was a detective and likely had many survival skills. I'd rather have him as an ally than an enemy. Either way, it would be easier to watch him for deceit if I kept him near.

"Sure," I said, "but when it comes to Hauntings, I make the calls and you listen."

Keeping his stare locked on mine, he said, "Fine. I'll have the backup team help everyone evacuate the building, but you and your friends are staying with me."

I wanted to argue further, but shut my mouth. It was a start.

I returned to my roommates and our dates while Mr. E went to the DJ and announced the evacuation over the speakers. For all the terror he rained on me, he spoke calmly and set off an organized emergency exit. Slowly, the penthouse began to clear. Mr. E pulled down some of the caution tape decorations to section off the kitchen, and I stayed with my back to the wall near my roommates and their dates. I didn't want them caught in my problems, but was grateful for their company.

I lifted my skirts to untie my emergency Haunting pack from my thigh. Jake nearly fainted while Hank gaped. Theo (the true gentleman) blushed and turned away.

"You brought *that* to the ball?" Emma shouted, pausing only a second in a bathroom dance.

"Of course. I take it everywhere," I said. "I had enough signs to warn me that something would happen tonight. Sorry, but you all need to toss your masks. Your faces need to be visible and recognizable."

Emma rolled her eyes dramatically, snapped off her elastic mask, then continued shifting her hips side to side. Hank apparently thought she was trying to lighten the mood by dancing as long as we were still in the ballroom, and he joined her. Heather removed her mask with the most reluctance, but eventually the identity concealers all found their way to the trash.

Unzipping my emergency pack, I pulled out my brother's book and passed it to my friends. "Read this. Your life will likely depend on it."

"'Rule number one,'" Heather read as Jake looked over her shoulder, "'abstain from drugs, sex, and violence.' How positively crass! What is this, Pansy?"

"It's the only thing my brother left for me, and it's the reason I survived Horror Zone. Keep reading." I rummaged through my pack, pulling out items that could save our lives and possibly destroy the Haunting. Just as silver bullets were known for killing werewolves, water was known for wounding poltergeists.

I removed my stakes to rummage for the aspergillum at the bottom of my pack. There wasn't enough holy water to combat multiple spirits. I'd need to save it and keep it handy in case normal water didn't work.

DON'T DATE THE HAUNTED

Heather flipped through a few pages to skim some of the main points. "'Always wear clothes you can run in.' 'Don't take showers or baths during Hauntings. Just forget hygiene until you're safe'? 'Don't be afraid to kill corrupted loved ones'? Pansy, you cannot honestly—"

"Yes, Heather, keep reading, but keep your voice down. If the Haunting is nearby, we don't want it to know what we know," I said, grabbing a cup from the bar and filling it with tap water.

Mr. E held the door open to the stairwell as the last few couples shuffled down, whining about their shoes and asking why they couldn't take the elevator. Mr. E spoke calmly as he called for backup security over his radio. The thundering sound of footsteps in the stairwell slowly calmed as the last of the masquerade participants evacuated.

I filled water cups for the rest of my friends as Mr. E approached us with slow and cautious steps.

"Alright," he said, "the building's nearly evacuated, Ms. Finster. Now, will you finally tell me what's going on?"

"I've told you most of what I know," I said. "We need to be somewhere secure."

"Such as the police station?" he asked. A cryptic smile crept up his face, like he imagined taking me in handcuffs.

I cleared my throat with a gulp. "Yes, actually. I will answer every question I can in the safety of the police station or the cathedral."

Mr. E gave me a quick, curious glare before gesturing me to go first down the stairwell. My little band of friends crowded around me. Heather returned my brother's book to me so she could focus on not tripping on her dress while descending the stairs. She and Emma left their water cups behind so they could hold their dresses. Supernaturals, our clothes would be the death of us all.

C. RAE D'ARC

I already knew the journey down the thirteen flights of stairs would be precarious. There wasn't a single light or window down the winding path. Condemn these modern buildings with glass elevators and concrete stairwells. The storm raged against the building, and a roaring echo of the wind filled the stairwell.

Heather whimpered. "Are you sure that we cannot take the elevator?"

Stairs were the number one cause for injuries in the common house, but only because common houses didn't have death-box elevators. Mr. E flipped out his flashlight to illuminate our trek down the black spiral.

I asked my friends, "Who has a phone light?"

"I have mine," Hank said, "but its batt'ry's nearly dead."

I grimaced. "Let's not use that four-letter 'D' word."

"Phones?" Jake scoffed. "We were on a date. I left my phone at home."

Heather sighed. "Like a proper gentleman."

I never thought I'd be grateful for a power outage as the shadows hid her googly eyes.

Emma offered her fancy touch phone as a second light. Then, we started downward.

The fine balance between stealth and speed was lost by my companions. Emma and Hank used her phone light to head our little group. My Contemporary roommate bounced with each pinched step of her don't-pee-hold-it-in dance. They were followed by the slow and thick heels of Heather and Jake. At least Theo descended the stairs beside me with the quiet grace of a swan. I had the stealth of the hunted while Mr. E followed like the hunter.

My Watcher insisted on taking the rear to make sure no one fell behind. I agreed, and preferred the middle position—

DON'T DATE THE HAUNTED

the first person always trips the traps, and the last person is easily picked off.

With Theo beside me, my mind wandered to our conversation on the balcony. My words and his pain ate at me. "Theo," I whispered, barely audible among Emma's nervous chatter and Heather's shoes. He didn't hear me. I reached for his hand with the lightest of touches. He glanced at me, but quickly returned his focus to the stairs. I hoped it was more to watch his steps than to avoid me. I gulped down my guilt and whispered, "You haven't said much, but you look like you have a lot on your mind. What are your thoughts?"

Taking a deep breath, his eyes catalogued everyone, analyzing only what he could see. "I remember Marcellette's aura when I passed her to the outside patio. It was almost black. We determined the shade of people's auras does not show a person's lifetime, yet I wonder. When the power cut, the auras of every person attending dimmed. However, now they have lightened, all except yours." He shook his head, as though a little shifting could put the pieces together. "I think it means something, though I cannot pin what exactly."

"Well," I said, reassuring him with my hand on his arm, "we'll figure it out. Whatever your auras show, it doesn't sound useless to me."

He flickered a half smile to me, but he was still broken from my lie. We turned our attention back to our feet.

I kept one hand steady on the railing while the other fumbled between hefting my skirts and clenching my water cup. I felt each step with my feet in the shifting shadows. I sighed with relief to reach the landing between each flight of stairs. I held the railing to swing left for the next set.

Down. Left, left. Down. Left, left.

Emma picked up speed, and the rest of us followed. We still had six more floors to descend.

Down. Left, left. Down. Left, left. Faster.

Heather yelped as her ankle twisted on a step. Crappy fancy dancing boots. I'd tell her to take them off if they weren't also solid protection from loose nails or other foot-stabbing traps. I urged her up and to move on. The sooner we were out, the safer we would be.

Down. Left, left. Down. Faster!

Three more levels. My head spun and vision tilted. I passed a couple discarded cups on the stairs. Condemnation, my friends either drank or spilled all their water?

"Pansy!" Theo cried. "Watch out!"

"Wha—"

An unseen foot tripped me. The railing support was just out of reach. I toppled forward into Jake.

Jake and I tumbled down the next flight of stairs. My cup sailed into the darkness as I braced myself for the crash. We hit Heather's legs from behind and she joined us at the bottom. Emma and Hank stumbled down the next set while trying to keep ahead of our avalanche. Hank slipped, grinding his arm against the wall to break his fall to the next landing. The stairwell echoed with a thunderous boom from outside and from maniacal laughter as our tumbling tapered.

"Who's there?" Mr. E shouted back at the echoes. The laughter rang familiar bells in my mind, though I couldn't remember from which of Dr. Hyde's poltergeists. The echoes slowly faded with each return. The fact that we weren't immediately attacked again gave me hope.

The poltergeist had limitations. That was why it waited for us to make ourselves vulnerable. It only had enough strength to trip me and make itself heard. We had a brief reprieve as it rejuvenated and waited for the next opportune moment.

I wiggled to collapse in a more comfortable position and pressed a palm to my bruised mandible. "Is everyone okay?"

DON'T DATE THE HAUNTED

"Ow," Jake moaned.

Theo and Mr. E hurried down the steps, the only people not caught in the dominoes. I sat up to survey our condition. Jake's foot pointed the wrong way. Dislocation.

"Hank," Theo asked, "are you alright?"

"I feel fine—nope, I'm bleedin'." He pulled a red hand away from his shoulder. He was more than bleeding. His arm looked like it got too friendly with a cheese grater.

Condemnation. My limited medical training kicked in. "Theo, thank the Supernaturals you still have your water. Go down and help Emma take off Hank's shirt. Emma, stay focused. Mr. E, I need you to hold Jake still. We need to reposition his foot. Heather, don't throw up."

My Regency roommate's already pale face had a tint of green. My directions unglued her eyes from Hank's mess of blood and skin. I shuffled to Jake as Theo and Emma struggled to remove Hank's shirt without touching the wound. Mr. E held Jake by the shoulders. I began to count, as if to pull Jake's foot on "three." On "two" I yanked his foot back into place. Jake screamed and the stairwell rang with terror.

"Start heading downstairs," I said, gesturing for Mr. E to brace Jake. "Take it slow, and don't put any weight on that foot. Heather, help them. Careful not to let anything or anyone trip you."

Next. I made my way down to Hank and pulled out my emergency first aid kit. My five-yard wrap would have enough to bandage his whole arm. Theo sat back and watched me work as Emma coddled Hank.

I grumbled, "I hate to waste water when it's our best weapon, but we need to clean this wound. Theo?"

Theo handed me his water, then whispered, "I saw something trip you."

I paused from my cleaning to gape at Theo.

"I saw it before," Theo said. "The black blur was in the picture Emma took of you and me at the Cathedral, then again during the ball. I knew not what it was, because never before had I seen an aura so black with no body. I assumed it was an ocular issue."

Hank grunted. "Why do ya always doubt yerself, Theo?"

"Wait, no body?" I asked. "You can confirm the Haunting is incorporeal, because you can *see* it?"

"Yes, I see the aura of it."

"That's incredible! Theo, your 'useless' ability might save us!"

A glimmer of hope shined in our foggy tunnel of doom. Theo could see the sometimes-invisible Haunting. I gave him a small smile, hoping he'd forgive me for my lie.

Emma smiled too as she hugged Hank. "See, babe? We're gonna be OK." Her hands subconsciously trailed down his bare chest as she stared into emptiness. I was almost finished with the wrap when Emma stiffened. "OMG, I'm gonna pee my pants—er, my dress."

"No bathrooms," I said.

"You expect me to pee in my dress?" She gawked. "Do you have any idea how much this cost?"

"Does it cost your life?" I jabbed back, tugging the wrap into a tight knot. I sat back and Hank shuffled to stand. Theo and Emma both reached to help him. As soon as Hank measured his weight on both feet, Theo stepped back to let Emma escort him down the next flight. She walked in tight steps while shifting her pelvis back and forth. We followed behind.

The stairwell echoed every footstep and creak of the building. The storm outside roared, the wind slammed with thunderous booms, trees cracked and scratched at walls. I never thought a "Level 1" sign could be so glorious.

DON'T DATE THE HAUNTED

We exited the stairwell to the hallway. No windows reflected the stormy night. No neon green exit signs glowed. I couldn't even see Theo standing next to me.

Chapter 16

BATHROOMS

Never open mirror cabinets (there will always be something in the reflection when it's closed or when you turn to leave)
Never be alone. Even in the bathroom. Always keep someone you trust within either sight or sound
Don't take showers/baths during Hauntings. Just forget hygiene until you're safe

- Oz's Haunting Survival Book

By instinct, I grabbed Theo's hand. I picked out the general direction of my friends as they talked over each other, playing blind man's bluff. I reached in the direction of Heather's panicked breathing.

"Nobody move," I shouted. We needed to locate everyone. I called out to my friends, "Reach for the walls, but don't walk anywhere."

Holding Theo's hand, I stepped away to reach farther. I bumped into someone and Heather yelped.

"It's okay, Heather, it's just me."

"Oh, Pansy, you gave me a fright!"

"Here, take my hand," I said, hoping to sound encouraging. She took my hand in hers, smashing my fingers with an icy grip. Her hand felt familiar, but I had an odd sense that something was wrong.

DON'T DATE THE HAUNTED

"How long has the power been out?" I said.

Suddenly, a light turned on: a single light from behind. It was a small pinprick compared to the encompassing blackness of the hallway. It was a light at the end of a tunnel.

"Who is that—"

"Don't go toward the light!" I cut Heather off. Heather tugged me away from the light. "Heather, where are you going? I said not to move!"

"What? You are the one pulling me forward," she said, her voice slightly further away than I would have thought.

"Heather! Pansy!" Theo shouted from behind. "A black aura stands between you!"

Chills crawled up my hand and down my spine. I wasn't holding Heather's hand. The poltergeist held us both as a trick.

The tunnel of light moved from my face and down my wrist. My hand grasped only air.

Immediately, I released my grip, but the icy invisible hand grabbed tighter. I tried to shake it, but it held on. The tunneled beam of light went berserk, waving around in jerked motions, confusing my vision.

Theo's hand gripped around mine as the cold one bolted forward. Theo's stationary hold was stronger.

I yelped with pain as the frozen grip ripped free.

Heather screamed. Her voice was even farther than before, and getting further fast.

"The black aura still has her!" Theo said. "It is taking her down the hall!"

I tugged him forward, shouting for him to lead the way. I stumbled, running blindly until Theo ran ahead.

"Grab Jake on your right!" Theo slowed down so I could connect with our friends. I reached out to my right and smacked my hand into Jake's outstretched arm.

Okay, so Theo could see our auras even in the dark. That was really helpful. Maybe we could survive this. Maybe.

The power flickered back on.

"There you are!" Jake said with a great sigh. "Where'd Heather go? Where is she?"

"Hey!" Mr. E shouted from behind us. "I was the only one with a flashlight and you almost left me behind?"

"Condemnation, Mr. E!" I shouted. "That was you? Don't blind me next time and stay with us!"

"Sorry," Theo said. "Should I have let you remain with Heather and the black aura? I wanted to kick it away, though I became solid instead."

"No," I said. "Thanks for your help. Did you see where it took her?"

Theo swung our hands forward to point down the hall. "It took her that way."

"Come on," I shouted, running down the hall. Reaching the end, I wasn't sure which way to turn. I didn't see any signs for the exits or elevators.

A door to our right slammed against its frame. Muffled screams and fists pounded on the other side. Two male voices argued inside.

"Stupid, worthless idiot!"

"Try all you want, but you can't possess two people at once."

"Shut up!"

Jake stopped short at the door. "Who else is in there?"

"It might be another trick," Mr. E. said.

A female screamed from behind the door, "Dear God! Save me!"

"That's definitely Heather!" Jake said, and grabbed the handle. He jiggled the handle against its lock as footsteps ran above us.

If Heather was beside us, who was above us?

Hank asked, "What'd ya reckon's goin' on up there?"

"We could split up," Mr. E suggested.

"No splitting up!" I shouted and Jake turned back, his face pained with betrayal. We had to choose, but I didn't want to be the one to make the choice. What if I was wrong? Then Heather's fate would be my fault. As if I didn't already blame myself for endangering everyone.

Gritting my teeth, I ran for the screaming door beside us.

"Heather?" I shouted.

"Pansy?" The shrill behind the door definitely sounded like Heather. "Help me! There is no light, and I cannot unlock the door!"

It would be the perfect trap from a Haunting. The other sounds from above morphed into heavy thuds. It sounded suspiciously like a body thrown to the floor. We had to be right. Jake and Theo slammed their shoulders against the door, hoping to break it down.

"Heather," I shouted through the door, "remind me what your mom said about kissing!"

The men around me paused to spare bewildered glances.

"Is this really the time for rules on propriety?" Heather asked, nearly crying. "I fear for my life, Pansy!"

"Just answer the question so we know it's you!" I said.

"She said—" she whimpered "—she said you only need two tries to determine whether or not someone is a good kisser."

Jake paused again. "Really? Because if I get you out of there alive, I'll give you a lot more than two tries!"

Heather hiccupped and it was all too easy to imagine her blushing behind the door.

"That's her," I said. "Get her out of there."

Even as I said it, the sounds upstairs became a rumbling drag. Mr. E stepped up and held Jake and Theo back.

"Where did you learn to break down doors?" he asked. "Don't you know that you'll only bust your shoulders and waste your strength that way?" The movement upstairs faded into silence. Mr. E warned Heather to step clear of the door, then angled himself to kick at the handle. The door broke open, and Heather leaped out.

"Supernaturals!" she said as she spread her arms around Jake. He caught her in an eager embrace, but didn't act on his threat to determine his kissing abilities. I figured their tight hug in front of their friends was equally forward from Heather's perspective.

"Supernaturals?" I asked her.

Heather blushed and shrugged. "You curse. I consider this an appropriate situation to warrant such expletives."

That was an understatement. "Heather, what happened in there?"

With hesitation, she stepped back from Jake, but they continued to hold hands. She blushed, somehow more conscious of her public affection than the terror she just escaped.

"It had pulled me with great strength and speed," she said. "I had to run simply to keep from falling. I somehow knew that had I slowed my pace, it would have hurt me."

I nodded. "Hauntings can have a way of pushing our instincts. What happened then?"

"It tossed me into the room like an uncouth master, then—" she swallowed "—it pressed itself against me, filling my mind with terrible thoughts of self-loathing and hate. It stopped to argue with...someone? I am unsure. I cried to God and the ghost locked me alone in the shadowy room. Please forgive my frantic manners; it appears I am all right."

"It tried to tempt you," I said, then laughed. "Only you, Heather. It tried to possess you, but you're too innocent! It became frustrated and locked you up instead."

"Then it went upstairs?" Theo asked. "We need to find and save whoever it attacked next."

"Gallant, but stupid idea," I said. "Searching for a sound after it stopped is nearly impossible. Besides, poltergeists are known for creating sounds of knocking doors and footsteps."

Heather's eyes went round and she visibly shivered.

Mr. E approached us with pursed lips and his pen to notepad.

"The three of you say you've interacted with this assumed poltergeist. Could you describe it for me?"

Theo spoke first. "Never before have I seen its likeness. It is a bodiless aura."

"Auras that only you claim to see," Mr. E said with a point. "You're sure it's not just a trick of the eyes?"

Theo rocked back. "You dare suggest that my ability is a delusion?"

"I'm suggesting, Lord Fromm," Mr. E said, "that perhaps your 'auras' aren't what you think? You said yourself that they don't mean or tell you anything."

I opened my mouth to argue, to explain our new theories and proof that his ability wasn't useless. Heather spoke first.

"Mr. E," she said, "I have not seen it, but I have felt it, and I believe in it as assuredly as though I had seen it."

"Thank you," I said to her. We weren't there to argue about Theo's ability. We had more urgent matters to discuss. "Mr. E, you have three witnesses now. We need you to accept there is an undead poltergeist and no normal method will kill it. We need your help to do that, but we need you to believe us first."

"Pansy," Theo said, "Heather's aura changed rapidly when the ghost was with her. Her shade of blue-green became incredibly dark. I no longer believe the auras are random."

"I agree," I said. "You said people's auras darkened after the blackout, and right before they were threatened."

"At first I thought it showed when a person was close to death. Your and Heather's auras were nearly black before. Now they are light again, though still darker than preferred."

I thought about the different times he mentioned when people's auras changed, and what it could mean. If it did mean something, Theo's supposedly useless ability could possibly save our lives.

"Theo, I don't think it shows when a person's close to death, but maybe close to danger."

"Or *in* danger," he said, nodding.

"Condominium!"

We jumped from Heather's strange cuss.

"You mean condemnation?" I asked.

"Oh," she blushed deeply. "How embarrassing!"

Jake laughed, his expression perplexed and humored. "How about you stay as the beautiful and refined woman you are?"

I cracked a smile. Although I wouldn't have chosen these people to fight a Haunting with me, I was glad to have them by my side. The possibilities of Theo's ability continued to roll through my mind. Though I found him intriguing before, there was a new sense of excitement to the man. His ability wasn't useless after all. Enlightenment reflected in his eyes, and that perfect smile edged up his cheeks. There was also an interesting thrill that came from our discussion. We learned and theorized together. The sense of teamwork was…alluring. It was like my inner self (if that even made sense) yearned for him and his inner self.

Okay, that sounded a little crazy.

Speaking of silly Romantic notions, where was Emma?

"Where's Emma?" I asked aloud.

Hank leaned as if to peer around a corner. "She went to find the outhouse."

Panic curled my blood. "When did you last see her?"

Not a second later, a scream fractured the air.

"Come on!" I yelled, running down the hall.

Mr. E puffed behind me. "Don't Horrors generally run away from the source of screams? I thought chasing after murderers was a Mystery characteristic."

"When trying to be a hero, it's a fifty/fifty shot, but don't let anyone fall behind!" I checked behind myself to make sure everyone followed.

As we grew closer, the sound of rushing water became clearer among the struggling screams. Hank ran faster than the rest of us, leading the path toward the bathrooms.

"Crap!" I cursed. "I told her no splitting up and no bathrooms!"

"What did you expect?" Jake said. "We're all on the verge of peeing our pants, and she had to go before this all started."

I huffed and ran faster. This wasn't the time for banter. Emma was in serious trouble. Hank hesitated when he reached the puddles outside the girl's lavatory. I splashed past him with Theo closely behind.

"Never hesitate to save the woman of your dreams," Theo shouted as he rammed into Hank, pushing him into the bathroom, "no matter where the dangers lie!"

Coming upon the scene, however, I wanted to hold Hank back. Every sink and toilet overflowed their basins. Emma trembled on the floor, drenched by the flood and spewing sinks. Somehow she kept her fancy phone dry from the splash zones. A silver stake protruded from her neck. Condemnation, that was *my* silver stake. How did it become lodged in Emma's neck? Did the poltergeist steal it from me? When?

C. RAE D'ARC

I remembered pulling my stakes from my emergency pack to find my aspergillum. Crap, had I forgotten to put it back? Was Emma's injury my fault?

Her arm lowered, losing strength. I dropped beside her, catching her arm and phone, assessing Emma's condition. My weapon was lodged in her neck at the deadliest angle. How had the poltergeist known the specific position for the jugular and carotid?

Regardless of all my classes, my emergency medical training dragged through my brain. I suddenly hated my studies that diagnosed the situation. Removing the stake would only make her death hurt more.

Hank dropped to his knees on Emma's other side, allowing the water to drench him and mask his tears.

"Emma," he sobbed, "what happened? Who did this to ya?"

Emma choked on her words. Instead she gestured limply toward her phone.

"You saw it?" I asked. "Did you take a picture of it?"

Her chin fell to her chest, like a nod that was too heavy.

As excited as I was to have a picture of the poltergeist, my heart gave out. "Emma, don't stress yourself. You—you'll be fine," I said. My denial didn't stop the truth.

She tried to speak, but words didn't come. Even her breath struggled.

Any of my apologies or hopeful words sounded pathetic and were outspoken by Hank. He grabbed her face. "Hold on, Emma! Don't die! You can't die! I love you! I love you, Emma!"

The harder he held on, the more she slipped away.

"We're goin' to run away to my country," he sobbed. "Live in a small town. Ya'd be the hottest chick for miles and I'd be the luckiest man in Novel."

Emma went still and Hank's hands trembled.

"We'd have nine kids. I know ya only want three, but I thought we could swing with...with three sets of triplets?" He tried to laugh at the idea, but instead sobs came.

Slowly, I stood. I might have been her paranoid roommate, but Hank was her lover. I backed away to give them some space.

Heather's chin shivered as she held back her wails. I reached to hug her first. Though she was taller, I pulled her face down to my shoulder and let her cry. Theo wrapped an arm around us and took the phone so I could place my hand on Heather's back. I mouthed a "Thank you" to him, and buried my face beside Heather's.

Why did this hurt so much? Emma was mean and selfish. Yet my heart ached almost as badly from Sean's death.

The answer came even as I debated with myself: she was like a sister to me. We argued and debated opinions, but we shared experiences and laughter. At the end of the day, we always tried to make things right.

Unlike many Hauntings, poltergeists didn't focus on locations, but on people. This poltergeist followed me from Horror and wanted me to suffer through those close to me. It wanted to torture me first. First Marcellette, then Heather, and now Emma. Even if I hadn't misplaced my silver stake, the poltergeist attacked Emma because of me. Her death, Sean's death, and Oz's death were my fault. How much guilt would burden me before it was my turn?

Fear shivered through me. This wasn't a mindless killer. It waited for the opportune moment by striking at the masquerade. It plotted. It wanted me to recognize and fear my inevitable death.

Between sobs, the rushing water, and my muddled mind, I only heard blurs of Mr. E's explanation as their voices drifted outside. "...dozen selfies...floating weapon...his face..."

A hand touched my shoulder and my reflexes swung out.

"Curses!" Theo shouted and raised his hands in defense. He stared at me with wide and shocked eyes. "Your aura just—" He blinked and refocused. "Sorry, I wondered if we ought to keep moving."

Right. That was probably wise. Theo went to convince Hank to leave Emma and the scene of the murder. I kept my arm around Heather and led us back to the hallway where Mr. E and Jake hunched over Emma's phone.

"Mr. E," I said, "could you arrange a forensic team to take care of Emma? They'll need to wait until after the Haunting's destroyed, or they might become casualties too."

Mr. E nodded, and gestured to the camera. "Speaking of the Haunting, you should come see this."

Heather and I joined Mr. E and Jake around the camera's viewing screen. I caught a quick glimpse of Emma's last selfie and the photo-bomber behind her. Immediately, I turned away, hands and knees shaking. I stabilized myself on the wall.

How? It couldn't—but I—it was—killed.

"Pansy?" Theo asked.

"I know—it's—how—?"

"What are you saying?" Mr. E said in his incriminating voice.

"It's—" I turned back to the rest of the group. "I've fought... this Haunting before."

"So ya know how to kill it?" Hank asked hopefully.

"I-I thought I had. I thought—I think its weakness is water."

"Interesting," Theo said, "considering the amount of water in the bathroom."

Mr. E stared at the camera screen. "I don't understand. Emma caught its picture before it stabbed her? How did she edit the photo to make the man translucent?"

DON'T DATE THE HAUNTED

"Because," I said, trying to be patient, "it's not just a man, it's a poltergeist."

Mr. E gave me a face that asked, *You're seriously going to try that on me?*

I exploded.

"For the Supernaturals, Mr. E! Look at the evidence!" I yelled, pointing at the phone. "The picture is as clear as day, but the man is nearly translucent! It's no ordinary ghost! It can bite people and it's bent on *killing* us! There is a real undead poltergeist coming after us! If you want to survive, I suggest you start believing in it, because if you don't, it will force you to believe with a knife in your stomach and its evil eyes as the last thing you see!"

I hadn't meant to burst out, to unleash my sorrow, stress, and confusion as anger, but I was overwhelmed. I needed to control myself, but I didn't know what to do. I was scared.

Warm arms wrapped around my shoulders. I recognized his cologne, but I looked up to confirm. Theo held me tightly, as if his arms could ward off the pressure around me.

"Pansy," he said, "we will overcome this. However, you need to breathe. You know these matters better than any of us. You are our best hope to overcome this."

I closed my eyes and forced myself to take longer, deeper breaths. It started to work. Until maniacal laughter broke out. The laughter echoed through the halls and revealed no source or sense of direction. We nearly scattered, each of us thinking to flee down different halls. It didn't help as thunder collapsed around the building and the lights flickered.

Heather screamed, but all I heard was the laughter, the freakishly familiar laughter. The memories shook me, rattled my bones, and chattered my teeth. I clapped my hands to my ears, but they were useless to block the noise. The laughter grew louder. I ran, unsure which way to go, but unable to stand still. Mr. E followed closely. I should have checked that the others weren't left behind, but the laughter consumed my every thought.

Get away! It was supposed to be dead!

I turned down another hall and skidded to a stop. A lone man stood with his back to us in the middle of the hallway.

"Pansy." Theo's voice shook from behind me. "His aura is black."

Mr. E stepped forward. "Sir, did you know this building's in emergency evacuation? I suggest—"

He stopped when the man's shoulders heaved in time with the imposing laughter.

"Turn around and put your hands in the air, where I can see them!" Mr. E shouted, leveling his gun.

No! I already knew who it was. His laughter was twisted, a mere echo of the man he used to be.

The man shuddered, turned, then smiled that perfect smile.

Sean.

Chapter 17

SACRIFICES

*You can't save everyone
Sacrifice is always required to defeat Hauntings
The Supernaturals allow Hauntings to go after those who can beat them*

- Oz's Haunting Survival Book

"Pansy," he said, and warmth flooded through me. I recognized his voice even after six months. His rusty-blond hair was groomed back to show off his chiseled face. He was nearly translucent, but his brown eyes swirled with the same shades of healthy soil. He wore a tuxedo with a golden vest, fancy bowtie, and even cufflinks. He was dressed for a wedding. Our wedding.

He shuddered and winced. His smile became twisted and his eyes dulled. He spoke with a gurgling garble. "Did you enjoy your inheritance?"

"No—no, you're dead!" I shouted.

"But I'm right here."

"Who are you?" Mr. E. asked. "Are you related to Mr. Chase?"

"It's not a relative," I said between clenched teeth. "It's an imposter with the spirit of my dead Haunting partner."

Sean tilted his head, as if confused. "If I'm dead, Pansy, how did I die?"

"You were injected with the poltergeist who still possesses you, even after death. How are you still here?"

Sean shook his head. "I might have lost control of my spirit that way, but that wouldn't kill my body. Tell me, Pansy, how did I die?"

He smiled. He knew the answer, but he wanted to hear me say it. Condemn him to Horror.

"Concussion and suffocation from drowning," my medical training explained.

Mr. E imitated Sean's confused head tilt with an extra layer of suspicion.

"In my own bathtub?" Sean asked. "That doesn't make sense, my dear. I would have struggled and escaped. Who kept me from escaping? Who killed me?" He still smiled, though his voice weighed heavier, bearing down on me for the truth.

"I did."

Mr. E narrowed his eyes on me and a small, victorious smile crept up his lips. Apparently, it didn't matter if he was meant to protect me. He was a Mystery who loved a confession. "Ms. Finster, you're under arrest for the murder—"

"Mr. E!" I shouted. "Look at him! He's animated and incorporeal! Either he's not dead, or he's undead! Either way, we have bigger problems right now!"

Mr. E turned back to Sean as his smile deepened to a sinister level. The specter faded before our eyes. Hanging pictures shook against the walls.

"That's not natural," Mr. E said.

"Welcome to Horror Zone, home of the Supernaturals," I said.

DON'T DATE THE HAUNTED

Mr. E tested a bullet through Sean's leg before he completely disappeared. It zipped through. I didn't wait for any such tests. I ran the other direction, pulling Theo along.

"You'll need to explain yourself," Mr. E said as he caught up to me.

I nodded. The only way to survive this was to tell everyone the truth.

Running pushed the cold tears across my face.

Six Months Earlier

The cool down after a Haunting was never easy. My heart went from terrified to relieved, then ecstatic to jumpy. Even after watching the crazy Dr. Hyde bleed to death before my eyes, I worried it wasn't over.

Maybe because his experiments still howled and writhed from their rooms. They used to be human. Now they were possessed by the spirits Dr. Hyde injected into them, trying to give them kinetic powers. One man threw himself at his door until he knocked himself unconscious. A young girl sat curled in the fetal position, screaming at the voices in her head. A third person writhed on the floor, scratching himself even as he bled. The fourth was our friend, Blake Washington. He was no more than a flying corpse, whirling itself and everything in its room in a vicious cycle.

When the paramedics arrived, they said there was nothing they could do for the four experiments. The Hauntings Investigations Unit set the entire cabin on fire, sending the souls with prayers to the Supernaturals for mercy. As interested as I was in the medical technicians, I was too exhausted to care about their work, other than their diagnosis on Sean.

"He should be okay," one said. "He's had a few recent injections, but based on his vitals and responses, we think they were only sedatives. Right now, he just needs some rest."

My own first aid was simple enough. I had a couple nasty cuts on my forehead and behind my knee that the paramedics struggled to bandage. Showering would be an issue.

I couldn't wait to relax at home and wash myself. That Haunting had been a long three days in the grungy woods. Sure, the campsite and cabin were fully furnished, but bathrooms were forbidden during Hauntings. Even if the camping trip was meant to lure a Haunting, I wasn't stupid enough to get naked around creatures with a taste for flesh.

I called Sean as I set out a fresh towel and change of clothes. "So, we should be clear for the next six months at least. It'll be nice to focus on graduation and the wedding, but let's never search for a Haunting like that again."

"We better be clear," he laughed. "I can't wait to plan our honeymoon, knowing we're in the remission months. You'll call the Bishop of Brimstone to set a date?"

"Yeah," I said, half distracted by my own thoughts.

No Hauntings for at least another six months. I tried to let that thought soak in, but it floated like a witch. I couldn't wait to soak myself. Showering was a regular relaxer for me after a Haunting, though I let out a small yelp as I struggled to remove my pants around my wounded knee.

"You okay?" Sean asked. His voice echoed as he stepped into his own bathroom.

"Yeah," I said through clenched teeth. "What about you? Whatever the crazy doctor gave you seems to have worn off."

He chuckled. "You worry about me too much. When we're married I can spend the rest of my life taking care of you instead."

DON'T DATE THE HAUNTED

I scoffed. "Your Romanticism's showing. But seriously, how are you feeling?"

"I feel—Holy horror!"

"Sean?" I pressed my phone to my ear and held my breath. What happened?

"Sorry," he said, and I breathed with relief. Until, "I thought I saw something in the mirror. Hold on a sec..."

His line went quiet. The silence put my mind on alert. "Hold on a sec" was synonymous with the famous last words: "I'll be right back." Every nerve in my body wanted to scream out and stop him. But I also knew it was no use. As I feared, the phone line died, and I immediately dialed the police. Even as I talked to the operator, I knew they wouldn't arrive in time. No way in horror I would stand by while my best friend struggled for his life.

Maybe it was just a scare, something to keep us on our toes. I was in denial.

I left the water running, yanked my pants back up despite the pain, threw open the window, and leapt out. My hair was a mess and I ran barefoot. Minor details that I hardly noticed. My knee threatened to trip me with every step, but I ran as fast as ever to Sean's trailer, knowing I wouldn't be fast enough.

We just finished a Haunting. We should have been clean. Why was this happening? We were going to get married and have each other's backs from then on!

I heard the screams from across the trailer park. I'd never heard Sean scream like that before. Rarely did any man scream like that. They were the screams of the dying—No! Those screams couldn't be from Sean! He was alive, taking a shower. We were going to graduate, get married, and save up to attend college in Romance!

Tears streamed down my face as I ran. I knew exactly which window led to Sean's bathroom, guided by the screams.

They were weak now, fading into a weird, gagged cough. I grabbed the largest stone nearby and threw it at the window, breaking it. Thankfully, his trailer wasn't elevated too high for me to reach my hand through the hole and unlock the frame. With the help of my adrenaline rush, I jerked it up and heaved myself through.

Sean lay alone in his boxers against the bathtub, struggling to breathe.

I climbed over the toilet to him. "Sean! What happened? Are you alright?"

"P-Pansy?" he croaked. His eyes met mine. They opened wider, but lacked a sense of brightness to them. He reached out to me and curled his hand around my neck. His touch was cold, and I shivered.

His eyes glazed past me, toward the ceiling. I turned upward to notice dozens of hygienic supplies floating in the air. What the horr—

Sean smacked my head sideways into the wall. At the same time, the objects crashed downward. The can of shaving cream struck my knee wound, and a heavy All-in-One shampoo+conditioner bottle pummeled my back. A ringing filled my ears as I struggled to make sense of what was happening.

Sean gripped my chin to yank my face back to him. "How 'bout a kiss for your lover?"

He crushed my lips with his. He kissed me angrily and pulled me tightly against him.

This isn't Sean! my muddled mind finally acknowledged. I bit his lip, and he jerked back in surprise. One look at his bleeding sneer and I knew I was in trouble.

This is not Sean! Condemnation, of all the times I left my emergency pack at home! I'd been so concerned with running to Sean's aid that I hadn't thought about my own!

DON'T DATE THE HAUNTED

Time to make do with what strength I had. I shoved my hands against his shoulders to push us apart. My right side was pelted by a foray of nail filers, clippers, and tweezers. Trimming scissors left a needle-thin cut down my arm. I shrieked in pain.

This wasn't a regular struggle between man and woman. It was mankind versus demon. I had to change my tactics, but—Supernaturals! It was hard to think straight!

He lurched forward and pushed me against the wall. He shoved his face under my chin, gripping my neck with his mouth. I screamed as he pricked my skin with his teeth and sucked hard. The piercing pain triggered my defensive reflexes.

I kicked my strong knee upward at his genitals. He jerked back, but kept that creepy smile.

It wasn't Sean's smile. The thought made me want to cry. If Sean was dead, this wasn't how I wanted to remember him. I struggled to imagine the real Sean's smile and laugh.

I kicked up again, but he rocked back to avoid it. Using his dodge, I shoved him to the side and caused him to teeter. Next, I threw my knee into his ribs to direct his teetering into the tub. A sick crack came from his skull, and a thud from the faucet. All the floating items in the bathroom tumbled to the floor.

Sean gasped as the wind was knocked out of him. His horrid sneer faded away. His mouth drooped with exhaustion and eyes squinted with pain. He struggled to focus on me.

"Kill me," he moaned.

My heart froze. Did I hear him right? Oz's words echoed in my mind, *Be willing to kill corrupted loved ones.* Could I actually do it?

"No," I cried. "You can still be saved. We can remove the spirit through exorcis—"

Sean shook his head. "He's not just taking over my body. Dr. Hyde fuzed our spirits. He's...taking..."

Sean's dry moans quickly shifted back to screams. The bathroom items lifted from the floor again.

I turned the shower on full blast and plugged the drain. The possessed man in the tub squirmed and sizzled as the water touched him.

This. Is. Not. Sean.

Still, it took every emotionless and impersonal fiber of my being to shove his head down into the gathered water. My best friend screamed of death again, gurgling and sizzling. Blood seeped from his pores and swirled in the water. Slowly, his struggling lessened. He seemed bloated, but also hollow somehow. I couldn't tell if the moisture that ran down my face was tears, condensation, or perspiration. Probably all three. I waited several minutes before turning off the water and releasing his head. My whole arm shook from the tension.

I ran back home and returned to my shower. No matter how hard I scrubbed, Sean's blood seemed stained on my skin. I lost count of how many times I vomited as Sean's blood streamed off my body and down the drain. The shower steamed the mirror, but felt cold on my skin. Only my free flowing tears were hot.

"So, you killed him in self-defense and as a mercy?" Mr. E asked, eyes darting to the room's corners every other second. Seeing the poltergeist had shaken him. He wasn't the type to respond well to insecurity and lack of confidence.

"Yes," I confessed, "in order to kill the poltergeist who possessed him. Normal poltergeists can be dispelled by exorcism, and the host may be saved as long as the host's spirit is still whole. But Sean's spirit was entangled. Dr. Hyde injected him before I arrived, but he was too heavily sedated to show the signs. Sean was already as good as dead before we went home. I killed Sean's body to keep the poltergeist from abusing it."

Mr. E narrowed skeptical eyes, like he considered which loopholes he could jump to arrest me. We all sat in an empty office room with a single chair, which we used to prop the door. The Tower was silent, save for the raging storm outside. We had a few minutes to plan before Sean's poltergeist regained its strength from its last attack. Sure, it could probably find us easier with the door open, but when the Haunting could slip through walls, it was better to safeguard against getting locked in a room. It was also better to have an empty room for fewer items to be thrown or used against us.

Theo rested a hand on my shoulder, his expression conflicted.

"I didn't lie to you, Theo," I said. "I lied to Mr. E because I knew he wouldn't believe the truth."

Mr. E muttered from the side, "You think that's a valid excuse?"

Jake shook his head. "Killing your own fiancé. I don't think I could have done it, even if I knew she was possessed by the devil."

"I didn't want to," I said, "but my brother taught me not to be afraid to kill any corrupted loved ones. Every Haunting requires sacrifice in some form."

Mr. E raised an eyebrow at me. "That's a bit heartless. You Horrors are a strange people."

I shrugged. Nothing I hadn't heard before.

Heather's face was a blank stare with wide eyes staring at the ground, like a shred of her innocence had been devoured by the hideous monster of truth. It was actually a bit comical, but I was in no mood to jest.

"Then," Theo began, "his weakness is water?"

"Yes," I said, and dug through my emergency pack to retrieve my aspergillum. "I have this too. Maybe the reason he came back is because I didn't destroy him with pure water. The holy water should have an extra effect on it because it's pure and blessed."

"How d'ya dunk a ghost?" Hank asked. "Won't it just go right through him? And there was water everywhere around Emm—in the ladies room."

"I don't know how it works," I said, "but it does. Maybe it's using tap water and the sewers to throw us off his weakness of holy water."

"Okay, then what's our plan?" Mr. E asked.

I considered the many fight strategies Oz taught me, how Sean and I killed Dr. Hyde, then the personal actions and psychology of our current enemy. "We'll need to surprise it. It'll see a trap. We also need to overwhelm it. Poltergeists are tricky because they can escape through walls and barriers. It needs to be drenched completely or it'll return again. Sean and I destroyed the poltergeist of Dr. Hyde by turning the lawn sprinklers on him."

"Innovative." Mr. E nodded with approval.

"I know we need to avoid bathrooms," Jake began, "but what if we set a trap there? Or a kitchen area?"

"No." I shook my head. "They're the best places for water, but it can easily trick us with mirrors and closed doors. The kitchen would be a better location if it wasn't also loaded with sharp knives, burning devices, and countless hiding places. Water might be its weakness, but the best way to surprise it is to start in a place that's dry, where it thinks it will have an advantage."

"Could we set off the fire alarm?" Mr. E asked.

DON'T DATE THE HAUNTED

"What?" I asked. That was a random question. The man stared at the ceiling. He pointed, and I followed his direction to an overhead sprinkler system.

"Genius!" I said.

"Will your sprinkling of holy water be enough?" Theo asked.

"We have to try," I said. "It's our best option. We can lure the poltergeist to a location of our choice, and set off the alarms."

"Fantastic," Theo said with little enthusiasm. "How will we lure it then?"

"Remember that rule book I told you all to read?"

"Yes," Heather said, squeezing her eyes as if to block out the memory.

"Well, now we're going to break those rules."

Chapter 18

FIGHTING

Think on your feet for hiding places, strategy, escape routes, etc.
Act fast
Be able to turn anything into a weapon
Surprise your Haunting by doing what they don't want/expect
Always carry a loaded gun and/or extra bullets

- *Oz's Haunting Survival Book*

    I counted down from three. Then, we burst into the hallway and bolted. Each of us ran with five matchsticks from my emergency pack. I held my aspergillum before me like a torch.
    This was always the part of Hauntings I hated most. Whether it was following the angry drunk foster father to discover his reason for drinking, or sneaking into the mad scientist's cabin lair to rescue your best friend, there was almost always a moment when a Horror had to give the Haunting an advantage while hoping to gain a bigger one.
    We scattered like ants crawling from a disturbed nest. Heather helped Jake limp near the elevators to stay within twenty feet of the closest emergency exit. Mr. E and Hank ran toward the first floor offices in search of a fire alarm. Theo and

DON'T DATE THE HAUNTED

I ran for the front lobby. I hated to split up, but at least we were all in pairs.

Our plan to set off the fire alarm offered a small relief. There were sprinkler heads everywhere. The emergency lights of the first floor weren't broken yet, though I worried. Had Sean's poltergeist escaped the building and now rained terror across the city? How would we fight it then?

Theo and I staggered to a halt in the front lobby. I scanned the ceiling for a smoke detector. The room was extra tall. I hoped the sprinklers still covered the area. Theo jogged around the desk with his back to the wall.

"Do you see anything?" I asked, panting to catch my breath.

"Not a black and bodiless aura in sight," Theo said. "There are two sprinkler heads near the hallway entry. You might need a table to stand directly below one."

"Okay," I said, "but let's be sure the table's wide and sturdy. Toppling off a table in a lobby sounds like a lame way to die."

Theo reached for my arm with gentle fingers. "I disapprove of this plan. Must you put yourself—"

"Yes," I said, touched by his concern. "The poltergeist crossed the continents to chase me. I'm its main target. It attacked our friends when they broke rules and made themselves vulnerable. To protect everyone else, I need to make myself more vulnerable. Plus, I have you with me." I gave him a wry smile. "You can warn me when I'm in danger."

Theo sighed with a slow caress down my arm. He nodded and started to remove the decorations from a thick end table. I helped him pull it under the sprinkler, glad we weren't stuck with only light or flimsy end tables.

Thunder crashed around us and a roar of wind surged through the halls. The emergency lights flickered. Heather released a cry of fright far down the hallway, and the lights cut out completely.

"This is it!" I shouted. The lobby's floor-to-ceiling windows offered us enough light to see shadows. A high pitched laugh pierced the air and echoed through the walls.

"Get into position," I told Theo, reluctant to have him step aside but knowing what needed to be done. I crouched on top of the table and asked, "Do you see him?"

"Negative!" Theo shouted over the maniacal laughter. "Wait—there! At the exit!"

Twisting around, I didn't see anything. Then, a faint reflection from the windows showed movement where no one stood.

"Its focus is on you, Pansy!" Theo said. "Your aura is darkening!"

Suddenly, the laughing cut off and the night went deadly still and quiet.

Sean's voice broke the silence like a shattering glass. "It sounds like your friend has a touch of the Supernatural." His voice was garbled, somehow muffled and echoed at the same time. "There's no use hiding when the only one who can see me isn't the one I want."

The possessed spirit materialized halfway between me and the exit. He wore a sinister version of Sean's perfect smile. His dull eyes gleamed with hate as he stared directly at me. Somehow I held my position, standing on the table. As the bait, I stood precariously on the table under a sprinkler head. I envied Theo's position on solid ground beneath a smoke detector.

Sean followed my gaze to Theo. Panic pricked my heart as I read the Haunting's intentions in those empty eyes. Theo lit his match.

Sean hesitated five feet away from me when screeching beeps threatened to burst my eardrums. The ceiling sprinkler heads switched on and fanned about. They spit at us, weak and pitiful. I wasn't sure if the one above me reached Sean, as it seemed to have no effect.

"Pansy!" Theo shouted. "Your aura darkened!"

Theo's shout stole Sean's attention again. This time, I used the distraction. I jumped from the table and launched myself at the poltergeist.

Swinging down my aspergillum, Sean noticed my movement and turned back toward me.

This was my one chance to finally end this!

I shook the handle to sprinkle some holy water on the evil when he shuddered. His eyes widened and smiled. That cursed perfect smile. For a second, I wasn't launching myself at a poltergeist determined to destroy my soul. I flew toward my ex-fiancé, and he smiled like he was eager to catch me in a lover's reunion leap.

This is not Sean!

The scream from my memories sounded a mile away, but it penetrated the fogginess of my mind. I squirted my last drops of water at the poltergeist. Was I too late? Was it enough?

Without warning, he swiped at me with inhuman speed. I barely had time to brace myself before his arms struck me. His fingers scratched like claws as he threw me across the room. I landed hard on the marble floor, rolling until I hit the receptionist desk. The sharp cuts in my side stung and bled freely.

I scrambled around the desk to retreat and called everyone back. Limited to the view of what was in front of me, I couldn't see if the water struck my target or what impact it had. I couldn't check my friends to ensure their safety. Nor could I tend to my wound from Sean's sharp swipe.

I couldn't turn around and witness the exploding anger that burst from Sean as he screamed. I didn't see the lamps and decorative plants fly from their tables. I didn't see the tables themselves be thrown like debris. I didn't see the couches and armchairs topple end over end.

All I saw was my little front desk of retreat as a vase soared over me and shattered against the wall ahead. All I felt was a sudden smack against my back as a table threw me forward. All I heard was that horrible scream and glass shattering all around.

Then, there was blackness and silence. Every light in the lobby was officially dead. I heaved myself up, unsure if I'd blacked out.

A single pitch rang through my ears, like a phone that refused to hang up.

Hands grabbed at my shoulders and I freaked.

He got me! If I wasn't already dead, I was so dead now!

Flipping myself around, I prepared to smack my attacker in the face with an added kick. Thankfully, I recognized the silhouette of Theo in the dim light. He stared down the hallway, oblivious to my near attack. I reached out and tried to say sorry, but no sound escaped me. His mouth moved, but I couldn't hear him. That condemned ringing filled my ears. He didn't grab at me again, but gestured wildly to stand and follow him.

My paranoia wondered if the poltergeist took over Theo and now directed me away from my friends, into a trap. The thought alone made my insides tighten and depress. I saw Heather's ragged form poke from the end of the hallway. She also appeared to shout unheard words and waved for us to come toward her.

Standing was a painful struggle of its own, but Theo pulled me up and into a tight hug. As much as I wanted to linger and ignore the world outside of his arms, the danger wasn't over.

Instead, we held hands as we ran to Heather. Assurance of each other's safety, right?

Rounding the corner of the hall, the ringing ebbed away and I could sense blurred noises. Theo held the door for Heather and me to enter a small office. Inside were the rest of my friends, huddled in the light of a stormy window. Despite the quick bloody bandage around Mr. E's arm, he shined his flashlight in Hank's eyes. Hank's hands rested on his forehead and stomach. Even from here, I saw the signs of a moderate concussion.

Muffled words entered my foggy brain as my hearing returned. They each talked about what they saw and how they escaped. Somewhere in the distance, a constant and annoying *drip…drip…drip…*splattered onto hard floor.

I went first to analyze Mr. E's bloody injury. I ripped off a section of my underskirts to rebandage a four-inch cut across his left deltoid.

"What happened?" he asked. "I thought for sure that explosion was his death. Then, we were bulldozed by a couch, of all things."

Theo shook his head. "The explosion was an eruption of his power. He has grown stronger, if anything. I saw his aura disappear below us."

"I thought I hit him, but maybe not." I grit my teeth. "I fumbled at the last minute and might have missed. Ugh! I really am a pansy!"

I harnessed my frustration to rip another piece from my underskirt for Mr. E's arm sling.

"You know," Heather said, "the pansy flower is actually quite resilient."

I stared at her, bewildered.

She shrugged. "It can grow all year long and may be used in herbal medicine." Heather smiled at me with an innocent smile that she knew best.

Still, I messed up. I had one chance, and I blew it. Now what were we going to do?

"Heather is right," Theo said, kneeling next to me. "You are stronger than you think. You fought head first against someone you loved. I cannot imagine how hard this must be on you." He waited for me to finish tying Mr. E's sling, then took my hand in his. "Remember, you are not alone in this, my flower. We fight together."

I almost fell into his arms again. How badly I wanted to cry on his shoulder and let him hold me, to forget there was a murderous ghost in the form of my ex-fiancé hunting us, to forget the pain of my past and the worries of my future, to become lost in his embrace.

The annoying *drip...drip...*broke my silly Romantic desire.

"Pansy," he said thoughtfully, "I am fairly certain that you struck him. It just had no effect. Are you sure his weakness is water?"

I shook my head. "I used water to destroy him before. I figured he wasn't completely destroyed because I hadn't used holy water."

I groaned and reconsidered the facts. Usually, when a malicious spirit took over a physical form, it had been invited by someone who took part in a deadly sin. Holy water cast the evil spirit out by cleansing the person. Except Sean and his poltergeist were forcibly fused together. This wasn't a normal poltergeist.

I spoke aloud as my thoughts connected. "Drowning Sean in the bathtub kept the poltergeist from controlling Sean's body. Now, it's controlling Sean's *spirit*. That's why it couldn't possess Heather when it pulled her away. It's already possessing Sean and can't possess multiple at once."

Hank rubbed his forehead, slowly recovering from his concussion. "A'right, let's rescue his spirit, and kill this thing right."

"How?" I asked.

"Sometimes," Mr. E said thoughtfully, "to catch a crook, you need to use crooks. Could we apply that to this case?"

I waved my hands to stop that thought. "Demons will yield to stronger and more evil forces, but making a pact with the devil will only cause more issues."

Mr. E flustered. "You thought I wanted to make a pact with the Devil? I just asked if we needed to release or utilize other demons to catch this one."

"No," I said firmly. "The cleanest way to destroy a Haunting is to keep other Hauntings out of it."

"Pansy?" Heather whimpered.

"What?" I asked, harsher than intended. Our plans crumpled to dust and I lashed out with my stress. Heather shrank back from my bite. *Drip...drip...*Releasing a deep breath, I tried again. "I'm sorry, what is it?"

"What about the Supernaturals?"

The question took me by surprise. Curious, I asked, "What about them?"

She shuffled with doubt. "Are they not the good that balances the wickedness of Hauntings? May we ask them for help?"

I shrugged. "You can always pray, but I won't promise they'll respond how you want. Most of the time they simply help us to help ourselves, such as prompting which path to take or giving you an idea to defend yourself."

"Oh." Heather's face fell, disappointed.

"If you want to pray, go ahead," I said, "but it's very rare for the Supernaturals to intervene."

"So, we're on our own?" Mr. E confirmed. "How else do you usually destroy a Haunting?"

Drip...drip...drip...

I took a deep breath and wished I wasn't the only one with experience.

"Different Hauntings have different weaknesses," I explained. "Wooden stakes for vampires, silver bullets for werewolves, or specific toxins for skeletons. Most poltergeists are dispelled with water, but this one seems to use water to grow stronger."

"What would a priest do?"

Everyone turned to Theo, who had spoken. He had a thoughtful hand under his chin, but his eyes showed sincere speculation and interest.

Hank balked. "What kind of random question is that?"

Theo shrugged. "Pansy has an aspergillum."

"Indeed." Mr. E narrowed his eyes at me. "Where did she get it?"

"I didn't steal it!" I said, then told myself to shut up. Just because everything he said sounded accusatory didn't mean it was. I explained, "The Bishop of Brimstone is a good friend of mine. He gave this to me last year, and I had him fill and bless it again before I left Horror."

Theo nodded. "A priest had the tools to destroy the first stage of the poltergeist. What would a priest do to dispel its second?"

"How would we know?" Mr. E crossed his arms. "Are any of you priests? We're no closer to destroying this thing, and who's to say it's not right behind us or one of these walls, listening to us, waiting for the perfect time to strike?"

DON'T DATE THE HAUNTED

"It probably is," I muttered. *Drip...drip...drip...*Now that I knew the poltergeist used water to strengthen its powers, each ominous drip sent shivers up my arms.

"I can see the spirit," Theo replied to Mr. E. "We are alone." The word "spirit" resurrected a different idea to my mind. *Baptism.* It rang through my head like Oz's survival instruction.

"Supernaturals," I cursed with my epiphany, "I know what a priest would do! I killed Sean with water, right? So he's been baptized by water, and now he uses it to his advantage. But he hasn't been baptized by fire yet, for the final cleansing. I bet fire's his new weakness." I nearly shouted with excitement, but managed to keep my voice at a whisper.

"A'right," Hank said, "but how do we trap him with fire? It ain't like we can dump a bucket of fire on his head when he's comin' to kill us."

I dug through my emergency pack and pulled out my little match box. I only had two match sticks left.

"We need a long lasting explosive," I said. "Something that will burn big and long enough to have effect. We need to confirm its destruction, or it'll escape. Hauntings have an eerie ability to escape when no one's watching."

"What if," Mr. E theorized, "we maximized our fire? Where's the closest aerosol can? Actually, I think I saw a water gun in one of the offices?"

"I don't know how much time we have..." I drifted as a chill washed over me.

Mr. E raised his eyebrow. "Does it matter if it's our only-"

"Pansy," a whisper crept through the room.

Everyone froze. *Drip...drip...drip...*

"Run?" Heather whined.

"Where?" I asked, barely a whisper. "Form a circle, cover each other's backs. Theo, do you see it?"

"No," he said, eyes darting every way. We scrambled into a huddled group, each of us wanting to be in the middle.

I saw it first. The face of my former best friend reflected in the window. From the reflection, it seemed like it was right among us.

"Theo!" I grabbed his arm.

"I see it," he said.

"I do too," said Mr. E, his voice shaking.

"Now we run!" I said, bolting for the door on the opposite side of the room. We had to backtrack toward the poltergeist to run for the exit down the hall. I started running for it anyway since it was our only escape.

"Wait!" Theo shouted from the back of the group. "That way crosses his path!"

"Not if we run fast enough!" I shouted back.

Heather screamed in a shrill panic. I forgot she wore heels and supported the limping Jake. I whirled around to see Jake collapse to the floor as Heather was pulled back into a side hallway, arms and hands scrambling. Jake shouted and reached helplessly for her. Theo and Hank doubled back to help.

Before I could run to their aid, something strong grabbed me from behind. Translucent arms wrapped around me, completely callous about where they grasped my body. I shouted. Surprise and terror gripped me with those icy hands. Mr. E lunged and tackled me to the ground. My perspective flew up to the ceiling as I hit the marble flooring with my coccyx then scapulae. Something tightened then snapped loose from around my neck.

Shouts echoed down the hall from Heather, Jake, Hank, and Theo. The translucent arms around me disappeared with a crazy cackle. Then, Theo's shouts became louder than the rest.

I struggled to get up as Mr. E still pinned me down.

"Get off of me," I said angrily, shuffling away.

DON'T DATE THE HAUNTED

"He can't take both of us!"

"It's not here anymore!"

Theo's shouts became frantic, then cut off.

"Theo!" I shouted. My mind traitorously concluded to the worst possible outcome. The others also shouted his name.

"It took Theo!" Hank called from down the hall. "They disappeared down the elevator!"

I stopped struggling as the words hit me. They cut my heart strings and plummeted my stomach down thirteen more floors.

Mr. E scrambled off me, his eyes full of true surprise and worry. I wanted to blame him, but he saved me from Sean's grasp.

Then, I found the broken chain that had been around my neck. The red pansy pendant had flown a few feet away and shattered. A surge of loss built in my throat.

This was a Haunting, I reminded myself. Casualties were expected. But Theo? Losing him ached my heart as much as losing Sean, or Oz. Was that love?

Regardless, if there was a chance to save him, I had to take it.

I wobbled over to my friends as quickly as I dared, regularly darting my head back to check for Sean's poltergeist.

"What?" I asked for confirmation. I struggled to keep angry tears back. "How did it take Theo?"

Heather, Jake, and Hank all sat on the floor, catching their breath from the tug o'war. Jake held Heather tightly, and for all her propriety, she clung right back.

"Theo," Hank said, "was helpin' me with Heather, when your old hitch disappeared. Then, it came back in a diff'rent spot and shoved Theo into the empty elevator shaft. The elevator arrived before we reached him, and now it's stuck like glue. If Theo's alive down there, he's trapped."

Jake shuddered. "How would we know?"

"We'll find him," I said. I refused to let another person disappear and die because of me. I refused to think of Theo's possible death and the heartache it caused. I refused to give up.

A trickling sound joined the ominous dripping behind the elevator doors.

Most Hauntings have a lair, or a place where they plot and revive.

"A basement," I pondered aloud. "I bet this building has a basement, and that's where we'll find Theo."

I examined my friends, feeling both pride and pity for them. They weren't used to this. They breathed heavily, tired and worn out. Even Mr. E, whom I assumed was more familiar with life and death situations, appeared spooked and a little lost. His mysteries, as creepy as they were, always had logical and tangible solutions.

We dealt with Hauntings here. This was my problem. It was up to me to fix it.

"Okay," I said, straightening. "Mr. E, I need you to take my friends to the police station. Keep them safe—"

"You think," he cut me off, "that we're going to leave you to find Lord Fromm on your own? Do you have any idea how fast the duke would have my head if he found out that his second eldest died under my watch?"

Heather shot a guilty face at Jake. That face said she'd had enough. Then, she turned to me with a determined stare.

"'Never split up,'" she quoted to me.

"I admire your courage," I said, "but you're all injured and need medical attention. I'm the one who brought this Haunting to Romance, and he made it clear that he'll hurt anyone to get to me. He's using Sean's knowledge and memories to attack. He knows my playbook, so the best way to surprise him will be to break my brother's rules."

Mr. E nodded and spread his arms to put his hands on the shoulders of Jake and Hank.

"We'll split up," he said. "Why don't you take Emma's phone and turn on the GPS? That way, when you find Theo we'll know your location to set a flame trap from another position?"

I wanted to shake my head, to argue "Get out while you can, and I hope you remember me as a good person," but the words wouldn't come. Instead, I accepted Emma's fancy GPS-equipped phone.

"Call me and stay on the line," I said. "If either end goes out, we'll know the other's in trouble." I unlatched my survival pack and pulled out my brother's book. I handed the book to Heather and the pack to Mr. E.

"Here," I said, "you'll need these."

"Won't you?" Mr. E countered.

I held up my little matchbook with a shrug. "If fire's his new weakness, this is all I need. If not, then I'm dry of solutions, and you're my best hope anyway."

Mr. E put a hand on my shoulder. "Let justice be served." He paused uncomfortably, then added, "With your Supernaturals."

His change of perspective encouraged a grim smile from me. I opened my mouth to reply, but cut off as the emergency lights died.

Chapter 19

COMBAT THE SEVEN DEADLY SINS WITH SEVEN VIRTUES

Wrath vs. Patience
Gluttony vs. Temperance
Greed vs. Charity
Sloth vs. Diligence
Lust vs. Self Control
Envy vs. Kindness
Pride vs. Humility

- *Oz's Haunting Survival Book*

"Go!" I shouted.

Mr. E's gruff voice affirmed, "Stay on the call as long as possible, alright?"

I nodded and forced myself to turn away from my companions. I ran back to the elevators and the stairwell that led to the basement.

Emma's phone light waved wildly across my path as I ran. It became my little beam of hope as I felt exposed in the Valley of the Shadows of Death. I was sure the desolate valley felt exactly like this: claustrophobic and trapped with nowhere to go but forward.

Theo needed me. I had to find the poltergeist's lair. If water was its new strength, then the lair was probably in the basement with the plumbing.

DON'T DATE THE HAUNTED

Emma's phone beeped and I nearly jumped out of my skin from fright. I quickly answered and distanced myself from the spot of disturbance in case the poltergeist was close.

"Hello?" I whispered.

"Alright, Ms. Finster, have you found the stairs?" Mr. E asked.

"Let me talk to her," Heather said as the phone was passed to her. "Are you alright, Pansy? Please say something to confirm your safety."

"Like what?"

"That works," Jake said from nearby.

"Okay, be alert," I puffed as I jogged. "I'll give you a commentary so you'll know if I'm in trouble, but stay quiet if you hear the poltergeist."

I didn't know if this building actually had a basement, but I assumed so with its creepiness. As soon as I thought the stairwell was around the corner, the hallways twisted and dead-ended. The storm continued to rage outside, causing me to jump as the building creaked around me. Whispers of my name and hushed screams drifted around each corner.

Every sense in my body wanted to scream at my stupidity—for leaving my friends, for trying to be the hero, for thinking I could win this one. I held tightly to Emma's phone and my matchbook and checked my back every couple of seconds. I allowed my back to be bare, knowing the poltergeist could move through walls anyway. Eventually, I found a door with a labeled picture of stairs.

"Okay, guys," I panted into the phone, "I think I found the basement. I'm going down."

"Be careful, Pansy," Heather replied. "We have you tracked and are searching for that water gun Mr. E spotted earlier. He said something about filling it with flammable liquid. Still, if you need immediate assistance, we will require a few minutes to reach you."

"You know you're still under my watch?" Mr. E huffed. "Don't you get yourself killed, understand? If you're going to die, do it on your own time, not mine."

I smirked at his odd statement of concern. He really did care.

As I opened the door to the basement, I heard a whisper in the wind. My instincts urged and repulsed at the same time to go down the concrete steps. I felt the wall for a light switch but found none. For all I knew, these weren't simply concrete steps, but cemetery stairs descending to Horror.

I gripped the phone light tightly to check the walls and ceiling for any disturbing signs. It was normal except that every surface seemed to sweat. The air was thick with moisture that I hoped was water, not something deadly or gross. I pocketed my matchbook to keep it dry. Grasping the slippery handrail, I carefully descended the stairwell. I couldn't see the bottom, and it didn't reveal itself even after the first several steps. I prayed to the Supernaturals that this wasn't a bottomless staircase.

I turned around, but the door had already disappeared into blackness. There was nowhere to go but down. The voices on the phone scattered as the basement broke our connection. I hung up. Part of me hoped my friends would come for me from the lost connection.

At last, the bottom of the staircase came into view. I was about to sigh in relief when my ears caught the sound of haunted moans. They were a man's, tired and in pain, as though the struggle to make himself heard required every bit of his strength. Shivers ran up my spine as I recognized the voice, but was unsure how.

Was it Sean? Or was it Theo? Or the poltergeist?

DON'T DATE THE HAUNTED

I followed the voice, sure I was walking straight into a trap. It led me around twists and turns of pipelined hallways. I clenched my teeth and forced my feet to walk through them.

The moaning became louder and clearer. I was sure I was almost there but couldn't see around the massive tanks.

I turned another corner and found the bottom of the glass elevator at the far end of the hall. I didn't know a lot about elevators, but I guessed the clamps around the pulley cords kept the cart locked on the floor above. Water streamed down the sides and filled two feet up the shaft. A man in a torn white tailcoat slumped at the bottom.

Theo had an ugly gash on his forehead that bled heavily down his face. His moans echoed in his cubic chamber accompanied by the water streams and an eerie *drip-drip-drip-drip-drip.*

He was alive!

"Theo!" I ran toward him.

"Pansy?" he replied with a tired moan. He shook his head, sprinkling the insides of the shaft from his blood and damp hair. "Wait—stop! Stay away from the water!"

I skidded to a stop right before splashing into a large puddle that flooded the path to the elevator. It was too wide for me to jump, even with a running start. With a closer analysis, I realized it wasn't ordinary water. It was thicker and reflected the room rather than revealing what was underneath. As I stared, a translucent head emerged from its center. I stepped back as the head grew a neck, chest, and torso. It was Sean—no, it was the poltergeist controlling Sean.

"You came alone. Interesting," it said. "Aren't you curious about the water?"

"Curious," I agreed, "but not stupid."

I took another step back. How was I supposed to kill it if it could escape in water? My trap didn't work, but its did.

Endangering Theo's life was enough to lure me wherever it wanted. My gut tightened as Theo struggled to his feet and above the rising water level.

"Let go of Theo!" I shouted. "This is between you and me, no one else."

The poltergeist cast his eyes about, like he was merely there to enjoy the architecture. "True, this is between us. This trap was meant for you, so I had to make rearrangements. Besides, aren't games more fun when we play with friends?"

He drifted to the elevator control box and pushed a button. Somewhere on a higher level, an elevator door opened. The *drip-drip-drip* into Theo's tank turned into another steady stream.

"No—wait!" I shouted.

The poltergeist grinned and drifted back to the middle of his puddle. "So you know the consequences now," he said, calmly rubbing his hands. "I spent too much time flooding the upper bathrooms to let this trap go to waste. Do what I say and your boyfriend might live."

I kept my eyes on the poltergeist but also kept Theo in clear periphery. "I already confessed I killed you. What more do you want from me?"

The poltergeist's chin quivered with deep hatred as his eyes sparked with flame. "Anguish."

Every inch of my skin urged me to scramble out of there. Somehow, I remained steady.

The poltergeist snarled, "You killed the only doctor who knew how to fuse spirits. You destroyed my one chance of returning to my own power. I wasn't too upset as long as I had a body to play with, but then you killed that too!" It trembled as it said, "What do I want with you? I want you back in Horror."

It twitched, shuddered, and struggled with itself. The poltergeist clenched its jaw and squeezed his eyes tight. "Gaaaagh—Don't go, Pansy!" For a second, his voice was crisp and human. The devil spirit snapped his head back and growled, "Shut up!"

What the horror? Had that been Sean? If their spirits were fused, did that mean they fought for control?

I remembered my glimpse of the picture from Emma's camera. I'd been too shocked by the image of Sean to notice. The photo caught the poltergeist gnashing his teeth not at Emma, but off to the side in pain like it struggled with itself. Sean probably tried to stop it. Except Sean's medical knowledge told it exactly where to strike and kill Emma.

Their spirits were in constant battle. My heart swelled with pride for Sean and his endurance to fight after all this time. Sean was a born Romantic. Did that mean he had more control in Romance? That would explain why the poltergeist wanted me to return to Horror, where he had more control. He wanted to restrain Sean and to kill me however he wanted.

My instincts told me to run. Run to the cathedral or police station and plan an attack while the poltergeist was weaker in Romance. I left Horror with no plans to return, but knowing what waited there urged me to stay all the more. I hadn't planned to make Romance my permanent home, but...I had fallen in love with Heartford. I fell in love with the peculiar people...with Theo.

He pounded his fists against his glass coffin, now up to his waist in water. He shouted at me, "You cannot go with him! Your aura went black as death as he said those words! What did your survival book say? Be willing to let anyone die?"

"Don't be afraid to kill corrupted loved ones," I quoted. "But you're not corrupted, Theo. You're—" My words clogged in my throat and I swallowed to start again. "You're the most trustworthy person I know."

"Then trust me when I say this," he said. His voice lowered and choked up, like his next words were a sacred secret. "I never experienced Love at First Sight until I met you. You cannot save me with your sacrifice because it would kill me to lose you."

My heart jumped in my chest and all sense of logic seeped away.

Theo loved me? I was ten feet away from a poltergeist bent on killing me, but I wanted to skip with delight! I found myself smiling—actually smiling!—like Sean had near the end of our last Haunting together. It was all I could manage to whisper back. "I'm still new to this, but I think I love you, too."

The poltergeist scoffed. "You committed to Sean, yet you killed him. Now it's time for you to kill this man."

"I won't kill Theo," I argued. "He's innocent of corruption!"

"Oh, you won't kill him directly, but his death will be your fault if you don't comply. You might as well push the buttons yourself," it snarled, the corners of its lips creeping upward. "I will follow your decision. If you deny me and run like you always do, this man will die, and I'll find another way to haunt you."

Theo gulped. I was sure if he could see his own aura, it suddenly dimmed.

"Who's to say you won't kill Theo anyway?" I asked. "If I go back to Horror right now, how can I trust you to set him free?"

"No, Pansy! You must run!" Theo shouted.

"Don't do it, Pansy!" Sean said before the poltergeist shuddered again. The demon spirit put out his hands like I'd caught him in a cheat. "I admit, you only have my word. Though at his current flow rate, your other friends should have plenty of time to find and release him without me to get in their way."

That wasn't too comforting.

"Honestly," the poltergeist smirked, "I'm surprised you stayed this long. The Pansy that Sean knew would have run for safety long before now. In fact, she wouldn't have split from her idiot friends to come back for this man in the first place."

"That's because you're wrong," I sneered. "Theo is innocent, but I'm tainted with your blood. That makes me the corrupted loved one who must be sacrificed." I took a step closer to the poltergeist, toward the transporting liquid. Fighting every muscle in my body, I took another step.

"Pansy, no!" Theo threw his whole body against the glass to no avail. The water splashed around his chest now. "Your aura blackens with each step! Go back! Get out of here!"

Any moment now, the poltergeist would lose patience and grab me. It would drag me down into that thick liquid, and I would drown into Horror. Still, I waited before each step. Any moment now...The hate in its eyes became tangible as chills crawled up my arms. My heel hit the edge of the glistening puddle.

"Sean," I said, "if I die in Horror because of this, it's not only to save Theo, but you too."

I prayed to the Supernaturals that the truth of my words would help Sean regain control.

The Haunting shuddered.

Now!

I pulled out my last two matches and struck one. Hope sparked as fire bloomed. I threw my little glowing fire at the base of the poltergeist. I watched as it burned a hole through his knee. He flinched back. Then, the small flame disappeared with only a sizzle into the puddle.

The poltergeist's evil version of the perfect grin widened.

He flew to the elevator box and pushed every button. My warning shout stuttered as water poured into the elevator shaft with a roar. Theo's head went under the surface in seconds.

The basement echoed with suffering cries: struggles from Theo, distress from me. He fought to swim for air until the water reached the bottom of the elevator and continued higher. He was trapped. The water might as well have engulfed me too, the way I felt suffocated and unable to clear my head. My heart literally ached to watch Theo struggle for his life. I was stuck behind that condemned liquid, trapped and helpless to save the man I valued more than my own life.

The poltergeist lunged for me with shocking speed and grabbed my ankle. I had just enough awareness to jump back as it yanked me to the ground. It held on and pulled with incredible strength. I had nothing to grab.

I shook my leg and kicked at it with my other foot, but my attacks simply passed through it. I kicked where it grabbed my ankle, but only struck myself. Its other hand reached forward and harnessed my second ankle.

I had no leverage now and slid toward the liquid, toward Horror. Screams escaped me as I clawed my fingers over the concrete, desperate to grab anything to hold me back. I rolled to my stomach for more traction against the floor. One more glance at the elevator shaft showed Theo's losing battle to breathe.

My feet dropped through the floor and my calves quickly followed.

Would I fall into Horror? How far was the drop? Probably enough to injure me so that I couldn't escape, but also to keep me alive for the poltergeist to have its way with me.

My likely and horrifying future flashed through my mind. This monster was going to torture me and rip me to shreds. There would be nothing left of me to remember.

DON'T DATE THE HAUNTED

That was my fate. The next few hours or days or even weeks would be the worst sort of torture. The poltergeist would make me beg for death. Theo was dead. Emma. Sean. Oz. Every person I ever cared for was dead. I was cursed to live and die alone.

The poltergeist yanked my stomach and chest into the puddle. My feet dangled, reaching for landing, but found none. I crunched my arms under my chest for more leverage as I fumbled with my final match stick.

I struck my last match. It didn't catch. I struck it again and again. The poltergeist climbed up to grab me around my shoulders and waist. No! If I didn't destroy the poltergeist now, it would kill me! It would continue to torture Sean's spirit as it haunted anyone it wanted!

Running footsteps echoed through the basement. Heather, Jake, Hank, and Mr. E ran for me. They were too late.

"Pansy!" Heather shouted as she rounded the corner.

The poltergeist's arms shuddered around me. Sean's voice broke through the garble. "Let go of her!"

Sean forced their fused spirits to retreat to the opposite side of the puddle.

I tried to pull myself up, but my arms slipped. My friends were still too far away to reach me in time. Mr. E threw a colorful object at me. It bounced with a plastic clatter, then slid within my reach. The water gun smelled of wine and had a metal extension at the nozzle.

What the horror?

"Torch it!" Hank shouted.

I had maybe half a second to analyze the plan.

What would this do to Sean? Would I destroy my best friend's soul? What if I failed to reach it?

I had to jump. I hadn't planned to return to Horror. I definitely didn't want to return to a poltergeist's torture chamber in a Regency dress with nothing but a water gun. But if it meant I could end this once and for all, I had to try.

Desperate, I struck my last match again. This time it lit. In one swooping motion, I grabbed the water-gun, and stabbed the match into the metal extension. I launched myself from the ledge while twisting my aim toward the Haunting. The flame stretched and engulfed the poltergeist. Screams of the condemned filled my ears. I needed to confirm its destruction, but my view of the poltergeist was blocked by my spraying fire.

Time passed in slow motion as I fell. All was black inside the hole. Even the light of my torch flame became lost in that abyss.

Pansy.

The familiar voice of my brother warmed me. Maybe if I had a promise to see my brother after death, I could handle whatever Horror threw at me. Again.

Lean yet strong arms caught me from underneath and slowed my fall. Then, they rushed me back up to the light of Romance. I was thrown back through the hole to land at the feet of my friends.

Only Heather seemed worried about me. The men stared past me, faces wide with surprise and wonder. Following their gazes, I cranked my neck to see the poltergeist looming over a ghost.

No, that wasn't right. The ghost was a plump spirit with the poltergeist's hateful expression. Then that meant—Sean?

The spirit of my best friend levitated and glowed a bit like a ghost. Yet he emanated more power and confidence. He spared a quick glance at me. In that brief moment, he flashed his familiar smile and caring eyes.

"*Get up,*" he said, in a voice that echoed through my body.

DON'T DATE THE HAUNTED

With the poltergeist distracted, I obeyed without another thought. As I pushed myself to my feet, a Supernatural rose with me to float before the poltergeist.

My heart stopped. I almost didn't recognize him without the scars of his life experiences. He had short, spiked hair and a thin triangular face. His figure was lean, but I knew the strength of those arms.

"Oz," I whispered.

He spared a quick smile to me before glaring at the poltergeist with terrifying fury.

They moved in a flash. They weren't simple ghosts, but neither were they poltergeists. They had a different sense of power and peace that emanated from them like their glow. I briefly wondered if the glow was similar to what Theo saw as auras.

Oz grabbed for the poltergeist while Sean zipped to the elevator shaft. I was sure Theo was dead, but I wanted to be with him all the same.

Sean must have known my thoughts as he waved his hand and the puddle shrank to the size of a manhole, clearing the way for me. I ran to Theo and Sean, passing the brawl between my Supernatural brother and the Haunting.

The poltergeist was furious and surprisingly quick, but Oz was quicker and more powerful. My brother fought faster than my eyes could track and radiated authority. With each strike the poltergeist trembled with less power.

Sean flexed his hands and muttered, "*Everything is so clear and easy without the corruption. My gifts were limited before, but now I know exactly what I can and should do.*" Then, he palmed the glass shaft. It shattered. The released water pushed me back before Theo smashed into me.

"Theo!" I lay his limp body on his back. His skin was too cold. I tilted his head to open his airway and began CPR chest compressions.

Sean stopped me. *"Hold on, I have something better. You were willing to sacrifice your life for this man,"* he said. *"I only ask for—"*

"Yes," I said, desperate for anything. "Whatever it takes to save him."

Sean laughed to himself. *"Here I thought I was the Romantic between the two of us."*

Before I could argue or wonder what he was doing, he put a hand over Theo's chest and touched his other hand to my heart. I had a brief moment to see Oz break through the poltergeist's defenses, stabbing through its chest and head with his bare hands. Everything exploded into white.

Chapter 20

NEVER SAY

"Be right back"—no you won't
"Where is it?"—behind you
"I promise to take care of you"—famous last words
"Glad that's over"—now it's back

- *Oz's Haunting Survival Book*

The light burned around and inside me. It was like slamming into a pool of cold water. Every inch of my body stung and bruised, yet it was also refreshing. The light cleared, and the feeling ebbed away. Sean came into view again, fainter than before. Oz was also dimmed, but the poltergeist was gone. Theo gasped and coughed for air.

"*He'll be alright,*" Sean said. I turned to him, and a heavy load of guilt fell on me. He held up a hand to stop my excuses. "*Thank you,*" he said, "*for saving me from the poltergeist infection.*" He then gestured to Theo. "*I'm glad you found someone to love. You can trust him.*"

From behind him, Mr. E stared wide at the whole scene. He held a small device in his hands, but I was surprised it wasn't his notepad and pen.

I wanted to say more but was unable to find the words. With a grim smile, Sean stood and floated to Oz.

"You're leaving?" I asked. The answer was obvious as Sean sank into the puddle, but a ridiculous hope inside of me wanted them to stay longer.

Oz floated to the ground, then walked over to me. Unbidden tears dripped from my eyes.

"*Pansy*," Oz said, his voice reverberating through me, "*what a strong woman you've become.*" He put his hand to my cheek, but all I felt was the memory of his warm touch.

"How are you here?" I asked.

"*I'm your guardian angel, of course. I go wherever you go.*"

"Why did you wait until now to help me?" I asked. "Where were you when I had to kill Sean?"

Oz smirked. "*I'm your guardian angel. God only has us intervene when the mortals can't do it alone. Did I mention what a strong woman you've become? Don't give me that look.*" He laughed, and my pout broke into a smile. "*I'm with you more than ever now that my mind's finally at peace.*"

I questioned him with my eyes.

"*I...*" He paused, as if ashamed. "*I heard voices and saw demons that weren't there. I couldn't trust my own mind. That's what really killed me in the end.*"

I gasped and unconsciously gripped Theo a little tighter. He coughed but sighed as I relaxed again.

Oz continued, "*I knew there was a werewolf after me, but I wouldn't go to the bathroom to wash my scent because of the demons in my head. I also refused to break any of my rules to lure the Haunting into a trap. You survived what I could not, but...it would tear me apart all over again if you fell into the same trap I did. Try to relax a bit, enjoy life a little. Can you do that for me? You escaped Horror and I'm here. Your Hauntings are over.*"

"Then don't leave me again," I pleaded like a child.

"*You don't see me, but you hear me, don't you? Reminding you of rules from my book?*"

"That's not you," I pouted, "those are just memories."

My brother's smile gleamed. *"There isn't a difference. I've always been there for you, and I always will be."*

"As will I." Theo coughed.

I smiled at the men I loved between my tears. Oz stepped back to the puddle, and I racked my brain for any reason to keep him longer. Again, my mind was blank. All I could think of were my feelings.

"I love you," I said.

"I love you, too."

Theo said the words, but I felt them echoed from Oz. He sank into the liquid, and the puddle shrank, seeming to disappear into the floor. When the last drop popped, my friends ran over to help Theo and me.

Mr. E, Heather, Jake, and Hank knelt down beside us. We all shared glances, wondering what to say after everything that happened.

Mr. E spoke first. "I've never heard of a teleporting liquid before. How did it get here and where did it go?"

I scoffed. "We just battled a fusion of a poltergeist with fire and angels. You honestly expect to understand the science of it all?"

"I suppose not," he grunted.

"It's been a really long night," I sighed. "Let's find some place to rest and we can talk about it with clear minds. This was the weirdest Haunting I've ever had."

"This was a fearsome Adventure," Theo agreed.

"Indeed, a most peculiar Case," Mr. E added.

"Most definitely," Heather concluded, "a haunted Romance."

A few days later, Brooke returned with good news that while the mutant did escape, her father survived the Experiment with only some cuts and a broken arm. The good news was blunted by Emma's funeral that afternoon. Hank was a mess in an arm sling, saying he'd planned to meet Emma's extended family at their wedding, not her funeral.

We shared tears and condolences, and while emotions were high, it was definitely the most beautiful and thoughtful funeral I'd ever attended. There were never so many flowers for Horror cremations. The President of Heartford University was even there to present a memorial bouquet. As our elected speaker, Heather gave a lovely eulogy, and Father Roosevelt spoke the benediction.

The family members glared darts at me. I couldn't blame them. Emma was killed by my Haunting. Her death was my fault.

Wanting to separate myself from the guilt and grievers, I left to wander the graveyard.

"Are you alright, my flower?"

I turned to find Theo walking quickly to catch up.

"I'm okay," I sighed, "unless my aura's dark?"

Theo flashed a light smile. "No, you are safe. Though I wonder what burdens your thoughts."

I didn't respond right away, but took his hand in mine, simply grateful for his presence. We wandered together between the gravestones.

"It was a beautiful funeral," I said. "Horrors are usually cremated to prevent zombification, but everything about the service was nice."

"Quite lovely," Theo agreed and waited for me to continue. I didn't until we passed a large bush to separate us from the family tears.

"I worry that everyone hates me. It's not enough to tell them I did my best, and you simply can't save everyone during Hauntings. I was the reason the Haunting came to Romance in the first place."

Theo's eyes became stern and concerned. He tugged me to a stop and into a hug. I wrapped my arms around his shoulders and buried my face into him.

I was ready to burst into tears, but none came. With Theo's comforting arms around me, I was too calm to cry. Theo held me like he'd never let go, and I didn't want him to. Wrapped in his arms, I'd never felt so relaxed in my life. I was unfamiliar with the notion that soothed my heart and struggled to define it.

Was it safety? Peace? Love? Or somehow a mixture of all three.

He gave me a squeeze then leaned back to face me directly.

"Sean was a Romantic, right? He may have come here anyway to gain strength over the poltergeist. I shudder to think what would have happened if you were not here to fight it."

"I hadn't thought of that," I said.

He fingered my chin upward until my eyes focused on his sincerity. "The fault lies not on you, Pansy. You just gave it a focus. You did all that you could to save those around you. All who were there know that you were the first to run to the rescue. I believe you are more worthy of the title Trusted than I am, as you sacrificed your own safety for others' multiple times."

"Based on my aura." I shrugged, like it was no big deal. "Though we still don't know what the lengths of your auras mean."

"True," he said, raising his palm to the side of my face, measuring a light only he could see. "Your aura no longer varies in length. It remains the shortest I have ever seen.

Perhaps we may continue our weekly discussions to discover why?"

"Sure," I said, closing the finger-width gap to lean my cheek against his palm.

He stroked a strand of my hair behind my ear. It wasn't long enough to stay, and I smirked as it slipped in front of my face again. He fingered it back and held it there, cupping my cheek. I allowed myself to appreciate the gesture and how handsome he was in his crisp black suit.

"What about you? Are you okay?" I asked. I was surprised only Heather and Jake asked for counseling after the incident. I was sure everyone was more scarred than they'd admit.

Theo paused, understanding my concern. "I am alive," he said, with a humorous hint of surprise. "And smiling," he added, "because of you."

As cheesy as it sounded, I couldn't help but grin back. I probably blushed too, but enjoyed his expression too much to notice. He smiled that infectious smile I loved, and his calm blue-green eyes seemed to recall the moment we confessed our affection for each other.

Not wanting to lose the moment, I slid my hand around his neck and lifted my lips up to his. I hesitated at the last second as habitual phrases shouted through my ever-alert mind: *Don't celebrate too soon! Don't let—*

They were silenced as Theo closed the distance. His beautiful smile met mine.

I didn't need two tries to determine his kissing skills. One was enough to know that I wanted a hundred more.

In that moment of complete bliss, I think I finally understood Emma. This was a peak for Romantics. My heart raced as quickly as an escape from a chainsaw murderer, but I was happy as...well, I knew nothing wonderful enough to compare.

All doubts washed away. This was love. I held onto the sensation with the same desperate yearning that I held onto Theo. This was the feeling that drove people mad and caused them to do the dumbest things, like walk into a poltergeist's lair alone, or wait patiently for a Contemporary Horror to fall for you. And it was worth it.

When our lips parted, I had to remind myself to breathe. I nestled into the nook below his chin. His heart pounded to the same pace as my own. It was a beautiful rhythm, full of life.

"I'm in love with you, Theodor the Trusted," I whispered, then leaned back to grin at him. Theo matched my expression.

We were a bush away from grieving families, and I didn't know how to express myself. People laughed when smiling wasn't enough, but laughing wasn't appropriate for the location. I took the better option of kissing Theo again.

After the funeral, I came home with two cheesecakes.

"What are those?" Heather asked.

"Theo and I kissed." I blushed. "I owe you and Emma cake."

Heather gave a mini squeal of delight and for the first time, I didn't check behind myself. Our eyes shared a sad message though. "Emma."

Ten minutes later, the dormitory was gathered in the front room. Heather was the last to grab a slice of cake. She paused and raised her slice.

"To our Psi sister, Emma."

The rest of us raised our slices in salute and echoed, "To Emma."

The next evening, I stood on the front porch and entryway to the Psi Dorms, staring across the street at the ominous

Tower. Several of its rooms were still taped off as crime scenes, but otherwise, the world moved on. I had finished giving my statements to the police, refilled my aspergillum with Father Roosevelt, and Theo and Jake became regular visitors to our dorm.

Mr. E walked out of the Tower, capping his pen and pocketing his notebook. Seeing me, he waved and crossed the street. He stopped in front of me, then stood there as he struggled with what to say. Eventually, he held out his hand. I took it, half expecting him to slap cuffs around my wrist. Instead, we shared a firm shake.

"I guess," he said, "I learned why we leave your continent alone concerning justice?"

I smiled in relief. It was weird to stand before this man and not feel intimidated. Especially since he now officially had a reason to take me in.

Mr. E pulled a small black device from his pocket and pressed a button on top.

"He'll be alright," Sean's voice said. "Thank you…for saving me from the poltergeist infection." There was another brief pause. "I'm glad you found someone to love. You can trust him."

I gaped. "You recorded the Supernaturals?"

"Somehow—" Mr. E shuffled uncomfortably "—I think he knew I was recording him, and I wonder why he didn't stop me?" He then gave a sly smile. "Did you notice that I recorded your confession?"

My exclamation of dismay cut off with a raise of his hand.

"Calm down, Ms. Finster. Wouldn't you say my witness and those of your friends' can convince Mystery's homicide department of your self-defense? It also helps that the victim himself thanked you, right?" He wiggled the recorder in his hand.

DON'T DATE THE HAUNTED

"Thank you," I said. "Without you, we might have never put Sean to rest."

He tilted his head. "Are you sure about that? You don't think that you and your friends would have figured it out eventually? You have a good team with you."

"You were part of that team," I said as a police officer crossed the street for Mr. E.

He smiled softly. "I'm flattered, but with the conclusion of your Haunting, aren't you cleansed? Will you ask me to stay for the remaining year as your Watcher?"

As much as I appreciated his help against the poltergeist, I didn't enjoy the feeling of someone constantly watching me. "No. Oz said my Hauntings are over. You can go home."

The officer came up from behind Mr. E and clapped him on the shoulder. "Did I hear that right? You're heading off?"

"Depends on exactly what you heard." Mr. E teased, then released a deep sigh. "Maybe sleeping in my own bed will arrest the nightmares of that night."

"Well, thanks for coming out, Nathan. We really appreciated your help on this one." The policeman shook his hand, then left.

I threw my hands up in defeat. "What the horror is your name?"

Mr. E had the audacity to smile mischievously.

"Every person has a different name for you!" I shouted. "How can anyone trust you if you never tell them your condemned name?"

"Ms. Finster, did you forget I'm from Mystery State? I don't outright lie to people, but do you think it's in my nature to tell whole truths? Why don't you think of them as clues?"

"Clues." I balked, still disbelieving the nerves of this man. "So they're all part of your name. How? I've heard you called John, Nate, Neil, Nathan…I mean, I can see how some of those are nicknames for Jonathan or Nathaniel, but neither of those start with E!"

Mr. E kept his smug smile, like he enjoyed the show of my frustration.

"It's Rumpelstiltskin, isn't it?"

He laughed jovially. "No, but maybe my parents had the same weird sense of combination? How many more clues do you need?"

I thought for a moment. A weird combination...

"Jonathaniel E?"

He laughed again, obviously enjoying this far more than I was. "You got my first name, but still don't know my last? How do you not know when you've been saying it all this time with a break between the syllables?"

"Mr-E—your last name is Mystery?"

He tipped his hat with a nod of a bow. "Mr. Jonathaniel Mystery at your service, Ms. Pansy Finster. Do you want congratulations? Why do you look surprised? There's a great deal of Cases involved in your continent, after all. How about you continue calling me Mr. E? Ambiguity is important for Mysteries, and we don't want to be redundant, do we?"

I simply stood there dumbfounded. No wonder he went by nicknames—he had so many options!

"I guess I know everything about you now," I said, trying to sound oppressive.

"I'll let you think that." He grinned. "Though could you guess what I have written on my notepad?"

"You mean you don't write my word-for-word responses to your interrogations?"

"Interviews," he corrected me with a laugh, "and why would I do that when I have a recorder?"

He said no more, but turned and dipped his fedora as goodbye.

DON'T DATE THE HAUNTED

"That man," I muttered. My thoughts were interrupted as Heather walked out, holding hands with Jake. Theo was right behind, but he walked past them to stand beside me.

"So, just to be sure, Pansy," Jake said, leaning against the porch railing, "we have at least six months of reprieve from Hauntings?"

I smiled and allowed Theo to wrap his arm around me. I took his hand to pull myself closer.

"At least," I said. "But that one was a crossover from Horror. Oz said my Hauntings are done."

Jake sighed with extreme relief. "Well, I'm glad—"

"Ah!" I shushed him with a finger to my lips. "Don't say you're glad it's over, because that only invites it back."

He laughed nervously and held tighter to Heather's hand. "We can't have that now."

"I think we'll be safe as long as we don't tempt them," I said for reassurance.

Theo leaned down to my ear. "Meaning your paranoia will return if ever the lights flicker."

"It's never *just* a power outage," I said.

Theo shook his head and chuckled, showing off that contagious smile of his.

Oz also asked me to relax a little. As difficult as that might be, I looked forward to a break from Hauntings. Supernaturals would know, I had enough to handle in the dramatic regions of Romance.

SNEAK PEEK OF THE SEQUEL

Chapter 1

ONCE UPON A TIME

> This phrase is a misconception,
> as history often repeats itself.
> It is usually paired with "in a kingdom far away."
> That is also a misnomer, as that kingdom is often Fairy.
>
> - *Thesis of Adventures*

THEO

My not-quite-useless ability to see blue-green auras revealed a light shade around my trembling hands. Unfortunately, my auras only revealed if I was in physical danger, not emotional. I balled my hands into fists and raised one to knock on Psi Dorm 201, located just south of Heartford University. I became increasingly familiar with this door over the past nineteen months. Behind it lived the love of my life—Pansy Finster, from Horror.

I attempted to dry my sweaty palms while smoothening my doublet. Only then did I notice my appearance.

Curses, I was a mess.

My undershirt poked free beneath my doublet. My black leather boots had scuff marks from my day's frantic activities, and my dress trousers needed more than their usual pressing. What was that white smear, and how long had it been there?

C. RAE D'ARC

I fingered through my dark brown hair in a failed attempt to tame it. The new ring on my middle finger caught on a couple strands. Every detail of my perfect plan had been defenestrated by that ring. Bullbeggar.

My frustrated scowl disappeared as soon as the door opened. Pansy stood before me. She was a welcome distraction from the anxiety, grief, and responsibilities. Just the sight of her lifted my heavy heart.

She wore a Contemporary yellow dress that matched her wardrobe of "comfortable and easy to run in." She also wore the blue pansy-flower necklace that I gave to her after her red one broke. Her straight, raven black hair just reached her bare shoulders, dark and soft as umber. Her blue-green aura was light and safe from dangers, and its unique shortness allowed me to analyze her angular features beneath the blurring glow. She smiled at me with delightful eyes of smoky quartz. Then, she took in my grungy appearance.

"Theo?" she asked. "Is something wrong?"

"Hey," I said, releasing a heavy breath. "Will you walk with me? Plans...have changed."

Pansy would have called that the understatement of the year if she knew how much they had changed.

I had planned everything to be perfect. In a few days, we were supposed to walk as graduates from Heartford University, then take a picnic on the Regency side of Romance's Heartbeat River next to a field of pansy flowers. We would eat tea sandwiches and biscuits until the sun set over the line of majestic evergreens. Then, I would ask the most romantic question.

As if only love mattered. As if I could provide for a woman without my father's blessing. As if we could live in Romance for the rest of our days without the responsibility of 1.55 million people.

DON'T MARRY THE CURSED

Curses, how would I convince Pansy to say yes to that? Even if she did, how would I convince Father to say yes to her? He tolerated our courtship (to put it nicely) while I was the "useless" second son. The ring on my middle finger changed my responsibilities and the scrutiny I would face.

I offered Pansy my elbow of escort as we walked out to the city streets of Heartford, Contemporary, Romance. I directed our walk away from the singular building known as the Tower. Over a year and a half had passed since the horrific masquerade that occurred within. I still remembered the fear of drowning in the trap set by Pansy's Haunting, though I drew a blank when the Supernaturals revived my life. I just remembered our auras turning black as my ability forewarned our deaths.

A diner's smells of spaghetti and breadsticks returned my thoughts to the present. Pansy and I walked past brick and marble townhouses that had been repurposed for businesses. Several showcased their products in their bay windows: wedding dresses, wedding cakes, wedding photography studios, wedding jewelry—the usual Romantic shops. This was hardly my first time passing these stores with Pansy beside me, though this was the first time my stomach churned at the sight of them.

We passed another shop that advertised tuxedos and tailcoats to buy or rent. My heart ached to recall my older brother in his ceremonial attire as Margen's Marquis. The uniform had been tailored for Greggory, and I knew it would drape loosely on me.

Pansy pursed her full lips in thought and glanced at me between steps. I failed to organize my thoughts for an entire block. When I rubbed the back of my neck, I found sweat. Disgraceful.

After the second block of silence, Pansy slid her hand down my arm until her fingers intertwined with mine. "Theo?" she asked again. "What's on your mind?"

"Hmm?" I blinked out of my anxious thoughts. Subconsciously, I had fiddled with the ring on my right hand. I clenched my fist to stop. "Just how plans never go according to plan."

Pansy smirked. "Always have a back up plan," she quoted from her brother's book about surviving Horror. As much as I wanted to join her smile, my frustrated frown remained. When I stayed silent, she prodded, "What plans went wrong?"

Just the most important part of our courtship.

We stepped into a city park. The paved pathway curved between deciduous trees in full bloom. A spring breeze smelled of sweet pollen and caused some white petals to float across our scene. Perhaps I could still provide Pansy with the perfect moment. If I could just calm my thoughts and nerves for half a minute.

I led Pansy to a metal bench along the path. We took a minute to sit, and my left arm wrapped around her shoulders as she snuggled into my side. I hoped she ignored my racing heartbeat. Then, with a deep breath, I willed myself to start from the beginning.

"I received news from Margen this morning."

"News?" she asked. "Did it explain why your dad's been quiet lately?"

"Nnno," I slurred, wondering for the hundredth time that day why my father's last letter dated two months ago. Was his silence connected to the sudden appearance of my brother's ring? Why did my weekly letters from the lords claim that all was well? Had they been fabricated? If so, why, and what were they hiding?

DON'T MARRY THE CURSED

I rested my right hand over Pansy's, and her eyes landed on the hulking piece of metal and stone on my middle finger. The ring was massive, made of gold and fortudo gems. It was crafted from King Sayer's mines, strong as dragon scales and more reflective than mirrors. I had not seen its likeness in a year, yet there was no mistaking the gray-blue tones.

"What's that?" Pansy asked.

"This was my brother's," I explained. "Marquis Greggory Fromm, the Wind Master, of Margen. I received it this morning."

"Your brother sent it to you?" Pansy bit her lip, unsure what to say. She settled with, "It's huge."

I chuckled. "Yes, I was never meant to wear it." Her eyebrows raised and prodded for an explanation. "See," I said, "this ring signified Greggory as the eldest and heir to my father's duchy. It can only be removed by the wearer or magically transferred to the next heir upon death."

Pansy straightened and frowned. "So, that means—"

"For this ring to appear on my finger, either my elder brother visited Romance, snuck into my apartment, then deliberately removed the ring from his hand to put it on mine, or" —I swallowed— "he is dead."

She gasped. "Supernaturals! I'm so sorry, Theo. You were close, weren't you?"

"Not as close as you and Oz. While you and I both idolize our older brothers, yours actually responded in kind. Greggory is..." I paused and struggled to think of my brother in the past tense. He was...everything I failed to be. "Greggory was a champion among swordsmen and master with his ability. He was the oldest and heir to the duchy with the power to change the very winds. He also had a stubborn attitude. We disagreed on multiple accounts regarding treatment of the lower classes and cursed beings. I figured the only way to gain influence and to support the people was through political knowledge." I took a deep breath and let it out slowly to rein my emotions. "However, I am now the Marquis of Margen. His duties have fallen to me, and I must return to Fantasy."

Greggory was dead. I was marquis. Curses! As the second eldest, I elected to study poli-sci to serve as Greggory's assistant and advisor, not to be the man himself. Margen titled me as "The Trusted" because the people thought my ability was useless, and I feared to strike my opponents even in the friendliest of skirmishes. I stroked my mental bruise from the time I froze in front of the whole town in a duel against my younger sister. How could I lead a duchy of magical warriors?

Regardless of the lightness of my aura, my fingers trembled. Two hands of grief—denial and fear—gripped me by the throat.

Pansy's brown eyes met mine with turmoil and worry. "Two questions then: when do you go and how soon will you be back?"

I placed a hand on her cheek and said the cursed words. "I must leave as soon as I am capable." In full honesty, that was the reason for my disarrayed attire. After swallowing the sudden appearance of Greggory's ring, I spent the day packing and preparing for my departure. "My Masters thesis on Adventures will be postponed. Concerning my return...I may not."

She leaned away from my touch. "So, you're leaving? It's that simple?"

No, it was hardly simple. The mere thought of saying goodbye to Pansy wrenched my core. Yet the thought of abandoning Margen to collapse—my homeland and inheritance—likewise tore me apart. If I could protect Margen from my younger brothers, or just a small piece of it, I had to try.

DON'T MARRY THE CURSED

Margen was the home of my heart, and Pansy was the keeper of it. How could I decide between the two?

I squeezed my eyes shut and whispered, "I dare not ask you to join me. I will protect Margen from my wayward younger brothers by taking the title of marquis and future duke...or I may die in my attempt."

"Not if I can help it."

"Sorry?" My eyes snapped open.

Pansy set her jaw. "Let me go with you. I can't stand aside and watch if you're in trouble. Let's see, how did you put it when you asked me to go to the ball with you? Oh! Will you let me be your sidekick?" She grinned.

My heart groaned. Was this how she felt when I asked her to go to the masquerade, and she begged me to understand how perilous it was?

"This is not the average Fairy Adventure. I know not what awaits me in Margen. This Adventure may be dangerous."

Regardless of the worry in my eyes, she laughed. "Compared to Hauntings? Seriously, Theo, no matter what we're up against, I've probably been through worse."

I opened my mouth to argue, then closed it, hoping she was right.

"Alright. You may accompany me under one condition," I said, then bolstered my courage for the audacious words about to leave my lips.

"Sure, what is it?" she asked.

"Marry me."

THE STORY CONTINUES...

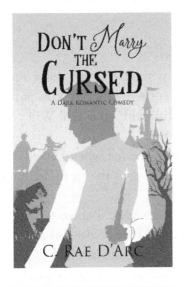

The state of Margen is Grimm...

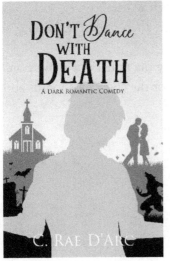

You can hide from your past, but can you outrun it?

ACKNOWLEDGEMENTS

If I knew how much time and work would be put into this book, I might have given up. I'm glad I didn't, though it's entirely due to the support of others.

Thanks, Lisa Gartner and Kendra Fugal for Alpha Reading, for probing questions like "How did Oz die?" and helping me to cut two minor characters. Thank you, Robyn Cheatham for staying up past 4:30 AM to read it all in one sitting (the first time). Sorry, I didn't base a roommate on you, but after seeing what happens to them, aren't you glad you weren't included?

With the help of my writing group, Miss Heather Appleton became a proper Regency resident. A special thanks to Rhiannon Hulse for urging the action forward and Shaela Kay of Blue Water Books for the perfect cover.

Thanks to Salt and Sage Editing I developed the poltergeist and blended my genres. A special thanks goes to Jeigh Meredith for the proofread. Noelle of Eschler Editing was so patient and good with me. After so many years of self-editing, I know I wasn't the easiest client. She encouraged me to kill some darlings and clarify the details to ultimately solidify the story. She also helped me define the genre of dark romantic comedy.

To the people who read my book when it wasn't fully polished: Jenny Roemmich, Lillie Dube, Kristen Holt, Abby Smith. Thanks for your final thoughts to encourage me.

As crazy as this may read, I'd also like to thank the literary agents who rejected my queries. They unknowingly pushed me forward to correct mistakes and research more.

There isn't a THANK YOU big enough for Michael Smith. You were my backboard as I bounced countless ideas off you. Thank you for putting up with my distracted thoughts as we sat at our computers or walked through neighborhoods. So much of this book (particularly Theo's ability, Oz's cause of death, and everything about the poltergeist) wouldn't be the same without you. You fill my life with Adventures and Romances.

Last of all, I thank God for the crazy thoughts He puts in my head. I firmly believe that if we do all we can with faith, then God will take care of us, though it's usually not how we expect.

ABOUT THE AUTHOR

    C. Rae D'Arc has been involved in every stage of a book's life. As a writer, editor, retailer, reader, and reviewer she has worked four part-time jobs at once. Thankfully, one of them actually paid her. She received her Bachelors in English from Brigham Young University, and now lives in the Tri-Cities of Washington with her husband and Aussie dog.
    PS. D'Arc is pronounced with one syllable.

You can check out more from C. Rae D'Arc on her website (craedarc.com),
Facebook (facebook.com/c.rae.darc), or
Instagram (instagram.com/craedarc)

Made in the USA
Middletown, DE
16 April 2024

53071915R00146